THE LEOPARD

Gordon Davey

THE
LEOPARD

By

GIUSEPPE DI LAMPEDUSA

Translated by Archibald Colquhoun

TWENTIETH CENTURY CLASSICS

This book was first published under the title
IL GATTOPARDO
by Feltrinelli Editore, Milan, in 1958
First published in Great Britain 1960

This edition published 1971 by
Book Club Associates
by arrangement with William Collins Sons & Co. Ltd.,

Reproduced and Printed in Great Britain by
Redwood Press Limited, Trowbridge & London

CONTENTS

TRANSLATOR'S NOTE

I AM most grateful for the chance of making a thorough revision of this translation. The Italian is so full of subtle word-play and irony both delicate and grandiose that at times I felt myself coping with some of the most allusive prose written since Manzoni.

Now Mr. John D. Christie has helpfully suggested a large number of corrections; many have come from Mr. Raymond Mortimer and Mr. and Mrs. Milton Waldman among others; and there has also been patient research by the librarians of the Italian Institute. Earlier portions were read aloud to the doyenne of English translators from Italian, Miss Beryl de Zoete. And I have had the advantage throughout of advice and encouragement from the author's widow, Principessa Alessandra di Lampedusa.

A word should be said about the Italian text. This was established for publication by Signor Giorgio Bassani, who first recognised the merit of the incomplete and anonymous manuscript from Palermo. The author himself died before his book was even set up in print, so had no chance of revising it. Another manuscript copy, with some variations, belongs to his co-heir and adopted son, now Duca di Palma, in Palermo.

To him and to many of the author's relatives, friends, and connections throughout Sicily I owe insights into island life that have greatly helped towards an understanding of this book. The present revised text might in fact almost be called a co-operative effort by admirers to present something closer to a worthy version.

❋   ❋   ❋

When this book opens the Bourbon state of Naples and

Sicily, called the Kingdom of the Two Sicilies, was about to end. King Ferdinand II ('Bomba') had just died; and the whole Italian peninsula would soon be one state for the first time since the fall of the Roman Empire.

The Risorgimento, as this movement for unification came to be known, had been gathering strength since the occupation of the north by the Austrians after the Napoleonic Wars, and had already come to a head once, in 1848. Leadership had now fallen mainly to Piedmont, the so-called Kingdom of Sardinia, ruled from Turin by Victor Emmanuel of Savoy, with Cavour as his prime minister.

Early in May 1860 the popular hero Garibaldi, acting against Cavour's wishes, sailed from near Genoa with a thousand volunteers for Sicily, to win the island from the Bourbons. The Redshirts, or 'Garibaldini,' landed at Marsala, defeated the Bourbon troops at Calatafimi, and within three weeks had occupied the capital, Palermo. Garibaldi, hailed as 'Dictator' of Sicily, gathered more volunteers, crossed to the mainland, swept up the coast and entered Naples in triumph. That autumn the Bourbon armies were defeated on the Volturno, the Piedmontese besieged the last Bourbon king, Francis II, in Gaeta, and Garibaldi handed over southern Italy to King Victor Emmanuel; he then withdrew to private life.

Plebiscites were held; every state in the peninsula agreed to join the new united kingdom, except the Papal States, which were occupied, for reasons of internal French politics, by troops of Napoleon III. In 1862 Garibaldi tried to force this issue and march on Rome. But on the slopes of Aspromonte in Calabria his men were routed and he himself wounded by Piedmontese troops.

This action by Italian government forces ended the revolutionary phase of the Risorgimento, which culminated officially in the declaration of Rome as capital of Italy in 1870.

A.C.

INTRODUCTION TO THE PRINCE

MAY, 1860

'Nunc et in hora mortis nostrae. Amen.'

The daily recital of the Rosary was over. For half an hour the steady voice of the Prince had recalled the Sorrowful and the Glorious Mysteries; for half an hour other voices had interwoven a lilting hum from which, now and again, would chime some unlikely word; love, virginity, death; and during that hum the whole aspect of the rococo drawing-room seemed to change; even the parrots spreading iridescent wings over the silken walls appeared abashed; even the Magdalen between the two windows looked a penitent and not just a handsome blonde lost in some dubious daydream as she usually was.

Now, as the voices fell silent, everything dropped back into its usual order or disorder. Bendicò, the Great Dane, grieved at exclusion, came wagging its tail through the door by which the servants had left. The women rose slowly to their feet, their oscillating skirts as they withdrew baring bit by bit the naked figures from mythology painted all over the milky depths of the tiles. Only an Andromeda remained covered by the soutane of Father Pirrone, still deep in extra prayer, and it was some time before she could sight the silvery Perseus swooping down to her aid and her kiss.

The divinities frescoed on the ceiling awoke. The troops of Tritons and Dryads, hurtling across from hill and sea amid clouds of cyclamen pink towards a transfigured Conca d'Oro and bent on glorifying the House of Salina, seemed suddenly so overwhelmed with exaltation as to discard the

most elementary rules of perspective; meanwhile the major
Gods and Goddesses, the Princes among Gods, thunderous
Jove and frowning Mars and languid Venus, had already
preceded the mob of minor deities -and were amiably
supporting the blue armorial shield of the Leopard. They
knew that for the next twenty-three and a half hours they
would be lords of the villa once again. On the walls the
monkeys went back to pulling faces at the cockatoos.

Beneath this Palermitan Olympus the mortals of the
Salina family were also dropping speedily from mystic
spheres. The girls resettled the folds in their dresses, exchanged blue-eyed glances and snatches of school-girl slang;
for over a month, ever since the outbreaks of the Fourth of
April, they had been home for safety's sake from their
convent, and regretting the canopied dormitories and collective cosiness of the Holy Redeemer. The boys were already scuffling with each other for possession of a medal
of San Francesco di Paola; the eldest, the heir, the young
Duke Paolo, longing to smoke and afraid of doing so in
his parents' presence, was squeezing through his pocket
the braided straw of his cigar-case. His gaunt face was
veiled in brooding melancholy; it had been a bad day;
Guiscard, his Irish sorrel, had seemed off form, and
Fanny had apparently been unable (or unwilling) to send
him her usual lilac-tinted billet-doux. Of what avail then,
to him, was the Incarnation of his Saviour?

Restless and domineering, the Princess dropped her rosary
brusquely into her jet-fringed bag, while her fine crazy
eyes glanced round at her slaves of children and her tyrant
of a husband, over whom her diminutive body yearned
vainly for loving dominion.

Meanwhile he himself, the Prince, had risen to his feet;
the sudden movement of his huge frame made the floor
tremble, and a glint of pride flashed in his light-blue eyes
at this fleeting confirmation of his lordship over both
humans and their works.

Now he was settling the huge scarlet missal on the chair
which had been put in front of him during his recitation
of the Rosary, putting back the handkerchief on which he

had been kneeling, and a touch of irritation clouded his
brow as his eye fell on a tiny coffee stain which had had
the presumption, since that morning, to fleck the vast white
expanse of his waistcoat.

Not that he was fat; just very large and very strong; in
houses inhabited by common mortals his head would touch
the lowest rosette on the chandeliers; his fingers could twist
a ducat coin as if it were mere paper; and there was constant coming and going between Villa Salina and a silver-
smith's for the straightening of forks and spoons which, in
some fit of controlled rage at table, he had coiled into a
hoop. But those fingers could also stroke and knead
with the most exquisite delicacy, as his wife Maria Stella
knew to her cost; while up in his private observatory at
the top of the house the gleaming screws, caps and studs of
telescopes, lenses and 'comet-finders' seemed inviolate beneath his gentle manipulations.

The rays of the westering sun, still high on that May
afternoon, lit up the Prince's rosy hue and honey-coloured
skin; these betrayed the German origin of his mother, the
Princess Carolina whose haughtiness had frozen the easy-
going court of the Two Sicilies thirty years before. But
in his blood also fermented other German strains particularly
disturbing to a Sicilian aristocrat in the year 1860, however
attractive his fair skin and hair amid all that olive and
black; an authoritarian temperament, a certain rigidity
of morals, and a propensity for abstract ideas; these, in
the relaxing atmosphere of Palermo society, had changed
respectively into capricious arrogance, recurring moral
scruples and contempt for his own relatives and friends,
all of whom seemed to him mere driftwood in the languid
meandering stream of Sicilian pragmatism.

In a family which for centuries had been incapable even
of adding up their own expenditure and subtracting their
own debts he was the first (and last) to have a genuine
bent for mathematics; this he had applied to astronomy, and
by his work gained a certain official recognition and a great
deal of personal pleasure. In his mind, now, pride and
mathematical analysis were so linked as to give him an

illusion that the stars obeyed his calculations too (as, in fact, they seemed to be doing) and that the two small planets which he had discovered (Salina and Speedy he had called them, after his main estate and a shooting-dog he had been particularly fond of) would spread the fame of his family throughout the empty spaces between Mars and Jupiter, thus transforming the frescoes in the villa from the adulatory to the prophetic.

Between the pride and intellectuality of his mother and the sensuality and irresponsibility of his father, poor Prince Fabrizio lived in perpetual discontent under his Jove-like frown, watching the ruin of his own class and his own inheritance without ever making, still less wanting to make, any move towards saving it.

That half hour between Rosary and dinner was one of the least irritating moments of his day, and for hours beforehand he would savour its rather uncertain calm.

With a wildly excited Bendicò bounding ahead of him he went down the short flight of steps into the garden. Enclosed between three walls and a side of the house its seclusion gave it the air of a cemetery, accentuated by the parallel little mounds bounding the irrigation canals and looking like the graves of very tall, very thin giants. Plants were growing in thick disorder on the reddish clay; flowers sprouted in all directions : and the myrtle hedges seemed put there to prevent movement rather than guide it. At the end a statue of Flora speckled with yellow-black lichen exhibited her centuries-old charms with an air of resignation; on each side were benches holding quilted cushions, also of grey marble; and in a corner the gold of an acacia tree introduced a sudden note of gaiety. Every sod seemed to exude a yearning for beauty soon muted by languor.

But the garden, hemmed and almost squashed between these barriers, was exhaling scents that were cloying, fleshy and slightly putrid, like the aromatic liquids distilled from the relics of certain saints; the carnations superimposed their pungence on the formal fragrance of roses and the oily

emanations of magnolias drooping in corners; and somewhere beneath it all was a faint smell of mint mingling with
a nursery whiff of acacia and a jammy one of myrtle;
from a grove beyond the wall came an erotic waft of early
orange-blossom.

It was a garden for the blind : a constant offence to
the eyes, a pleasure strong if somewhat crude to the nose.
The *Paul Neyron* roses, whose cuttings he had himself
bought in Paris, had degenerated; first stimulated and then
enfeebled by the strong if languid pull of Sicilian earth,
burnt by apocalyptic Julys, they had changed into objects
like flesh-coloured cabbages, obscene and distilling a dense
almost indecent scent which no French horticulturist would
have dared hope for. The Prince put one under his nose
and seemed to be sniffing the thigh of a dancer from the
Opera. Bendicò, to whom it was also proffered, drew back
in disgust and hurried off in search of healthier sensations
amid dead lizards and manure.

But the heavy scents of the garden brought on a gloomy
train of thought for the Prince : 'It smells all right here now;
but a month ago . . .'

He remembered the nausea diffused throughout the
entire villa by certain sweetish odours before their cause
was traced : the corpse of a young soldier of the Fifth
Regiment of Sharp-shooters who had been wounded in the
skirmish with the rebels at San Lorenzo and come up there
to die, all alone, under a lemon tree. They had found him
lying face downwards in the thick clover, his face covered
in blood and vomit, crawling with ants, his nails dug into
the soil; a pile of purplish intestines had formed a puddle
under his bandoleer. Russo the agent had discovered this
object, turned it over, covered its face with his red handkerchief, thrust the guts back into the gaping stomach with
some twigs, and then covered the wound with the blue flaps
of the cloak; spitting continuously with disgust, meanwhile,
not right on, but very near the body. And all this with
meticulous care. 'Those swine stink even when they're dead.'
It had been the only epitaph to that derelict death.

After bemused fellow-soldiers had taken the body away

(and yes, dragged it along by the shoulders to a cart so that the puppet's stuffing fell out again), a *De Profundis* for the soul of the unknown youth was added to the evening Rosary; and now that the conscience of the ladies in the house seemed placated, the subject was never mentioned again.

The Prince went and scratched a little lichen off the feet of the Flora and then began to stroll up and down; the lowering sun threw an immense shadow of him over the grave-like flowerbeds.

No, the dead man had not been mentioned again; and anyway soldiers presumably become soldiers for exactly that, to die in defence of their king. But the image of that gutted corpse often recurred, as if asking to be given peace in the only possible way the Prince could give it; by justifying that last agony on grounds of general necessity. And then around would rise other even less attractive ghosts. Dying for somebody or for something, that was perfectly normal, of course : but the person dying should know, or at least feel sure, that someone knows for whom or for what he is dying; the disfigured face was asking just that; and that was where the haze began.

'He died for the King, of course, my dear Fabrizio, obviously,' would have been the answer of his brother-in-law Màlvica had the prince asked him, and Màlvica was always the chosen spokesman of most of their friends. 'For the King, who stands for order, continuity, decency, honour, right; for the King, who is sole defender of the Church, sole bulwark against the dispersal of property, the "Sect's" eventual aim.' Fine words, these, pointing to all that lay dearest and deepest in the Prince's heart. But there was, even so, something that didn't quite ring true. The King, all right. He knew the King well or rather the one who had just died; the present one was only a seminarist dressed up as a general. And the old King had really not been worth much. 'But you're not reasoning, my dear Fabrizio,' Màlvica would reply, 'one particular sovereign may not be up to it, yet the idea of monarchy is still the same.'

That was true, too; but kings who personify an idea should not, cannot, fall below a certain level for generations; if they do, my dear brother-in-law, the idea suffers too.

He was sitting on a bench, inertly watching the devastation wrought by Bendicò in the flowerbeds; every now and again the dog would turn innocent eyes towards him as if asking for praise at labour done : fourteen carnations broken off, half a hedge torn apart, an irrigation channel blocked. How human ! 'Good Bendicò, come here.' And the animal hurried up and put its earthy nostrils into his hand, anxious to show it had forgiven this silly interruption of a fine job of work.

Those audiences! All those audiences granted him by King Ferdinand at Caserta, at Capodimonte, at Portici, Naples, anywhere at all.

Beside the chamberlain on duty, chatting as he guided with a cocked hat under an arm and the latest Neapolitan slang on his lips, they would move through innumerable rooms of superb architecture and revolting décor (just like the Bourbon monarchy itself), plunge into dirty passages and up ill-kept stairs, and finally emerge into an ante-chamber filled with waiting people; closed faces of police spies, avid faces of petitioners. The chamberlain apologised, pushed through this mob, and led him towards another ante-chamber reserved for members of the Court; a little blue and silver room of the period of Charles III. After a short wait a lackey tapped at the door and they were admitted into the August Presence.

The private study was small and consciously simple, on the white-washed walls hung a portrait of King Francis I and one, with an acid ill-tempered expression, of the reigning Queen; above the mantelpiece was a Madonna by Andrea del Sarto looked astounded at finding herself in the company of coloured lithographs representing obscure Neapolitan saints and sanctuaries; on a side table stood a wax statuette of the Child Jesus with a votive light before it; and the modest desk was heaped with papers, white, yellow and blue; the whole administration of the kingdom here attained its final phase, that of signature by His Majesty (D.G.).

Behind this paper barricade was the King. He was already standing so as not to be seen getting up; the King with his pallid heavy face between fairish side-whiskers, with his rough cloth military jacket under which burst a purple cataract of trousers. He gave a step forward with his right hand out and bent for the hand-kiss which he would then refuse.

'Well, Salina, blessings on you!' His Neapolitan accent was far stronger than the chamberlain's.

'I must beg Your Majesty to excuse me for not wearing court dress; I am only just passing through Naples; but I did not wish to forgo paying my respects to Your Revered Person.'

'Nonsense, Salina, nonsense : you know you're always at home here at Caserta.

'At home, of course,' he repeated, sitting down behind the desk and waiting a second before indicating to his guest to sit down too.

'And how are the little girls?' The Prince realised that now was the moment to produce a play on words both salacious and edifying.

'Little girls, Your Majesty? At my age and under the sacred bonds of matrimony?'

The King's mouth laughed as his hands primly settled the papers before him. 'Those I'd never let myself refer to, Salina. I was asking about your little daughters, your little princesses, Concetta, now, that dear godchild of ours, she must be getting quite big, isn't she, almost grown up?'

From family he passed to science. 'Salina, you're an honour not only to yourself but to the whole kingdom! A fine thing, science, unless it takes to attacking religion!' After this, however, the mask of the Friend was put aside, and in its place assumed that of the Severe Sovereign. 'Tell me Salina, what do they think of Castelcicala down in Sicily?'

Salina had never heard a good word for the Lieutenant-General of Sicily from either Royalists or Liberals, but not wanting to let a friend down he parried and kept to generalities. 'A great gentleman, a true hero, maybe a little old for the fatigues of the Lieutenant-Generalcy . . .'

The King's face darkened; Salina was refusing to act the spy. So Salina was no use to him. Leaning both hands on his desk he prepared the dismissal: 'I've so much work! the whole Kingdom rests on these shoulders of mine.' Now for a bit of sweetening: out of the drawer came the friendly mask again. 'When you pass through Naples next, Salina, come and show your Concetta to the Queen. She's too young to be presented, I know, but there's nothing against our arranging a little dinner for her, is there? Sweets to the sweet, as they say. Well, Salina, 'bye and be good!'

On one occasion, though, the dismissal had not been so amiable. The Prince had made his second bow while backing out when the King called after him, 'Hey, Salina, listen. They tell me you've some odd friends in Palermo. That nephew of yours, Falconeri . . . Why don't you knock some sense into him?'

'But, Your Majesty, Tancredi thinks of nothing but women and cards.'

The King lost patience; 'Take care, Salina, take care. You're responsible, remember, you're his guardian. Tell him to look after that neck of his. You may withdraw.'

Repassing now through the sumptuously second-rate rooms on his way to sign the Queen's book, he felt suddenly discouraged. That plebeian cordiality had depressed him as much as the police grins. Lucky those who could interpret such familiarity as friendship, such threats as royal might. He could not. And as he exchanged gossip with the impeccable chamberlain he was asking himself what was destined to succeed this monarchy which bore the marks of death upon its face. The Piedmontese, the so-called *Galantuomo* who was getting himself so talked of from that little out-of-the-way capital of his? Wouldn't things be just the same? Just Torinese instead of Neapolitan dialect; that's all.

He had reached the book. He signed : Fabrizio Corbera, Prince of Salina.

Or maybe the Republic of Don Peppino Mazzini? 'No, thanks. I'd just be plain Signor Corbera.'

And the long jog back to Naples did not soothe him. Nor even the thought of an appointment with Cora Danolo.

This being the case, then, what should he do? Just cling to the status quo and avoid leaps in the dark? Then he would have to put up with more rattle of firing-squads like that which had resounded a short time before through a squalid square in Palermo; and what use were they, anyway? 'One never achieves anything by going bang! bang! Does one, Bendicò?'

'Ding! Ding! Ding!' rang the bell for dinner. Bendicò rushed ahead with mouth watering in anticipation. 'Just like a Piedmontese!' thought Salina as he moved back up the steps.

Dinner at Villa Salina was served with the slightly shabby grandeur then customary in the Kingdom of the Two Sicilies. The number of those taking part (fourteen in all, with the master and mistress of the house, children, governesses and tutors) was itself enough to give the dining-table an imposing air. Covered with a fine but mended lace cloth, it glittered under a powerful carcel-lamp hung precariously under the Murano chandelier. Daylight was still streaming through the windows, but the white figures in painted bas-relief against the dark backgrounds of the door-mantels were already lost in shadow. The silver was massive and the glass splendid, bearing on smooth medallions amid cut Bohemian ware the initials F.D. (*Ferdinandus dedit*) in memory of royal munificence; but the plates, each signed by an illustrious artist, were mere survivors of many a scullion's massacre and originated from different services. The biggest, vaguely Capodimonte, their wide almond-green borders engraved with little gilt anchors, were reserved for the Prince, who liked everything round him to be on his own scale except his wife.

When he entered the dining-room the whole party was

already assembled, only the Princess sitting, the rest
standing behind their chairs. Opposite his own chair,
flanked by a pile of plates, swelled the silver flanks of the
enormous soup tureen with its cover surmounted by a
prancing Leopard. The Prince ladled out the *minestra*
himself, a pleasant chore, symbol of his proud duties as
paterfamilias. That evening, though, there came a sound
that had not been heard for some time, a threatening
tinkle of the ladle against a side of the tureen; sign of
great though still controlled anger, one of the most terrifying sounds in the world, as one of his sons used to call it
even forty years later. The Prince had noticed that the
sixteen-year-old Francesco Paolo was not in his place. The
lad entered at once ('Excuse me, Papa') and sat down. He
was not reproved, but Father Pirrone, whose duties were
more or less those of sheep-dog, bent his head and muttered
a prayer. The bomb did not explode, but the gust from its
passage had swept the table and ruined the dinner all the
same. As they ate in silence the Prince's blue eyes, nar-
rowed behind half-closed lids, stared at his children one
by one and numbed them with fear.

But, 'A fine family,' he was thinking. The girls plump,
glowing, with gay little dimples, and between the forehead and nose that frown which was the hereditary mark of
the Salina; the males slim but wiry, wearing an expression
of fashionable melancholy as they wielded knives and forks
with subdued violence. One of them had been away for two
years. Giovanni, the second son, the most loved, the most
difficult. One fine day he had vanished from home and
there had been no news of him for two months. Then
a cold but respectful letter arrived from London with
apologies for any anxiety he had caused, reassurances about
his health, and the strange statement that he preferred a
modest life as clerk in a coal depot to a pampered (read:
'fettered') existence in the ease of Palermo. Often a twinge
of anxiety for the errant youth in that foggy and heretical
city would prick the Prince's heart and torture him. His
face grew darker than ever.

It grew so dark that the Princess, sitting next to him,

put out her childlike hand and stroked the powerful paw
reposing on the tablecloth. A thoughtless gesture, which
loosed a whole chain of reactions in him; irritation at being
pitied, then a surge of sensuality, not however directed towards her who had aroused it. Into the Prince's mind flashed
a picture of Mariannina with her head deep in a pillow. He
raised a dry voice : 'Domenico,' he said to a lackey, 'go and
tell Don Antonio to harness the bays in the brougham;
I'll be going down to Palermo immediately after dinner.'
A glance into his wife's eyes, which had gone glassy, made
him regret his order : but as it was quite out of the question
to withdraw instructions already given, he persevered and
even added a jeer to his cruelty; 'Father Pirrone, you will
come with me; we'll be back by eleven; you can spend a
couple of hours at your Mother-house with your friends.'

There could obviously be no valid reason for visiting
Palermo at night in those disordered times, except some low
love-adventure; and taking the family chaplain as companion was sheer offensive arrogance. So at least Father
Pirrone felt, and was offended, though of course he acqui-
esced.

The last medlar had scarcely been eaten when the
carriage wheels were heard crunching under the porch;
in the hall, as a lackey handed the Prince his top hat and
the Jesuit his tricorne, the Princess, now on the verge of
tears, made a last attempt to hold him—vain as ever :
'But Fabrizio, in times like these . . . with the streets full
of soldiers, of hooligans . . . why, anything might happen.'

'Nonsense,' he snapped, 'nonsense, Stella; what could
happen? Everyone knows me; there aren't many men as
tall in Palermo. I'll see you later.' And he placed a hurried
kiss on her still unfurrowed brow which was level with his
chin. But, whether the smell of the Princess's skin had called
up tender memories, or whether the penitential steps of
Father Pirrone behind him evoked pious warnings, on reaching the carriage door he very nearly did countermand the
trip. At that moment, just as he was opening his mouth to
order the carriage back to the stables, a loud shriek of 'Fabrizio, my Fabrizio !' followed by a scream, reached him

from the window above. The Princess was having one of her fits of hysteria. 'Drive on,' said he to the coachman on the box holding a whip diagonally across his paunch. 'Drive on, down to Palermo and leave Father at his Mother-house,' and he banged the carriage door before the lackey could shut it.

It was not dark yet and the road meandered on, very white, deep between high walls. As they came out of the Salina property they passed on the left the half-ruined Falconeri villa, owned by Tancredi, his nephew and ward. A spendthrift father, married to the Prince's sister, had squandered his whole fortune and then died. It was one of those total ruins which engulfed even the silver braid on liveries; and when the widow died the King had conferred the guardianship of her son, then aged fourteen, on his uncle Salina. The lad, scarcely known before, had become very dear to the irascible Prince, who perceived in him a riotous zest for life and a frivolous temperament contradicted by sudden serious moods. Though the Prince never admitted it to himself, he would have preferred the lad as his heir to that booby Paolo. Now, at twenty-one, Tancredi was enjoying life on the money which his uncle never grudged him, even from his own pocket. 'I wonder what the silly boy is up to now?' thought the Prince as they drove past Villa Falconeri, whose huge bougainvillaea cascaded over the gates like swags of episcopal silk, lending a deceptive air of gaiety to the dark.

'What is he up to now?' For King Ferdinand, in speaking of the young man's undesirable acquaintances, had been wrong to mention the matter but right in his facts. Swept up in a circle of gamblers and so-called 'light' ladies, all dominated by his slim charm, Tancredi had actually got to the point of sympathising with the 'Sect' and getting in touch with the secret National Committee; maybe he drew money from them as well as from the Royal coffers. It had taken the Prince a great deal of labour and trouble, visits to a sceptical Castelcicala and an over-polite Manis-

calco, to prevent the youth getting into real trouble after
the 4th of April 'riots.' That hadn't been too good; on
the other hand Tancredi could never do wrong in his uncle's
eyes : so the real fault lay with the times, these confused
times in which a young man of good family wasn't even
free to play a game of faro without involving himself with
compromising acquaintanceships. Bad times.

'Bad times, Your Excellency.' The voice of Father Pirrone sounded like an echo of his thoughts. Squeezed into a
corner of the brougham, hemmed in by the massive Prince,
subject to that same Prince's bullying, the Jesuit was suffering in body and conscience, and, being a man of parts
himself, was now transposing his own ephemeral discomfort into the perennial realms of history. 'Look, Excellency,'
and he pointed to the mountain heights around the Conca
d'Oro still visible in the last dusk. On their slopes and
peaks glimmered dozens of flickering lights, bonfires lit
every night by the rebel bands, silent threats to the city
of palaces and convents. They looked like lights that
burn in sick rooms during the final nights.

'I can see, Father, I can see,' and it occurred to him
that perhaps Tancredi was beside one of those ill-omened
fires, his aristocratic hands stoking on twigs being burnt
to damage just such hands as his. 'A fine guardian I am,
with my ward up to any nonsense that passes through his
head.'

The road was now beginning to slope gently downhill
and Palermo could be seen very close, plunged in total
darkness, its low shuttered houses weighed down by the
huge edifices of convents and monasteries. There were
dozens of these, all vast, often grouped in twos or threes,
for women and for men, for rich and poor, nobles and
plebeians, for Jesuits, Benedictines, Franciscans, Capuchins,
Carmelites, Liguorians, Augustinians . . . Here and there
squat domes rose higher, in flaccid curves like breasts
emptied of milk; but it was the religious houses which gave
the city its grimness and its character, its sedateness and also
the sense of death which not even the vibrant Sicilian light
could ever manage to disperse. And at that hour, at night,

they were despots of the scene. It was against them really that the bonfires were lit on the hills, stoked by men who were themselves very like those living in the monasteries below, as fanatical, as self-absorbed, as avid for power or rather for the idleness which was, for them, the purpose of power.

This was what the Prince was thinking as the bays trotted down the slope; thoughts in contrast to his real self, caused by anxiety about Tancredi and by the sensual urge which turned him against the restrictions embodied by religious houses.

Now the road was crossing orange groves in flower, and the nuptial scent of the blossoms absorbed the rest as a full moon does a landscape; the smell of sweating horses, the smell of leather from the carriage upholstery, the smell of Prince and the smell of Jesuit, were all cancelled out by that Islamic perfume evoking houris and fleshly joys beyond the grave.

It even touched Father Pirrone. 'How lovely this would be, Excellency, if . . .'

'If there weren't so many Jesuits,' thought the Prince, his delicious anticipations interrupted by the priest's voice. At once he regretted this rudeness of thought, and his big hand tapped his old friend's tricorne.

Where the suburbs began, at Villa Airoldi, the carriage was stopped by a patrol. Voices from Apulia, voices from Naples, called a halt, bayonets glittered under a wavering lantern; but a sergeant soon recognised the Prince sitting there with his top hat on his knees. 'Excuse us, Excellency, pass on.' And a soldier was even told to get up on to the box so that the carriage would have no more trouble at other block posts. The loaded carriage moved on more slowly, round Villa Ranchibile, through Torrerosse and the orchards of Villafranca, and entered the city by Porta Maqueda. Outside the Caffè Romerese at the *Quattro Canti di Campagna* officers from units on guard were sitting laughing and eating huge ices. But that was the only sign of life in the entire city; the deserted streets echoed only to the rhythmic march of pickets on their rounds, passing with white bandoleers crossed over their chests. On each side were continuous monastery walls, the Monastery of the Mountain, of the Stigmata, of the Cross-Bearers, of the Theatines, massive, black as pitch, immersed in a sleep that seemed like the end of all things.

'I'll fetch you in a couple of hours, Father. Pray well.'

And poor Pirrone knocked confusedly at the door of the Jesuit Mother-house, Casa Professa, as the brougham wheeled off down a side street.

Leaving the carriage at his palace, the Prince set off for his destination on foot. It was a short walk, but through a quarter of ill repute. Soldiers in full equipment, who had obviously just slipped away from the patrols bivouacked in the squares, were issuing with shining eyes from little houses on whose balconies pots of basil explained their ease of entry. Sinister-looking youths in wide trousers were quarrelling in the guttural grunts Sicilians use in anger. In the distance echoed shots from nervous sentries. Once past this district his route skirted the Cala; in the old fishing port decaying boats bobbed up and down, desolate as mangy dogs.

'I'm a sinner, I know, doubly a sinner, by Divine Law and by Stella's human love. There's no doubt of that, and to-morrow I'll go and confess to Father Pirrone.' He smiled to himself at the thought that it might be superfluous, so certain must the Jesuit be of his sins of to-day. And then a spirit of quibble came over him again. 'I'm sinning, it's true, but I'm sinning so as not to sin worse, to stop this sensual nagging, to tear this thorn out of my flesh and avoid worse trouble. That the Lord knows.' Suddenly he was swept by a gust of tenderness towards himself. 'I'm just a poor, weak creature,' he thought as his heavy steps crunched the dirty gravel. 'I'm weak and without support. Stella! oh, well, the Lord knows how much I've loved her; but I was married at twenty. And now she's too bossy, as well as too old.' His moment of weakness passed. 'But I've still got my vigour; and how can I find satisfaction with a woman who makes the sign of the Cross in bed before every embrace and then at the critical moment just cries, "*Gesummaria*!" When we married and she was sixteen I found that rather exalting; but now . . . seven children I've had with her, seven; and never once have I seen her navel. Is that right?' Now he was almost shouting, whipped by this odd anguish, 'Is it right? I ask you all!' And he turned to the portico of the Catena. 'Why, she's the real sinner!'

Comforted by this reassuring discovery he gave a firm knock at Mariannina's door.

Two hours later he was in his brougham on the way home with Father Pirrone beside him. The latter was worried; his colleagues had been telling him about the political situation which was, it seemed, much tenser than it looked from the detached calm of Villa Salina. There was fear of a landing by the Piedmontese in the south of the island, near Sciacca; the authorities had noticed a silent ferment among the people; at the first sign of weakening control the city rabble would take to looting and rape. The Jesuit Fathers were thoroughly alarmed and three of them, the oldest, had left for Naples by the afternoon packet-boat, taking their archives with them. 'May the Lord protect us and spare this holy Kingdom!'

The Prince scarcely listened. He was immersed in sated ease tinged with disgust. Mariannina had looked at him with her big opaque peasant's eyes, had refused him nothing, and been humble and compliant in every way. A kind of Bendicò in a silk petticoat. In a moment of particularly intense pleasure he had heard her exclaim 'My Prince!' He smiled again with satisfaction at the thought. Much better than '*mon chat*' or '*mon singe blond*' produced in equivalent moments by Sarah, the Parisian slut he had frequented three years ago when the Astronomical Congress gave him a gold medal at the Sorbonne. Better than '*mon chat*', no doubt of that; much better than '*Gesummaria!*'; no sacrilege at least. A good girl, Mariannina; next time he visited he'd bring her three lengths of crimson silk.

But how sad too : that manhandled, youthful flesh, that resigned lubricity; and what about him, what was he?

A pig, just a pig! Suddenly there occurred to him a verse read by chance in a Paris bookshop while glancing at a volume by someone whose name he had forgotten, one of those poets the French incubate and forget next week. He could see once more the lemon-yellow pile of unsold copies, the page, an uneven page, and heard again the verses ending a jumble of a poem :

> ... *donnez-moi la force et le courage*
> *de contempler mon coeur et mon corps san dégoût.*

And as Father Pirrone went worrying on about a person called La Farina and another called Crispi, the Prince dozed off into a kind of tense euphoria, lulled by the trotting of the bays on whose plump flanks quivered the light from the carriage lamps. He woke up at the turning by Villa Falconeri. 'Oh, he's a fine one too, tending bonfires that'll destroy him!'

In the matrimonial bedroom, glancing at poor Stella with her hair well tucked into her nightcap, sighing as she slept in the great brass bed, he felt touched. 'Seven children she's given me and she's been mine alone.' A faint whiff of valerian drifted through the room, last vestige of her crisis of hysterics. 'Poor little Stella,' he murmured pityingly as he climbed into bed. The hours passed and he could not sleep; a powerful hand was stoking three fires in his mind; Mariannina's caresses, those French verses, the threatening pyres on the hills.

Towards dawn, however, the Princess had occasion to make the sign of the Cross.

Next morning the sun lit on a refreshed Prince. He had taken his coffee and was shaving in front of the mirror in a red and black flowered dressing-gown. Bendicò was leaning a heavy head on one of his slippers. As he shaved his right cheek he noticed in the mirror a face behind his own, the face of a young man, thin and elegant with a shy, quizzical look. He did not turn round and went on shaving. 'Well, Tancredi, where were you last night?'

'Good morning, Nuncle. Where was I? Oh, just out with friends. An innocent night. Not like a certain person I know who went down to Palermo for some fun!'

The Prince concentrated on shaving the difficult bit between lips and chin. His nephew's slightly nasal voice had such a youthful zest that it was impossible to be angry; but he might allow himself a touch of surprise. He turned and with his towel under his chin looked his nephew up and down. The young man was in shooting kit, a long tight jacket, high leggings. 'And who was this person, may I ask?'

'Yourself, Nuncle, yourself. I saw you with my own eyes, at the Villa Airoldi block-post, as you were talking to the sergeant. A fine thing at your age! With a priest too! Old rips!'

Really this was a little too insolent. Tancredi thought he could allow himself anything. Dark blue eyes, the eyes of his mother, his own eyes, gazed laughingly at him through half-closed lids. The Prince was offended; the boy didn't know where to stop; but he could not bring himself to reprove him: and anyway he was quite right. 'Why are you dressed up like that, though? What's on? A fancy-dress ball in the morning?'

The youth went serious; his triangular face took on an unexpectedly manly look. 'I'm leaving, Uncle, leaving in an hour. I came to say good-bye.'

Poor Salina felt his heart tighten. 'A duel?' 'A big duel, uncle. A duel with Francis-by-the-Grace-of-God. . . . I'm off into the hills at Ficuzza; don't tell a soul, specially Paolo. Great things are in the offing and I don't want to stay at home. Anyway I'd be arrested at once if I did.'

The Prince had one of his visions: a savage guerrilla skirmish, shots in the woods, and Tancredi, his Tancredi, lying on the ground with his guts hanging out like that poor soldier. 'You're mad, my boy, to go with those people! They're all *mafia* men, all crooks. A Falconeri should be with us, for the king.'

The eyes began smiling again. 'For the King, yes, of course. But which King?' The lad had one of those sudden

serious moods which made him so mysterious and so endearing. 'Unless we ourselves take a hand now, they'll foist
a republic on us. If we want things to stay as they are,
things will have to change. D'you understand?' Rather
moved, he embraced his uncle. 'Well, good-bye for now.
I'll be back with the tricolour.' The rhetoric of those friends
of his had touched Tancredi a little too; and yet, no, there
was a tone in that nasal voice which undercut the em-
phasis.

What a boy! Talking rubbish and contradicting it at the
same time. And all that Paolo of his had on his mind probably at that moment was Guiscard's digestion! This was
his real son! The Prince jumped up, pulled the towel from
his neck and rummaged in a drawer. 'Tancredi, Tancredi,
wait!' He ran after his nephew, slipped a roll of gold pieces
into his pocket, and squeezed his shoulder.

The other laughed. 'You're subsidising the Revolution
now! Thank you, Nuncle, see you soon; and my respects to
my aunt.' And off he rushed down the stairs.

Bendicò was called from following his friend with joyous
barks through the Villa, the Prince's shave was over, his
face washed. The valet came to help him into shoes and
clothes. 'The tricolour! Tricolour indeed! They fill their
mouths with these words, the scamps. What's it got, that
geometric emblem, that aping of the French, compared to
our white banner with its golden lily in the centre? What
hope can those clashing colours bring 'em?' It was now the
moment for the monumental black satin cravat to be wound
round his neck : a difficult operation during which political
worries were best suspended. One turn, two turns, three
turns. The big delicate hands smoothed out the folds,
settled the overlaps, pinned into the silk the little head of
Medusa with ruby eyes. 'A clean waistcoat. Can't you see
this one's dirty?' The valet stood up on tiptoe to help
him into a frockcoat of brown cloth; he proffered a
handkerchief with three drops of bergamot. Keys, watch
and chain, money, the Prince put in a pocket himself. Then
he glanced in a mirror; no doubt about it, he was still
a fine-looking man. 'Old play-boy indeed! A bad joke,

that one of Tancredi's! I'd like to see him at my age,
all skin and bone as he is!'

His vigorous steps made the windows tinkle in the
rooms he crossed. The house was calm, luminous, ornate;
above all it was his own. On his way downstairs he suddenly understood that remark of Tancredi 'if we want
things to stay as they are . . .' Tancredi would go a long
way : he'd always thought so.

The estate office was still empty, lit silently by the sun
through closed shutters. Although the scene of more frivolity
than anywhere else in the villa, its appearance was of calm
austerity. On white-washed walls, reflected in wax-polished
tiles, hung enormous pictures representing the various Salina
estates; there, in bright colours contrasting with the gold
and black frame, was Salina, the island of the twin mountains, surrounded by a sea of white-flecked waves on which
pranced beflagged galleons; Querceta, its low houses
grouped round the rustic church on which were converging
groups of bluish-coloured pilgrims; Ragattisi tucked under
mountain gorges : Argivocale, tiny in contrast to the vast
plains of corn dotted with hard-working peasants; Donnafugata with its baroque palace, goal of coaches in scarlet
and green and gilt, loaded with women, wine and violins;
and many others, all protected by a taut reassuring sky
and by the Leopard grinning between long whiskers. Each
picture was jocund—each illustrating the enlightened rule,
direct or delegated, of the House of Salina. Ingenuous
masterpieces of rustic art from the previous century;
useless though at showing boundaries, or detailing tenures
or tenancies; such matters remained obscure. The wealth
of centuries had been transmuted into ornament, luxury,
pleasure; no more; the abolition of feudal rights had
swept away duties with privileges; wealth, like old wine,
had let the dregs of greed, even of care and prudence, fall
to the bottom of the barrel, preserving only verve and
colour. And thus eventually it cancelled itself out; this
wealth which had achieved its own object was now com-
posed only of essential oils—and like essential oils soon

evaporated. Already some of the estates which looked so gay
in those pictures had taken wing, leaving behind only
bright-coloured paintings and names. Others seemed like
those September swallows which though still present are
already grouped stridently on trees, ready for departure.
But there were so many; endless, they seemed.

In spite of this the sensation felt by the Prince on
entering his own office was, as always, an unpleasant one.
In the centre of the room towered a huge desk, with dozens
of drawers, niches, sockets, hollows and folding shelves;
its mass of yellow wood and black inlay was carved and
decorated like a stage set, full of unexpected, uneven
surfaces, of secret drawers which no one knew now how to
work except thieves. It was covered with papers and,
although the Prince had taken care that most of these
referred to the starry regions of astronomy, there were quite
enough of others to fill his princely heart with dismay.
Suddenly he was reminded of King Ferdinand's desk at
Caserta, also covered with papers needing decisions by
which the King illuded himself to be influencing the
course of fate, actually flowing on its own in another
valley.

Salina thought of a medicine recently discovered in the
United States of America which could prevent suffering
even during the most serious operations and produce
serenity amid disaster. Morphia was the name given to this
crude substitute for the stoicism of the ancients and for
Christian fortitude. With the late King, poor man, phantom
administration had taken the place of morphia; he, Salina,
had a more refined recipe : astronomy. And thrusting away
the memory of lost Ragattisi and precarious Argivocale,
he plunged into reading the latest number of the *Journal
des Savants*. '*Les dernières observations de l'Observatoire
de Greenwich présentent un intérêt tout particulier . . .*'

But he was soon exiled from these stellar realms. In
came Don Ciccio Ferrara, the accountant. He was a
scraggy little man who hid the deluded and rapacious mind
of a Liberal behind reassuring spectacles and immaculate
cravats. That morning he looked brisker than usual;

obviously the same news which had depressed Father Pirrone had acted as a tonic on him. 'Sad times, Excellency,' he said after the usual ritual greetings. 'Big troubles ahead, but after a bit of bother and a shot or two things will turn out for the best : then glorious new days will dawn for this Sicily of ours; if it weren't that so many fine lads are sure to get killed, we should be really pleased.'

The Prince grunted and expressed no opinion. 'Don Ciccio,' he said then, 'the Querceta rents need looking into : we haven't had a thing from them for two years.'

'The books are ready, Your Excellency.' It was the magic phrase. 'I only have to write to Don Angela Maza to send out collectors : I will prepare the letter for your signature this very day.'

He went to turn over the huge register. In them, with two years' delay, were inscribed in minute writing all the Salina accounts, except for the really important ones. When he was alone again the Prince waited a little before soaring back through the clouds. He felt irritated not so much by the events themselves as by the stupidity of Don Ciccio, whom he sensed at once to represent the class which would now be gaining power. 'What the fellow says is the very contrary of the truth. Regretting the fine lads who're sure to die ! there'll be very few of those, if I'm any judge of the two adversaries; not a single casualty more than is strictly necessary for a victory bulletin, whether compiled at Naples or Turin. But he does believe in "glorious new days for this Sicily of ours" as he puts it; these have been promised us on every single one of the thousand invasions we've had, by Nicias onwards, and they've never come. And why should they come, anyway? What will happen next? Oh, well. Just negotiations punctuated by a little harmless shooting, then all will be the same though all will be changed.' Into his mind had come Tancredi's ambiguous words, which he now found himself really understanding. Reassured, he ceased turning over the pages of the scientific review and looked up at the scorched slopes of Monte Pellegrino, scarred like the face of misery by eternal ravines.

Soon afterwards appeared Russo, whom the Prince found the most significant of his dependants. Clever, dressed rather smartly in a striped velvet jacket, with greedy eyes below a remorseless forehead, the Prince found him a perfect specimen of a class on its way up. He was obsequious too, and even sincerely friendly in a way, for his cheating was done in the certainty of exercising a right. 'I can imagine how Your Excellency must be worried by Signorino Tancredi's departure; but he won't be away long, I'm sure, and all will end well.' Again the Prince found himself facing one of the enigmas of Sicily; in this secret island, where houses are barred and peasants refuse to admit they even know the way to their own village in clear view on a hillock within a few minutes' walk, here, in spite of the ostentatious show of mystery, reserve is a myth.

He signed to Russo to sit down and stared him in the eyes. 'Pietro, let's talk to each other man to man. You're involved in all this too, aren't you?' No, came the answer, not actually; he had a family and such risks were for young men like Signorino Tancredi. 'I'd never hide anything from Your Excellency, who's like a father to me.' (Yet three months before he had hidden in his cellar three hundred baskets of lemons belonging to the Prince, and he knew that the Prince knew.) 'But I must say that my heart is with them, those bold lads.' He got up to let in Bendicò, who was making the door shake under his friendly impetus. Then he sat down again. 'Your Excellency knows we can stand no more; searches, questions, nagging about every little thing, a police-spy at every corner of the street; an honest man can't even look after his own affairs. Afterwards, though, we'll have liberty, security, lighter taxes, ease, trade. Everything will be better; the only ones to lose will be the priests. But the Lord protects poor folk like me, not them.'

The Prince smiled. He knew that he, Russo, was at that moment trying through intermediaries to buy the estate of Argivocale. 'There will be a day or two of shooting and trouble, but Villa Salina will be safe as a rock; Your

Excellency is our father, I have many friends here. The Piedmontese will come cap in hand to pay Your Excellencies their respects. And then you are also the uncle, the guardian of Don Tancredi!'

The Prince felt humiliated, reduced to the rank of one protected by Russo's friends; his only merit, as far as he could see, was being uncle to that urchin Tancredi. 'In a week's time I'll find my life's only safe because I keep Bendicò.' He squeezed one of the dog's ears so hard that the poor creature whined, honoured doubtless but in pain.

Shortly afterwards a remark of Russo's relieved the Prince. 'Everything will be better, believe me, Excellency. Honest and able men will have a chance to get ahead, that's all. The rest will be as it was before.' All that these people, these petty local Liberals wanted, was to find ways of making more money themselves. No more. The swallows would take wing a little sooner, that was all. Anyway there were still plenty in the nest.

'You may be right. Who knows?' Now he had penetrated all the hidden meanings; the enigmatic words of Tancredi, the rhetorical ones of Ferrara, the false but revealing ones of Russo, had yielded their reassuring secret. Much would happen, but all would be play-acting; a noisy, romantic play with a few spots of blood on the comic costumes. This was a country of arrangements, with none of that frenzy of the French; and anyway, had anything really serious happened in France, except for June of '48? He felt like saying to Russo, but his innate courtesy held him back, 'I understand now; you don't want to destroy us, who are your "fathers." You just want to take our places. Gently, nicely, maybe even putting a few thousand ducats in our pockets. And what then? Your nephew, my dear Russo, will sincerely believe himself a baron; maybe you, because of your name, will become descendant of a grand duke of Muscovy instead of some red-skinned peasant, which is what that name of yours means. And long before that your daughter will have married one of us, perhaps Tancredi himself, with his blue eyes and his willowy hands.

She's good-looking, anyway, and once she's learned to wash
. . . For all will be the same, just as it is now : except for
an imperceptible change round of classes. My Court
Chamberlain's gilt keys, my cherry-coloured cordon of St.
Januarius will stay in a drawer and end up in some glass
case of Paolo's son. But the Salina will remain the Salina;
they may even get some sort of compensation; a seat in
the Sardinian Senate, that pistachio ribbon of St. Maurice.
Both have tassels, after all.'

He got up. 'Pietro, talk to your friends, will you? There
are girls here. They mustn't be alarmed.'

'I felt that, Excellency, and have already spoken of it—
Villa Salina will be quiet as a convent,' and he smiled with
amiable irony.

Don Fabrizio went out followed by Bendicò; he wanted
to go up and see Father Pirrone, but the dog's yearning
look forced him out into the garden; for Bendicò had
thrilling memories of the fine work he'd put in the night
before, and wanted to finish it off like a good artist. The
garden was even more odorous than the day before, and
under the morning sun the gold of the acacia tree clashed
less. 'What about our King and Queen, though, what about
them? And what about the principle of legitimacy?' The
thought disturbed him a moment, he could not avoid it. For
a second he felt like Màlvica. Those Ferdinands, those
Frances that had been so despised, seemed for a moment like
elder brothers, trusting, just, affectionate, true kings. But the
defence forces of his inner calm always on the alert in the
Prince were already hurrying to his aid, with the musketry
of law, the artillery of history. 'What about France? Isn't
Napoleon III illegitimate? And aren't the French quite
happy under that enlightened Emperor, who will surely lead
them to the highest of destinies? Anyway, let's face it. Was
our Charles III so definitely within his right? Was his
Battle of Bitonto so unlike that of Bisacquino or Corleone
or any of these battles in which the Piedmontese are now
sweeping our troops before them? One of those battles
fought so that all should remain as it was? And anyway,
even Jupiter was not legitimate King of Olympus.'

At this, of course, Jupiter's *coup d'état* against Saturn was bound to bring his mind back to the stars.

Leaving Bendicò panting from his own dynamism, he climbed the stairs again, crossed rooms in which his daughters sat chatting to friends from the Holy Redeemer (at his passage the silken skirts rustled as the girls rose), went up a long ladder and came into the bright blue light of the observatory. Father Pirrone, with the serene air of a priest who has said Mass and drunk black coffee with Monreale biscuits, was sitting immersed in algebraical formulae. The two telescopes and three lenses were lying there quietly, dazed by the sun, with black pads over the eyepieces, like well-trained animals who knew their meal was only given them at night.

The sight of the Prince drew the priest from his calculations and reminded him of his humiliation of the night before. He got up, and then, as he bowed politely, found himself saying, 'Is Your Excellency coming to confession?' The Prince, whose sleep that night and conversations that morning had driven the episode of the previous night from his mind, looked amazed. 'Confession? It's not Saturday.' Then he remembered and smiled, 'Really, Father, there wouldn't even be need, would there? You know it all already.'

This insistence on his enforced complicity irritated the Jesuit. 'Excellency, the efficacy of confession not only consists in telling our sins, but in being sorry for them. And until you do so and show me you do so, you will remain in mortal sin, whether I know what your sins are or not.' He blew a meticulous whiff at a bit of fluff on his sleeve and plunged back into his abstractions.

Such was the calm produced in the Prince's mind by the political discoveries of that morning that he smiled at what would at other times have seemed to him gross impertinence. He opened one of the windows of the little tower. The countryside spread below in all its beauty. Under the leaven of the strong sun everything seemed weightless; the sea in the background was a dash of pure colour, the mountains which had seemed so alarmingly full of hidden men during the night now looked like masses of vapour on the point of dissolving, and grim Palermo itself lay crouching quietly around its monasteries like a flock of sheep around their shepherds. Even the foreign warships anchored in the harbour in case of trouble spread no sense of fear in the majestic calm. The sun, still far from its blazing zenith on that morning of the 13th of May, was showing itself the true ruler of Sicily; the crude brash sun, the dragging sun, which annulled every will, kept all things in servile immobility, cradled in violence and arbitrary dreams.

'It'll take any number of Victor Emmanuels to change this magic potion for ever being poured for us.'

Father Pirrone had got up, adjusted his sash and moved towards the Prince with a hand out. 'Excellency, I was too brusque. Let me not trespass on your kindness, but do please listen and come to confession.'

The ice was broken. And the Prince could tell Father Pirrone of his own political intuitions. But the Jesuit was far from sharing his relief and even became acid again. 'Briefly, then, you nobles will come to an agreement with the Liberals, and yes, even with the Masons, at our expense, at the expense of the Church. Then of course, our property, which is the patrimony of the poor, will be seized and carved up among the most brazen of their leaders; and who will then feed all the destitute sustained and guided by the Church to-day?' The Prince was silent. 'How will those desperate masses be placated? I'll tell you at once, Excellency. They will be flung first a portion, then another portion and eventually all the rest of your estates. And so God will have done His justice, even by means of the Masons. Our Lord healed the blind in body; but what will be the fate of the blind in spirit?'

The unhappy priest was breathing hard; sincere horror at the foreseen dispersal of Church property was linked with regret at his having lost control of himself again, with fear of offending the Prince, whom he genuinely liked and whose blustering rages as well as disinterested kindness he knew well. So he sat down warily, glancing every now and again at Don Fabrizio, who had taken up a little brush and was cleaning the knobs of a telescope, apparently absorbed. A little later he got up and cleaned his hands thoroughly with a rag; his face was quite expressionless, his light eyes seemed intent only on finding any remaining stain of oil in the cuticles of his nails. Down below, around the villa, all was luminous and grandiose silence, emphasised rather than disturbed by the distant barking of Bendicò baiting the gardener's dog at the far end of the lemon-grove, and by the dull rhythmic beat from the kitchen of a cook's knife chopping meat for the approaching meal. The sun had absorbed the turbulence of men as well as the harshness of earth. The Prince moved towards the priest's table, sat down and began drawing pointed little Bourbon lilies with a carefully sharpened pencil which the Jesuit had left behind in his anger. He looked serious but so serene that Father Pirrone no longer felt on tenterhooks.

'We're not blind, my dear Father, we're just human beings. We live in a changing reality to which we try to adapt ourselves like seaweed bending under the pressure of water. Holy Church has been granted an explicit promise of immortality; we, as a social class, have not. Any palliative which may give us another hundred years of life is like eternity to us. We may worry about our children and perhaps our grandchildren; but beyond what we can hope to stroke with these hands of ours we have no obligations. I cannot worry myself about what will happen to any possible descendants in the year 1960. The Church, yes, She must worry for She is destined not to die. Solace is implicit in Her desperation. Don't you think that if now or in the future She could save herself by sacrificing us She wouldn't do so? Of course She would, and rightly.'

Father Pirrone was so pleased at not having offended the Prince that he did not take offence either. Of course that word 'desperation' applied to the Church was quite inadmissible, but long habit as confessor had made him capable of appreciating Don Fabrizio's disillusioned mood. He must not let the other triumph, though. 'Now, Excellency, you have a couple of sins to confess to me on Saturday; one of the flesh yesterday, one of the spirit to-day. Remember!'

Both soothed, they began discussing a report which they would soon be sending to a foreign observatory, at Arcetri. Supported, guided, it seemed, by calculations which were invisible at that hour yet ever present, the stars cleft the ether in those exact trajectories of theirs. The comets would be appearing as usual, punctual to the fraction of a second, in sight of whoever was observing them. They were not messengers of catastrophe as Stella thought; on the contrary, their appearance at the time foreseen was a triumph of the human mind's capacity to project itself and to participate in the sublime routine of the skies. 'Let's leave the Bendicòs down there running after rustic prey, and the cooks' knives chopping the flesh of innocent beasts. From up in this observatory the bluster of the one and the blood on the other merge into tranquil harmony. The real problem is how to go on living this life of the spirit in its most sublimated moments, those moments that are most like death.'

So reasoned the Prince, forgetting his own recurrent whims, his own cavortings of the night before. During those moments of abstraction he seemed more intimately absolved, in the sense of being linked anew with the universe, than by any blessing of Father Pirrone. For half an hour that morning the gods of the ceilings and the monkeys on the walls were again put to silence. But in the drawing-room no one noticed.

When the bell for luncheon called them downstairs, both had regained their serenity, due to understanding the political scene and to setting that understanding aside. An atmosphere of unusual relaxation had spread over the house. The midday meal was the chief one of the day, and went, God be thanked, quite smoothly. This in spite of one of the ringlets framing the face of the twenty-year-old Carolina, the eldest daughter, dropping into her soup plate because apparently of an ill-secured pin. Another day the incident might have had dreadful consequences, but now it only heightened the gaiety; and when her brother, sitting next to her, took the lock of hair and pinned it on his neckerchief where it hung like a scapular, even the Prince allowed himself a smile. Tancredi's departure, destination and reasons were now known to all, and everyone talked of them, except Paolo who went on eating in silence. No one was really worrying about him, in fact, but the Prince, who showed no signs of the anxiety he still felt deep down, and Concetta who was the only one with a shadow on her pretty forehead. 'The girl must have her eye on the young scamp. They'd make a fine couple. But I fear Tancredi will have to aim higher, by which of course I mean lower.'

To-day, as political calm had cleared the mists generally veiling it, the Prince's fundamental good nature showed on the surface. To reassure his daughter he began explaining what useless muskets the royal army had; the barrels of those enormous pieces had no rifling, he said, so bullets coming from them would have very little penetration; technical comments thought up on the spur of the moment, understood by few and convincing none but consoling all, including Concetta, as they managed to transform war into a neat little diagram of fire-trajectories from the very squalid chaos that it really was.

At the end of the meal appeared a rum jelly. This was the Prince's favourite pudding, and the Princess had been careful to order it early that morning in gratitude for favours granted. It was rather threatening at first sight, shaped like a tower with bastions and battlements and smooth slippery walls impossible to scale, garrisoned by red and green cherries and pistachio nuts; but into its transparent and quivering flanks a spoon plunged with astounding ease. By the time the amber-coloured fortress reached Francesco Paolo, the sixteen-year-old son who was served last, it consisted only of shattered walls and hunks of wobbly rubble. Exhilarated by the aroma of rum and the delicate flavour of the multi-coloured garrison, the Prince enjoyed watching the rapid demolishing

of the fortress beneath the assault of his family's appetite.
One of his glasses was still half-full of Marsala. He raised it,
glanced round the family, gazed for a second into Concetta's
blue eyes, then said : 'To the health of our Tancredi.' He
drained his wine in a single gulp. The initials F.D., which
before had stood out clearly on the golden colour of the
full glass, were no longer visible.

In the estate office, to which he returned after luncheon,
the sunlight was oblique, and the pictures of his estates,
now shadowed, sent no messages of reproof. 'Blessings on
Your Excellency,' muttered Pastorello and Lo Nigro, the
two tenants of Ragattisi who had brought the portion of
their rent they paid in kind. They were standing very
straight with stunned-looking eyes in faces carefully shaven
and burnt dark by sun. They gave out a smell of flocks
and herds. The Prince talked to them cordially in his very
stylised dialect, inquired about their families, the state
of their livestock, the outlook for the crops. Then he asked,
'Have you brought anything?' And when the two answered
yes, that it was in the room next door, the Prince felt a
twinge of shame as he realised that the interview was a
repetition of his own audiences with King Ferdinand.
'Wait five minutes and Ferrara will give you the receipts.'
He put into their hands a couple of ducats each, worth
more, probably, than what they had brought. 'Drink my
health, will you?' and then went and looked at their
produce : on the ground were four *caciocavallo* cheeses,
each weighing roughly ten kilos; he gave them a careless
glance; he loathed that particular cheese; there were
six baby lambs, the last of the year's litter, with their
heads lolling pathetically above the big gash through which
their life-blood had flowed a few hours before. Their bellies
had been slashed open too, and iridescent intestines hung
out. 'May God receive his soul,' he thought, remembering
the gutted soldier of a month before. Four pairs of chickens
tied by the claws were twisting in terror under Bendicò's
restless snout. 'Another example of pointless alarm,' he

thought, 'the dog is no danger to them at all; he wouldn't even touch one of their bones as it would give him a belly-ache.'

All this blood and panic revolted him, however. 'Pastorello, take the chickens into the coop, will you, as there's no need of them in the larder; and another time take the baby lambs straight into the kitchen, will you; they make a mess here. And you, Lo Nigro, go and tell Salvatore to come and clean up and take away the cheeses. And open the window to let out the smell.'

Then Ferrara came and made out the receipts.

When the Prince went upstairs again, he found Paolo, his heir, the Duke of Querceta, waiting for him in his study on the red sofa where he proposed to take his siesta. The youth had screwed up all his courage to talk to him. Short, slim, olive-skinned, he seemed older than the Prince himself. 'I wanted to ask you, papa, how we're to behave with Tancredi when we next meet him.'

The Prince understood at once and felt a twinge of annoyance. 'What d'you mean? Has anything changed?'

'But papa, you can't possibly approve; he's gone to join those swine who're making trouble all over Sicily; things like that just aren't done.'

Personal jealousy, a bigot's resentment of his agnostic cousin, a dullard's at the other's zest, had taken political guise. The Prince was so indignant that he did not even ask his son to sit down. 'Better to make a fool of oneself than spend all day staring at horses' dung! I'm even fonder of Tancredi than I was before. And anyway what he's doing isn't as silly as all that. If in the future you're able to go on putting Duke of Querceta on your cards, and if you inherit any money when I'm gone, you will owe it to Tancredi and to others like him. Out with you now, and don't mention the subject to me again! I'm the only one who gives orders here.' Then he became kindlier and substituted irony for anger. 'Be off now, son, as I want to have a snooze. Go and talk politics with Guiscard, you'll understand each other.'

And as a shaken Paolo closed the door behind him, the Prince took off his frock-coat and boots, made the sofa creak under his weight and slid calmly off to sleep.

When he awoke, his valet came in with a newspaper and a letter on a tray. They had been sent up from Palermo by his brother-in-law Màlvica, brought by a mounted groom a short while before. Still a little dazed from his afternoon nap, the Prince opened the letter. 'My dear Fabrizio, I am writing to you in a state of utter collapse. Such dreadful news in the paper. The Piedmontese have landed. We are all lost. To-night I and my whole family will take refuge on a British man-o'-war. You will want to do the same, I am sure; if you wish I can reserve a berth or two for you. May God save our beloved King! As always, Ciccio.'

He folded up the letter, put it in his pocket and began laughing out loud. That ass Màlvica! He'd always been a rabbit. Not understanding a thing, and now panic-struck. Abandoning his palace to the mercy of servants; this time he'd really find it empty on his return. 'That reminds me, Paolo must go and stay down at Palermo; a house empty at a moment like this means a house lost. I'll tell him at dinner.'

He opened the newspaper. 'On the 11th of May an act of flagrant piracy culminated in the landing of armed men at Marsala. The latest reports say that the band numbers about eight hundred, and is commanded by Garibaldi. When these brigands set foot on land they were very careful to avoid any encounter with the royal troops, and moved off, as far as can be ascertained, in the direction of Castelvetrano, threatening peaceful citizens and spreading rapine and devastation, etc., etc. . . .'

The name of Garibaldi disturbed him a little. That adventurer all hair and beard was a pure Mazzinian. He had caused a lot of trouble already. 'But if that *Galantuomo* King of his has let him come down here it means they're sure of him. They'll curb him!'

Reassured, he combed his hair and had his shoes and

frock-coat put on again. He thrust the newspaper into a drawer. It was almost time for Rosary, but the drawing-room was still empty. He sat down on a sofa, and as he waited noticed how the Vulcan on the ceiling was rather like the lithographs of Garibaldi he had seen in Turin. He smiled. 'Cuckold!'

The family was gathering. Silken skirts rustled. The youngest were still joking together. Behind the door could be heard the usual echo of controversy between servants and Bendicò determined to take part.

A ray of sunshine full of dust specks lit up the malicious monkeys.

He knelt down. '*Salve Regina, Mater misericordiae.*'

2

DONNAFUGATA

'THE TREES! The trees!'

This shout from the leading carriage eddied back along the following four, almost invisible in clouds of white dust; and at every window perspiring faces expressed tired gratification.

The trees were only three, in truth, and eucalyptus at that, scruffiest of Mother Nature's children. But they were also the first seen by the Salina family since leaving Bisacquino at six that morning. It was now eleven, and for the last five hours all they had set eyes on were bare hillsides flaming yellow under the sun. Trots over level ground had alternated briefly with long slow trudges uphill and then careful shuffles down; both trudge and trot merging, anyway, into the constant jingle of harness bells, imperceptible now to the dazed senses except as sound equivalent of the blazing landscape. They had passed through crazed-looking villages washed in palest blue; crossed dry beds of torrents over fantastic bridges; skirted sheer precipices which no sage and broom could temper. Never a tree, never a drop of water; just sun and dust. Inside the carriages, tight shut against that sun and dust, the temperature must have been well over 120 degrees. Those desiccated trees yearning away under bleached sky bore many a message; that they were now within a couple of hours from their journey's end; that they were entering the family estates; that they could lunch, and perhaps even wash their faces in the verminous waters of the well.

Ten minutes later they reached the farm buildings of

Rampinzeri; a huge pile, only used one month in the year by labourers, mules and cattle gathered there for the harvest. Over the great solid yet staved-in door a stone Leopard pranced in spite of legs broken off by flung stones; next to the main farm building a deep well, watched over by those eucalyptuses, mutely offered various services : as swimming pool, drinking trough, prison or cemetery. It slaked thirst, spread typhus, guarded the kidnapped and hid the corpses both of animals and men till they were reduced to the smoothest of anonymous skeletons.

The whole Salina family alighted from their various carriages. The Prince cheered by the thought of soon reaching his beloved Donnafugata, the Princess irritated and yet inert, part restored, however, by her husband's serenity; tired girls; boys excited by novelty and untamed by the heat; Mademoiselle Dombreuil, the French governess, utterly exhausted, remembering years spent in Algeria with the family of Marshal Bugeaud, moaning '*Mon Dieu, mon Dieu, c'est pire qu'en Afrique!*' and mopping at her turned-up nose; Father Pirrone, whose breviary-reading had lulled him into a sleep which had shortened the whole trip and made him the spryest of the party; a maid and two lackeys, city folk worried by the unusual aspect of the countryside; and Bendicò, who had rushed out of the last carriage and was baying at the funereal suggestions of rooks swirling low in the light.

All were white with dust to the eyebrows, lips or pigtails; whitish puffs arose around those who had reached the stopping-place and were dusting each other down.

Amid this dirt Tancredi's elegant spruceness stood out all the more. He had travelled on horseback and, reaching the farm half an hour before the carriages, had time to shake off dust, brush up and change his white cravat. While drawing some water from that well of many uses he had glanced for a second into the mirror of the bucket and found himself in good order, with the black patch over his right eye now more reminiscent than protective of a wound received three months before in the fighting at Palermo; with that other dark blue eye which seemed to have assumed the task of expressing enough sly gaiety for its mate in temporary eclipse; and with, above his cravat, a scarlet thread alluding discreetly to the red shirt he had once worn. He helped the Princess to alight, dusted the Prince's top hat with his sleeve, distributed sweets to his girl cousins and quips to the boys, almost genuflected before the Jesuit, returned the passionate hugs of Bendicò, consoled Mademoiselle Dombreuil, laughed at all, enchanted all.

The coachmen were walking the horses slowly round to freshen them up before watering, the lackeys laying tablecloths out on straw left over from the threshing, in the oblong of shade from the building. Luncheon began near the accommodating well. All round quivered the funereal countryside, yellow with stubble, black with burnt patches; the lament of cicadas filled the sky. It was like a death-rattle from parched Sicily at the end of August vainly awaiting rain.

An hour later they were all on the road again, refreshed. Although the horses were tired and going slower than ever, the last part of the journey seemed short; the landscape, no longer unknown, had lost its more sinister aspects. They began recognising places they knew well, arid goals of past excursions and picnics in other years—the Dragonara ravine, the Misilbesi cross-roads; soon they would reach the shrine of Our Lady of Graces, turning-point of their longest walks from Donnafugata. The Princess had dozed off, the Prince, alone with her in the wide carriage, was beaming.

Never had he been so glad to be going to spend three months at Donnafugata as he was now, in that late August of 1860. Not only because at Donnafugata he loved the house, the people, the sense of feudal ownership still surviving there, but also because, unlike other times, he felt no regret for his peaceful evenings in the observatory, his occasional visits to Mariannina. The truth was he had found the spectacle offered by Palermo in the last three months rather nauseating. He would have liked to have had the fun of being the only one to understand the situation and accept

that red-shirted 'bogey-man' Garibaldi; but he had to admit
that second-sight was not a Salina monopoly. Everyone in
Palermo seemed pleased; everyone except a mere handful of
grumblers : his brother-in-law Màlvica, who had got himself
arrested by Garibaldi's police and spent ten days in prison;
his son Paolo, just as discontented but slightly more prudent,
and now left behind at Palermo deep in some silly plot or
other. Everyone else was making a great show of joy;
wearing tricolour cockades on lapels, marching about in
processions from morning till night, and above all talking,
haranguing, declaiming; and if in the very first days of the
occupation all this was given some sense of purpose by
the acclamations greeting the few wounded passing through
the main streets and by the shrieks of Bourbon police 'rats'
being tortured in the side alleys, now that the wounded
had recovered and the surviving 'rats' enrolled in the new
police this hubbub, inevitable though he realised it to be,
began to seem pointless and petty.

But he had to admit that all this was a mere surface
manifestation of ill-breeding; the fundamentals of the
situation, economic and social, were satisfactory, just as
he had foreseen. Don Pietro Russo had kept his promises
and not a shot had been heard near Villa Salina; and
though a whole service of Chinese porcelain had been stolen
from the palace in Palermo, that was merely due to the
idiocy of Paolo, who had had it packed into a couple of
cases which he had then left out in the palace courtyard
during the shelling; a positive invitation for the packers
themselves to cart it off.

The 'Piedmontese' (as the Prince continued to call them
for reassurance, just as others called them 'Garibaldini' in
exaltation or 'Garibaldeschi' in vilification) had paid a call
at the house, if not precisely cap in hand as he had been
told, at least with a hand at the visors of those red caps
of theirs, as floppy and faded as those of any Bourbon
officer.

About the 20th of June, announced twenty-four hours
beforehand by Tancredi, appeared a general in a red tunic
with black froggings. He was followed by an aide-de-camp

and asked most politely for admission in order to admire
the frescoes on the ceilings. In he was ushered without ado,
as there had been sufficient warning to clear from one of
the drawing-rooms a portrait of King Ferdinand II in full
regalia and substitute for it a neutral *Pool of Bethsaida*; an
operation combining advantages political and aesthetic.

The general was a quick-witted Tuscan of about thirty,
talkative and inclined to show off; he had been well behaved and agreeable, had treated the Prince with all
proper respect and even called him 'Excellency,' in utter
contradiction to one of the Dictator's first decrees; the
aide-de-camp, a new recruit of nineteen, was a Milanese
count, who fascinated the girls with his glittering boots
and his slurred 'r's. With them came Tancredi, promoted,
or rather created, captain on the field of battle; a little
drawn from the pain of his wound he stood there red-shirted
and irresistible, showing an easy intimacy with the victors,
an intimacy demonstrated by a mutual use of the familiar
tu, lavished with childish fervour by the two officers from
the mainland and returned in kind by Tancredi, though
with a faint nasal twang that to the Prince seemed full of
muted irony. While greeting them from heights of imper-
turbable courtesy, the Prince had in fact been much
amused and quite reassured. So much so that three days
later the two 'Piedmontese' had been invited to dinner;
Carolina then had made a fine sight at the piano accom-
panying the singing of the general, who had risked, in
homage to Sicily, Bellini's *'Vi ravviso, o luoghi ameni'* with
Tancredi demurely turning over the pages of the score as
if false notes didn't exist. The young Milanese count,
meanwhile, was leaning over a sofa, chatting away about
orange blossom to Concetta and revealing to her the existence of a writer she had never heard of, Aleardo Aleardi;
she was pretending to listen though worrying really about
the look of her cousin, whom the candlelight on the piano
made even more languid than he was in reality.

It had been an idyllic evening and was followed by
others equally cordial; during one of these the general
was asked to try and obtain an exemption from the order

expelling Jesuits for Father Pirrone, described as very aged and very ill; the general, who had taken a liking to the good priest, pretended to believe in his wretched state and agreed; he talked to political friends, pulled a string or two, and Father Pirrone stayed. Which went to confirm the Prince more than ever in the accuracy of his predictions.

The general was also most helpful about the complicated permits necessary in those troubled times for anyone wanting to move from place to place; and it was largely due to him that the Salina family was able to enjoy its annual sojourn in the country in that year of revolution. The young captain asked for a month's leave and set off with his uncle and aunt. Even apart from permits, the preparations for the Salina family's journey had been lengthy and complicated. Cryptic negotiations had to be conducted in the agent's office with 'persons of influence' from Girgenti, negotiations ending in smiles, handclasps and the tinkle of coin. Thus a second and more useful permit had been obtained; though this was no novelty. Piles of luggage and food had to be collected too, and cooks and servants sent on three days ahead; then there was one of the smaller telescopes to be packed and Paolo persuaded to stay behind in Palermo. After this they were able to move off; the general and the little lieutenant came to wish them all Godspeed and bring them flowers; and as the carriages moved off from Villa Salina two scarlet-covered arms continued to wave for a long time; at a carriage window appeared the Prince's black top hat, but the little hand in black lace mittens which the young count had hoped to see remained in Concetta's lap.

The journey had lasted more than three days and been quite appalling. The roads, the famous Sicilian roads which had cost the Prince of Satriano the Lieutenant-Generalcy, were no more than tracks, all ruts and dust. The first night at Marineo, at the home of a notary and friend, had been more or less bearable, but the second at a little inn at Prizzi had been torture, with three of them to a bed, besieged by repellent local fauna. The third was at Bisacquino; no bugs there but to make up for that the Prince had found thirteen flies in his glass of *granita*, while a strong smell of excrement drifted in from the street and the privy next door, and all this had caused him most unpleasant dreams; waking at very early dawn amid all that sweat and stink he had found himself comparing this ghastly journey with his own life, which had first moved over smiling level ground, then clambered up rocky mountains, slid over threatening passes, to emerge eventually into a landscape of interminable undulations, all the same colour, all bare as despair. These early morning fantasies were the very worst that could happen to a man of middle age; and although the Prince knew that they would vanish with the day's activities he suffered acutely all the same, as he was used enough to them by now to realise that deep inside him they left a sediment of sorrow which, accumulating day by day, would in the end be the real cause of his death.

With the rising of the sun those monsters had gone back to their lairs in his unconscious; nearby now was Donnafugata and his palace, with its many-jetted fountains, its memories of saintly forebears, the sense it gave him of everlasting childhood. Even the people there were pleasant, simple and devoted. At this point a thought occurred : would they be just as devoted as before, after recent events? 'We'll soon see.'

Now at last they were nearly there. Tancredi's mischievous face appeared at the carriage window-sill. 'Uncle, Aunt, get ready, in five minutes we'll be there.' Tancredi was too tactful to precede the Prince into the town. He slowed his horse to a walk and proceeded in silence beside the leading carriage.

Beyond the short bridge leading into the town were waiting the authorities, surrounded by a few dozen peasants. As the carriages moved on to the bridge the municipal band struck up with frenzied enthusiasm *Noi siamo zingarelle* from 'Traviata,' the first odd and endearing greeting by Donnafugata to its Prince in recent years; after this at a warning by some urchin on the look-out the bells of the

Mother Church and of the Convent of the Holy Ghost filled the air with festive sound.

'Thanks be to God, everything seems as usual,' thought the Prince as he climbed out of his carriage. There was Don Calogero Sedàra the mayor, with a tricolour sash bright and new as his job tight around his waist; Monsignor Trottolino, the arch-priest, with his big red face; Don Ciccio Ginestra, the notary, all braid and feathers, dressed up as captain of the National Guard; there was Don Totò Giambono, the doctor, and there was little Nunzia Giarritta, who offered the Princess a rather messy bunch of flowers, picked half an hour before in the palace gardens. There was Ciccio Tumeo, the Cathedral organist, who was not strictly speaking of sufficient standing to be there with the authorities but had come along all the same as friend and hunting companion of the Prince, and had had the excellent notion of bringing along with him, for the Prince's pleasure, his red pointer bitch Teresina, with two little brown spots above its eyes; a daring rewarded with a special smile from Don Fabrizio.

The latter was in high good humour and sincerely amiable; he and his wife had alighted to express their thanks, and against the tempestuous music of Verdi and the crashing of bells embraced the mayor and shook hands with all the others. The crowd of peasants stood there silent, but their motionless eyes emitted a curiosity that was in no way hostile, for the poor of Donnafugata really did have a certain affection for their tolerant lord who so often forgot to ask for their little rents of kind or money; also, used as they were to seeing the be-whiskered Leopard on the palace façade, on the Church front, above the baroque fountains, on the majolica tiles in their houses, they were glad to set eyes now on the real animal in nankeen trousers, distributing friendly shakes of the paw to all, his features amiably wreathed in feline smiles. 'Yes, indeed; everything is the same as before, better, in fact, than before.' Tancredi, too, was the object of great curiosity; though everyone had known him for a long time, now he seemed to them transfigured; no longer did they see him as a mere unconventional youth, but as an aristocratic liberal, companion of Rosolino Pilo, wounded hero of the battle of Palermo. He was swimming in this noisy admiration like a fish in water; these rustic admirers were really rather fun; he talked to them in dialect, joked, laughed at himself and his wounds; but when he said 'General Garibaldi' his voice dropped an octave and he put on the rapt look of a choir-boy before the Monstrance; then to Don Calogero Sedàra, of whom he had vaguely heard as being active during the period of the liberation, he said in booming tones, 'Ah, Don Calogero, Crispi said lots of nice things to me about you.' After which he gave his arm to his cousin Concetta and moved off, leaving everyone abuzz.

The carriages, with servants, children and Bendicò, went on to the palace; but according to ancient usage, before the others set foot in their home they had to hear a *Te Deum* in the Duomo. This was anyway only a few paces off, and they moved there in procession, the new arrivals dusty but imposing, the authorities gleaming but humble. Ahead walked Don Ciccio Ginestra, the prestige of his uniform cleaving a path; he was followed by the Prince giving an arm to the Princess, and looking like a sated and pacified lion; behind them came Tancredi with on his right Concetta, who found this walk towards a church beside her cousin most upsetting and conducive to weepiness: a state of mind in no way alleviated by the dutiful young man's strong pressure on her arm, though its only purpose, alas, was to save her from potholes and ruts. The others followed in disorder. The organist rushed off so as to have time to deposit Teresina at home and be back at his resonant post at the moment of entry into the church. The bells were clanging away ceaselessly, and on the walls of the houses the slogans of 'Viva Garibaldi,' 'Viva King Vittorio,' 'Death to the Bourbon King,' scrawled by an inexpert brush two months before were fading away as if wanting to merge back into the walls. Squibs were exploding all round as they moved up the steps, and as the little procession entered the church Don Ciccio Tumeo, who had arrived panting but in time, broke impetuously into the strains of Verdi's *Amami, Alfredo*.

The nave was packed with curious idlers between its squat columns of red marble; the Salina family sat in the choir, and during the short ceremony Don Fabrizio got up and made an impressive bow to the crowd; meanwhile the Princess was on the verge of swooning from heat and exhaustion; Tancredi, pretending to brush away flies, grazed more than once Concetta's blonde head. All was in order and after a short address by Monsignor Trottolino, they all genuflected to the altar, turned towards the doors and issued into the sun-dazed square.

At the bottom of the steps the authorities took their leave, and the Princess, acting under instructions whispered to her during the ceremony, invited the mayor, the arch-priest and the notary to dine that same evening. The arch-priest was a bachelor by profession and the notary one by vocation, so that for them the question of consorts did not arise; the invitation to the mayor was rather languidly extended to his wife; she was some peasant woman, of great beauty, but considered by her own husband as quite unpresentable in public for a number of reasons; thus no one was surprised at his saying that she was indisposed; but great was the amazement when he added, 'If Your Excellencies will allow I'll bring along my daughter Angelica, who's been talking for the past month of nothing but her longing to be presented to you now that she's grown up.' Consent was, of course, given; and the Prince, who had seen Tumeo peering at him from behind the others' shoulders, called out to him, 'You come too, of course, Don Ciccio, and bring Teresina.' And he added, turning to the others, 'And after dinner, at nine o'clock, we shall be happy to see all our friends.' For a long time Donnafugata commented on these last words. And the Prince, who had found Donnafugata unchanged, was found very much changed himself, for never before would

he have issued so cordial an invitation : and from that
moment, invisibly, began the decline of his prestige.

The Salina palace was next door to the Mother Church.
Its short façade with seven windows on the square gave
no hint of its vast size, which extended three hundred yards
back; the buildings were of different styles, but all harmon-
iously grouped round three great courtyards ending in a
large garden. At the main entrance in the square the
travellers were subjected to new demonstrations of welcome.
Don Onofrio Rotolo, the family's local steward, took no
part in the official greetings at the entry of the town.
Educated under the rigid rule of the Princess Carolina, he
considered the '*vulgus*' as non-existent and the Prince as
resident abroad until the moment when he crossed
the threshold of his own palace. So there he stood, exactly
two steps outside the gates; very small, very old, very
bearded, with a much younger and plumper wife standing
beside him, flanked by lackeys and eight rangers with
golden Leopards on their caps and in their hands eight
shot-guns of uncertain damaging power. 'I am happy to
welcome Your Excellencies to your home. And I beg to
hand back the palace in the exact state in which it was left
to me.'

Don Onofrio Rotolo was one of the rare persons held in
esteem by the Prince, and perhaps the only one who had
never cheated him. His honesty bordered on mania, and
spectacular tales were told of it, such as the glass of *rosolio*
wine once left half-full by the Princess at the moment of
departure, and found a year later in exactly the same place
with its contents evaporated and reduced to a state of sugary
lees, but untouched. 'For it is an infinitesimal part of the
Prince's patrimony and must not be dispersed.'

After a proper exchange of greetings with Don Onofrio
and Donna Maria the Princess, who was on her feet still
only by sheer strength of will, went straight to bed, the
girls and Tancredi hurried off to the tepid shade of the
gardens, while the Prince and his steward went on a tour
of the vast apartments. Everything was in perfect order;

the pictures were clear of dust in their heavy frames, the old gilt bindings emitted discreet gleams, the high sun made the grey marbles glitter round the doorposts. Everything was in the state it had been for the last fifty years. Away from the noisy turbine of civil dissent Don Fabrizio felt refreshed, full of serene confidence, and glanced almost tenderly at Don Onofrio trotting along beside him. 'Don Onofrio, you're like one of those djinns standing guard over treasure, really you are; we owe you a great debt of gratitude.' In an earlier year the sentiment might have been the same but the words themselves would never have come to his lips; Don Onofrio looked at him in gratitude and surprise; 'My duty, Your Excellency, it's just my duty,' and to hide his emotion he scratched the back of his ear with the long nail on the little finger of his left hand.

After this the steward was put to the torture of tea. Don Fabrizio had two cups brought, and with death in his heart Don Onofrio had to swallow one. After this he began to recount the chronicles of Donnafugata : he had renewed the lease for the Aquila land two weeks before, on rather worse terms; he had had to meet heavy expenses for the repairs of the roof in the guest wing; but in the safe, at His Excellency's disposal, was the sum of three thousand two hundred and seventy-five ounces of gold, after paying all expenses, taxes and his own salary.

Then came the private news, all of which turned round the great novelty of the year : the rapid rise to fortune of Don Calogero Sedàra; six months ago a mortgage arranged by the latter with Baron Tumino had fallen in, and he had gained possession of the estate; thus by the loan of a thousand ounces of gold he now owned a property which yielded five hundred ounces a year; in April Don Calogero had also been able to buy, for practically nothing, a certain piece of land which contained a vein of much sought-after stone that he intended to exploit; he had also made some very profitable sales of grain at the period of confusion and famine after the landings. The voice of Don Onofrio filled with rancour. 'I've totted it up roughly on my fingers : Don Calogero's income will very shortly be equal to that

of Your Excellency's here at Donnafugata.' With riches
had also grown political influence. He had become head
of the liberals in the town and also in the districts round;
when the elections were held he was sure to be returned
as deputy to Turin. 'And what airs they give themselves;
not he, who is far too shrewd to do that, but his daughter
who's just got back from college in Florence and goes
around town in a crinoline with velvet ribbons hanging from
her hat.'

The Prince was silent; the daughter, yes, that must be
the Angelica who would be coming to dinner to-night; he
was curious to see this dressed-up shepherdess; it was not
true that nothing had changed: Don Calogero was as
rich as he was! But deep down he had foreseen such
things; they were the price to be paid.

Don Onofrio was disturbed by his master's silence, and
imagined he had put the Prince out by telling him petty
local gossip.

'Excellency, I ordered a bath to be prepared for you, it
should be ready by now.' Don Fabrizio suddenly realised
that he was tired; it was almost three o'clock, and he had
been up and about for nine hours under that torrid sun
and after that ghastly night. He felt his body covered in
dust to the remotest creases. 'Thank you, Don Onofrio,
for thinking of it; and for everything else. We shall meet
to-night at dinner.'

He went up the internal staircase, passed through the
tapestry hall, through the blue, the yellow drawing-rooms;
lowered blinds filtered the light; in his study the Boulle
clock ticked away discreetly. 'What peace, my God, what
peace!' He entered the bathroom: small, whitewashed,
with a rough tiled floor and a hole in the middle to let
the water out. The bath itself was a kind of oval trough,
vast, of enamelled iron, yellow outside and grey in, propped
on four heavy wooden feet. Hanging on a nail was a dressing-gown; fresh linen was laid out on a rush chair; and on
another a suit which still showed creases from packing.
Beside the bath lay a big piece of pink soap, a brush, a

knotted handkerchief containing bran which would emit a sweet scent when soaked, and a huge sponge, one of those sent by the Salina agent. Through the unshaded window beat the savage sun.

He clapped his hands; two lackeys entered, each holding a pair of quivering pails, one of cold, the other of boiling water; they went to and fro a number of times; the trough filled up; he tried the temperature with a hand; it was all right. He ordered the servants out, undressed, got in. Under his huge bulk the water brimmed over a little. He soaped himself, rubbed himself; the warmth did him good, relaxed him. He was almost dozing off when he heard a knock at the door; Mimi, his valet, entered timidly. 'Father Pirrone is asking to see Your Excellency at once. He is waiting outside for Your Excellency to leave the bathroom.' The Prince was surprised; if there had been some accident he had better know at once. 'No, no, let him come in now.'

Don Fabrizio was alarmed by this haste of Father Pirrone; and partly from this and partly from respect for the priestly habit, he hurried to leave the bath expecting to get into his bath-robe before the Jesuit entered; but he did not succeed, and Father Pirrone came in at the very moment when, no longer veiled by soapy water, not yet shrouded by his bath-sheet, he was emerging quite naked, like the Farnese Hercules, and steaming as well, while water flowed in streams from neck, arms, stomach, and legs like the Rhône, the Rhine, the Danube and the Adige crossing and watering Alpine ranges. The sight of the Prince in a state of nature was quite new to Father Pirrone; the Sacrament of Penance had accustomed him to naked souls, but he was far less used to naked bodies; and he who would not have blinked an eyelid at hearing the confession, say, of an incestuous intrigue, found himself flustered by this innocent but vast expanse of naked flesh. He stuttered an excuse and made to back out; but Don Fabrizio, annoyed at not having had time to cover himself, naturally turned his irritation against the priest. 'Now, Father, don't be silly; hand me that bath-robe, will you, and help me to dry, if you don't mind.'

Then suddenly he remembered a discussion they had once had and went on : 'And take my advice, Father, have a bath yourself.' Satisfied at being able to give advice on hygiene to one who so often gave it to him on morals, he felt soothed. With the upper part of the bath-robe in his hands at last he began drying his hair, whiskers and neck, while with the lower end the humiliated Father Pirrone rubbed his feet.

When the peak and slopes of the mountain were dry, the Prince said, 'Now take a seat, Father, and tell me why you're in such a hurry to talk to me.' And as the Jesuit sat down he began some more intimate moppings on his own.

'Well, Excellency, I've been given a most delicate commission. One who is very dear to you indeed has opened her heart to me and charged me to tell you of her feelings, trusting, perhaps wrongly, that the consideration with which I am honoured . . .' Father Pirrone hesitated and hovered from phrase to phrase.

Don Fabrizio lost patience. 'Well, come on, Father, who is it? The Princess?' And his raised arm seemed to be threatening : in fact he was drying an armpit.

'The Princess is tired; she's asleep and I have not seen her. No, it is the Signorina Concetta.' Pause. 'She is in love.' A man of forty-five can consider himself still young till the moment comes when he realises that he has children old enough to fall in love. The Prince felt old age come over him in one blow; he forgot the huge distances still tramped out shooting, the *Gesummaria* he could still evoke from his wife, his freshness now at the end of a long and arduous journey. Suddenly he saw himself as a white-haired old man walking beside herds of grandchildren on billy-goats in the public gardens of Villa Giulia.

'Why ever did the silly girl go and tell you such a thing? Why not come to me?' He did not even ask who the man was; there was no need to.

'Your Excellency hides his fatherly heart almost too well under the mask of authority. It's quite understandable that the poor girl should be frightened of you and so fall back on the family chaplain.'

Don Fabrizio slipped on his long drawers and snorted; he foresaw long interviews, tears, endless bother. The silly girl was spoiling his first day at Donnafugata with her fancies.

'I know, Father, I know. Here no one really understands me. It's my misfortune.' He was sitting now on a stool with the fuzz of fair hair on his chest dotted with pearly drops of water. Rivulets were snaking over the tiles, and the room was full of the milky smell of bran and the almond smell of soap. 'Well, what should I say, in your opinion?'

The Jesuit was sweating in the heat of the little room, and now that his message had been delivered would have liked to go but he was held back by a feeling of responsibility. 'The wish to found a Christian family is most agreeable to the eyes of the Church. The presence of Our Lord at the marriage of Cana . . .'

'Let's keep to the point, shall we? I wish to talk about this marriage, not about marriage in general. Has Don Tancredi made any definite proposal, by any chance, and if so, when?'

For five years Father Pirrone had tried to teach the boy Latin; for seven years he had put up with his quips and pranks; like everyone else he had felt his charm. But Tancredi's recent political attitudes had offended him; his old affection was struggling now with a new rancour. He did not know what to say. 'Well, not a real proposal, exactly, no. But the Signorina Concetta is quite certain : his attentions, his glances, his remarks, have all become more and more open and frequent and quite convinced the dear creature; she is sure that she is loved; but, being an obedient and respectful daughter, she wishes me to find out from you what her answer is to be if a proposal does come. She thinks it imminent.'

The Prince felt a little reassured; how ever did a chit of a girl like that think she had acquired enough experience to be able to judge so surely the behaviour of a young man;

particularly of a young man like Tancredi? Perhaps it was just imagination, one of those 'golden dreams' which convulse the pillows of schoolgirls? The danger might not be so near.

Danger. The word resounded so clearly in his mind that he gave a start of surprise. Danger. But danger for whom? He had a great affection for Concetta; he liked her perpetual submission, the placidity with which she yielded to the most unwelcome of paternal suggestions: a submission and placidity, incidentally, rather overvalued by him. His natural tendency to avoid any threat to his own calm had made him miss the steely glint which crossed her eyes when the whims she was obeying were really too vexing. Yes, the Prince was very fond of this daughter of his. But he was even fonder of his nephew. Conquered for ever by the youth's affectionate chaff he had begun during the last few months to admire his intelligence too; that quick adaptability, that worldly penetration, that innate artistic subtlety with which he could use the demagogic terms then in fashion while hinting to initiates that for him, the Prince of Falconeri, it was only a momentary pastime; all this amused Don Fabrizio, and in people of his character and standing the fact of being amused makes up four-fifths of affection. Tancredi, he considered, had a great future; he could be the standard-bearer of a counter-attack which the nobility, under changed trappings, could launch against the new social state. To do this he lacked but one thing; money; this Tancredi did not have, none at all. And to get on in politics, now that a name counted less, would need a lot of money; money to buy votes, money to do the electors favours, money for a dazzling style of living. Style of living . . . And would Concetta, with all those passive virtues of hers, be capable of helping an ambitious and brilliant husband to climb the slippery slopes of the new society? Timid, reserved, bashful as she was? Wouldn't she always remain just the pretty schoolgirl she was now, a leaden weight on her husband's feet?

'Can you see Concetta, Father, as ambassadress in Vienna or Petersburg?'

The question took Father Pirrone quite unawares. 'What has that to do with it? I don't understand.'

Don Fabrizio did not bother to explain; he plunged back into his silent thoughts. Money? Concetta would have a dowry, of course. But the Salina fortune would have to be divided into seven parts, unequal at that, in which the girls' would be the smallest. Well, then? Tancredi needed much more; Maria Santa Pau, for instance, with four estates already hers and all those uncles, priests and misers; or one of the Sutèra girls, so ugly but so rich. Love. Of course, love. Flames for a year, ashes for thirty. He knew what love was. . . . Anyway, Tancredi would always find women falling for him like ripe pears.

Suddenly he felt cold. The water on him had evaporated and the skin of his arms was icy. The ends of his fingers were crinkling. Oh, dear, what a lot of bothersome talk it would all mean. That must be avoided . . . 'Now I have to go and dress, Father. Tell Concetta, will you, that I am not in the least annoyed, but that we'll talk about all this later when we're quite sure it's not all just the fancy of a romantic girl. *Au revoir,* Father.'

He got up and passed into the dressing-room. From the Mother Church next door rang a lugubrious funeral knell. Someone had died at Donnafugata, some tired body unable to withstand the deep gloom of Sicilian summer had lacked stamina to await the rains. 'Lucky person,' thought the Prince, as he rubbed lotion on his whiskers. 'Lucky person, with no worries now about daughters, dowries and political careers.' This ephemeral identification with an unknown corpse was enough to calm him. 'While there's death there's hope,' he thought; then he saw the absurd side of letting himself get into such a state of depression because one of his daughters wanted to marry. *'Ce sont leurs affaires, après tout,'* he thought in French, as he did when his cogitations persisted in playing pranks. He settled in an arm-chair and dropped off into a doze.

An hour later he awoke refreshed and went down into the garden. The sun was already low and its rays, no longer

overwhelming, were lighting amiably on the araucarias, the
pines, the lusty ilexes, which were the glory of the place.
From the end of the main alley, sloping gently down
between high laurel hedges framing anonymous busts of
broken-nosed goddesses, could be heard the gentle drizzle
of spray falling into the fountain of Amphitrite. He moved
swiftly towards it, eager to see it again. The waters came
spurting in minute jets, blown from shells of Tritons and
Naiads, from noses of marine monsters, spattering and
pattering on the greenish surface, bouncing and bubbling,
wavering and quivering, dissolving into laughing little
gurgles; from the whole fountain, the tepid water, the
stones covered with velvety moss, emanated a promise of
pleasure that would never turn to pain. Perched on an
islet in the middle of the round basin, modelled by a crude
but sensual hand, a vigorous smiling Neptune was embrac-
a willing Amphitrite; her navel, wet with spray and gleaming in the sun, would be the nest, shortly, for hidden kisses
in subaqueous shade. Don Fabrizio paused, gazed, remembered, regretted. He stood there a long while.

'Uncle, come and look at the foreign peaches. They've
turned out fine. And leave these indecencies which are not
for men of your age.'

Tancredi's affectionate mocking voice called him from
his voluptuous torpor. He had not heard the boy come;
he was like a cat. For the first time he felt a touch of rancour prick him at the sight of Tancredi; this fop with
the pinched-in waist under his dark blue suit had been
the cause of those sour thoughts of his about death two
hours ago. Then he realised that it was not rancour, just
disguised alarm : he was afraid the other would talk to him
about Concetta. But his nephew's approach and tone was
not that of one preparing to make amorous confidences to
a man like himself. Don Fabrizio grew calm again; his
nephew was looking at him with the affectionate irony
which youth accords to age. 'They can allow themselves to
be a bit nice to us, as they're so sure to be free of us
the day after our funerals.' He went with Tancredi to
look at the 'foreign peaches.' The grafting with German

cuttings, made two years ago, had succeeded perfectly; there was not much fruit, a dozen or so, on the two grafted trees, but it was big, velvety, luscious-looking; yellowish, with a faint flush of rosy pink on the cheeks, like those of modest little Chinese girls. The Prince felt them with the delicacy for which his fleshy fingers were famous. 'They seem quite ripe. A pity there are too few for to-night. But we'll get them picked to-morrow and see what they're like.'

'There! that's how I like you, uncle; like this, in the part of *agricola pius*—appreciating in anticipation the fruits of your own labours; and not as I found you a short while ago, gazing at all that shameless naked flesh.'

'And yet Tancredi these peaches are also products of love, of coupling.'

'Of course, but legal love, blessed by you as their master, and by Nino the gardener as notary. Considered, fruitful love. As for those,' he went on, pointing at the fountain whose shimmer could just be discerned through a veil of ilexes, 'd'you really think they've been before a priest?'

The conversation was taking a dangerous turn and Don Fabrizio hastily changed its direction. As they moved back up towards the house Tancredi began telling what he had heard of the love-life of Donnafugata: Menica, the daughter of Saverio the keeper, had let herself be put with child by her young man; the marriage would be rushed on now. Calicchio had just avoided being shot by an angry husband.

'But how d'you know such things?'

I know, uncle, I know. They tell me everything; they know I'll sympathise.'

When they reached the top of the steps, which rose from the garden to the palace with gentle turns and long landings, they could see the dusky horizon beyond the trees; over towards the sea huge, inky clouds were climbing up the sky. Perhaps the anger of God was satiated and the annual curse over Sicily nearly over? At that moment those clouds loaded with relief were being stared at by thousands of other eyes, sensed in the womb of the earth by billions of seeds.

'Let's hope the summer is over and that the rains are finally here,' said Don Fabrizio; and with these words the haughty noble to whom rain would only be a personal nuisance showed himself a brother to his roughest peasants.

The Prince had always taken care that the first dinner at Donnafugata should bear the stamp of solemnity: children under fifteen were excluded from table, French wines were served, there was punch *alla Romana* before the roast; and the flunkeys were in powder and knee-breeches. On just one detail did he compromise; he never wore evening dress, lest he embarrass guests who would, obviously, possess none. That evening, in the 'Leopard' drawing-room, as it was called, the Salina family were awaiting the last arrivals. From under lace-covered shades the oil-lamps spread circumscribed yellow light: the vast equestrian portraits of past Salinas were as imposing and shadowy as their memories. Don Onofrio had already arrived with his wife, and so had the arch-priest who, with his light mantle folded back on his shoulders in sign of gala, was telling the Princess about tiffs at the College of Mary. Don Ciccio, the organist, had also arrived (Teresina had already been tied to the leg of a scullery table) and was recalling with the Prince their fantastic bags in the Dragonara ravines. All was placid and normal when Francesco Paolo, the sixteen-year-old son, burst into the room and announced: 'Papa, Don Calogero is just coming up the stairs. In *tails*!'

Tancredi, intent on fascinating the wife of Don Onofrio, realised the import of the news a second before the others. But when he heard that fatal word he could not contain himself and burst into convulsive laughter. No laugh, though, came from the Prince on whom, one might almost say, this news had more effect than the bulletin about Garibaldi's landing at Marsala. That had been an event not only foreseen but also distant and invisible. Now, with his sensibility to presages and symbols, he saw revolution in that white tie and two black tails moving at this moment up the stairs of his own home. Not only was he, the Prince, no longer the major land-owner in Donnafugata, but he now found himself forced to receive, when in afternoon dress himself, a guest appearing in evening clothes.

His distress was great; it still lasted as he moved mechanically towards the door to receive his guest. When he saw him, however, his agonies were somewhat eased. Though perfectly adequate as a political demonstration it was obvious that, as tailoring, Don Calogero's tail-coat was a disastrous failure. The stuff was excellent, the style modern, but the cut appalling. The Word from London had been most inadequately made flesh in a tailor from Girgenti to whom Don Calogero had gone with his tenacious avarice. The wings of his cravat pointed straight to heaven in mute supplication, his huge collar was shapeless, and, what is more, it is our painful but necessary duty to add that the mayor's feet were shod in buttoned boots.

Don Calogero advanced towards the Princess with a hand outstretched and still gloved. 'My daughter begs you to excuse her, she was not quite ready. Your Excellency knows how females are on these occasions,' he added, expressing in his near dialect a thought of Parisian levity, 'but she'll be here in a second; it's only a step from our place, as you know.'

The second lasted five minutes; then the door opened and in came Angelica. The first impression was of dazed surprise. The Salina family all stood there with breath taken away; Tancredi could even feel the veins pulsing in his temples. Under the first shock from her beauty the men were incapable of noticing or analysing its defects, which were numerous; there were to be many for ever incapable of this critical appraisal. She was tall and well-made, on an ample scale; her skin looked as if it had the flavour of fresh cream which it resembled, her childlike mouth that of strawberries. Under a mass of raven hair, curling in gentle waves, her green eyes gleamed motionless as those of statues, and like them a little cruel. She was moving slowly, making her wide white skirt rotate around her, and emanating from her own beauty. Only many months later was it known that at the moment of that victorious entry of hers she had been on the point of fainting from nerves.

She took no notice of the Prince hurrying towards her, she passed by Tancredi grinning at her in a daydream; before the Princess's arm-chair she bent her superb back in a slight bow, and this form of homage, unusual in Sicily, gave her for an instant the fascination of exoticism as well as that of local beauty.

'Angelica, my dear, it's so long since I've seen you. You've changed a lot; not for the worse!' The Princess could not believe her own eyes; she remembered the rather ugly and uncared-for thirteen-year-old girl of four years ago and could not make her tally with this voluptuous maiden before her. The Prince had no memories to re-organise; he only had forecasts to overturn; the blow to his pride dealt by the father's tail-coat was now repeated by the daughter's looks; but this time it was not a matter of black stuff but of milk-smooth white skin; and well-cut, yes, very well indeed! Old war horse that he was, the bugle-call of feminine beauty found him ready and he turned to the girl with the tone of gracious respect which he would have used to the Duchess of Bovino or the Princess of Lampedusa; 'How lucky we are, Signorina Angelica, to have gathered such a lovely flower in our home; and I hope that we shall have the pleasure of seeing you here often.'

'Thank you, Prince; I see that you are as kind to me as you have always been to my dear father.' The voice was pretty, low-pitched, a little too careful perhaps; Florentine schooling had cancelled the sagging Girgenti accent; the only Sicilian characteristic still in her speech was the harsh consonants, which anyway toned in well with her clear but emphatic type of beauty. In Florence she had also been taught to drop the 'Excellency.'

About Tancredi there seems little to be said; after being introduced by Don Calogero, after manœuvring the search-light of his blue eyes, after just managing to resist implanting a kiss on Angelina's hand, he had re-sumed his chat with the Signora Rotolo without taking

in a word that the good lady said. Father Pirrone, in a
dark corner, was deep in meditation over Holy Scripture,
which that night appeared only in the guise of Delilahs,
Judiths and Esthers.

The central doors of the drawing-room were flung open
and the butler declaimed mysterious sounds announcing
that dinner was ready : *'Prann' pronn'.'* The heterogeneous
group moved towards the dining-room.

The Prince was too experienced to offer Sicilian guests,
in a town of the interior, a dinner beginning with soup,
and he infringed the rules of *haute cuisine* all the more
readily as he disliked it himself. But rumours of the bar-
baric foreign usage of serving an insipid liquid as first
course had reached the notables of Donnafugata too insistently for them not to quiver with a slight residue of
alarm at the start of a solemn dinner like this. So when
three lackeys in green, gold and powder entered, each
holding a great silver dish containing a towering macaroni
pie, only four of the twenty at table avoided showing
pleased surprise; the Prince and Princess from foreknowl-
edge, Angelica from affectation and Concetta from lack of
appetite. All the others (including Tancredi, I regret to
say) showed their relief in varying ways, from the fluty
and ecstatic grunts of the notary to the sharp squeak of
Francesco Paulo. But a threatening circular stare from the
host soon stifled these improper demonstrations.

Good manners apart, though, the aspect of those monumental dishes of macaroni was worthy of the quivers of
admiration they evoked. The burnished gold of the crusts,
the fragrance of sugar and cinnamon they exuded, were but
preludes to the delights released from the interior when the
knife broke the crust; first came a spice-laden haze, then
chicken livers, hard boiled eggs, sliced ham, chicken and
truffles in masses of piping hot, glistening macaroni, to which
the meat juice gave an exquisite hue of suède.

The beginning of the meal, as happens in the provinces,
was quiet. The arch-priest made the sign of the Cross and
plunged in head first without a word. The organist absorbed the succulent dish with closed eyes; he was grateful

to the Creator that his ability to shoot hare and woodcock could bring him ecstatic pleasures like this, and the
thought came to him that he and Teresina could exist for
a month on the cost of one of these dishes; Angelica, the
lovely Angelica, forgot little Tuscan black-puddings and
part of her good manners and devoured her food with
the appetite of her seventeen years and the vigour given
by grasping her fork half-way up the handle. Tancredi,
in an attempt to link gallantry with greed, tried to imagine
himself tasting, in the aromatic forkfuls, the kisses of his
neighbour Angelica, but he realised at once that the experi-
ment was disgusting and suspended it, with a mental
reserve about reviving this fantasy with the pudding;
the Prince, although rapt in the contemplation of Angelica
sitting opposite him, was the only one at table able to
notice that the *demi-glace* was overfilled, and made a
mental note to tell the cook so next day; the others ate
without thinking of anything, and without realising that the
food seemed so delicious because sensuality was circulating
in the house.

All were calm and contented. All except Concetta. She
had of course embraced and kissed Angelica, told her not
to use the formal third person and insisted on the familiar
tu of their infancy, but under her pale blue bodice her
heart was being torn to shreds; the violent Salina blood
came surging up in her, and beneath a smooth forehead
she found herself brooding over day-dreams of poisoning.
Tancredi was sitting between her and Angelica distributing,
with the punctiliousness of one who feels in the wrong,
his glances, compliments and jokes equally between both
neighbours; but Concetta had an intuition, an animal intuition of the current of desire flowing from her cousin
towards the intruder, and the little frown between her
nose and forehead deepened; she wanted to kill as much
as she wanted to die. But being a woman she snatched at
details; Angelica's little finger in the air when her hand
held her glass; a reddish mole on the skin of her neck;
an attempt, half repressed, to remove with a finger a shred
of food stuck in her very white teeth, she noticed even more

sharply a certain coarseness of spirit; and to these details, which were really quite insignificant as they were cauterised by sensual fascination, she clung as trustingly and desperately as a falling builder's boy snatches at a leaden gutter; she hoped that Tancredi would notice too and be revolted by these obvious traces of difference in breeding. But Tancredi had already noticed them, and, alas! with no result. He was letting himself be drawn along by the physical stimulus of a beautiful woman to his fiery youth, and also by the (as-it-were) numerical excitement aroused by a rich girl in the mind of a man ambitious and poor.

At the end of dinner the conversation became general; Don Calogero told in bad Italian but with knowing insight some inside stories about the conquest of the province by Garibaldi: the notary told the Princess of a little house he was having built 'out of town'; Angelica, excited by light, food, Chablis and the obvious admiration she was arousing in every man around the table, asked Tancredi to describe some episodes of the 'glorious battle' for Palermo. She had put an elbow on the table and was leaning her cheek on her hand. Her face was flushed and she was perilously attractive to behold; the arabesque made by her forearm, elbow, finger and hanging white glove seemed exquisite to Tancredi and repulsive to Concetta. The young man, while continuing to admire, was describing the campaign as if it had all been quite light and unimportant; the night march on Gibilrossa, the scene between Bixio and La Masa, the assault on Porta di Termini. 'It was the greatest fun, signorina. Our biggest laugh was on the night of the 28th of May. The general needed a look-out post at the top of the convent at Origlione; we knocked, banged, cursed, knocked again: no one opened; it was an enclosed convent. Then Tassoni, Aldrighetti, I and one or two others tried to break down the door with our rifle buts. Nothing doing. We ran to fetch a beam from a shelled house nearby and finally, with a hellish din, the door gave way. We went in; not a soul in sight, but from a corner of the passage we heard des-

perate screams; a group of nuns had taken refuge in
the chapel and were all crouching round the altar; I
wonder *what* they feared at the hands of those dozen
excited young men! They looked absurd, old and ugly
in their black habits, with starting eyes, ready and prepared for . . . martyrdom. They were whining like bitches.
Tassoni, who's a card, shouted : "Nothing doing, sisters,
we've other things to think of; but we'll be back when
you've some novices." And we all laughed fit to burst. Then
we left them there, their tongues hanging out, to go and
shoot at Royalists from the terraces above. Ten minutes
later I was wounded.'

Angelica laughed, still leaning on her elbow, and showed
all her pointed teeth. The joke seemed most piquant to
her; that hint of rape perturbed her; her lovely throat
quivered. 'What fine lads you must have been ! How I wish
I'd been with you !' Tancredi seemed transformed; the
excitement of the story, the thrill of memory, mingling
with the agitation produced by the girl's air of sensuality,
changed him for an instant from the gentle youth he was
in reality into a brutal and licentious soldier.

'Had you been there, signorina, we'd have had no need
to wait for novices.'

Angelica had heard a lot of coarse talk at home; but
this was the first time (and not the last) when she found
herself the object of a sexual innuendo; the novelty of it
pleased her, her laughter went up a tone, became strident.

At that moment everyone rose from the table; Tancredi bent to gather up the feather fan dropped by
Angelica; as he rose to his feet he saw Concetta with face
aflame and two little tears in the corners of her lids. 'Tancredi, one tells nasty tales like that to a confessor, not to
young ladies at table; anyway when I'm there.' And she
turned her back on him.

Before going to bed Don Fabrizio paused a moment
on the little balcony of his dressing-room. Beneath lay the
shadowed garden, sunk in sleep; in the inert air the
trees seemed like fused lead; from the overhanging bell-

tower came an elfin hoot of owls. The sky was clear of clouds; those which had greeted the dusk had moved away, maybe towards less sinful places, condemned by divine wrath to lesser penalties. The stars looked turbid and their rays scarcely penetrated the pall of sultry air.

The soul of the Prince reached out towards them, towards the intangible, the unattainable, which gives joy without laying claim to anything in return; as on many other occasions, he tried to imagine himself in those icy tracts, a pure intellect armed with a note-book for calculations: difficult calculations, but ones which would always work out. 'They're the only truly disinterested, the only really trustworthy creatures,' thought he in his worldly idiom; 'who worries about dowries for the Pleiads, a political career for Sirius, marital joys for Vega?' It had been a bad day; he realised it now, not only from a pressure in the pit of his stomach, but from the stars too; instead of seeing them disposed in their usual groupings he noticed a single pattern up there every time he raised his eyes: two stars above, the eyes; one beneath, the tip of a chin: mocking symbol of a triangular face which his mind projected into the constellations when it was disturbed. Don Calogero's tail-coat, Concetta's love, Tancredi's blatant infatuation, his own cowardice; even the threatening beauty of that girl Angelica; bad things; rubble preceding an avalanche. And Tancredi! The lad was right, agreed, and he would help him too; but Don Fabrizio had to admit that it was all slightly ignoble. And he himself was like Tancredi. 'Enough of that now, let's sleep on it.'

Bendicò in the shadow rubbed a big head against his knee; 'You see; you, Bendicò, are a bit like them, like the stars; happily incomprehensible, incapable of producing anxiety.' He raised the dog's head, which was almost invisible in the darkness. 'And then with those eyes of yours at the same level as your nose, with your lack of chin, such a head can't possibly evoke malignant spectres in the sky.'

Centuries-old tradition required that the day following

their arrival the Salina family should visit the Convent of
the Holy Ghost to pray at the tomb of Blessed Corbèra,
forebear of the Prince and foundress of the convent, who
had endowed it, there lived a holy life and there died a holy
death.

The Convent of the Holy Ghost had a rigid rule of en-
closure and entry was severely forbidden to men. That
was why the Prince particularly enjoyed visiting it, for he,
as direct descendant of the foundress, was not excluded:
and of this privilege, shared only with the King of Naples,
he was both jealous and childishly proud.

This faculty of canonical intrusion was the chief, but
not the only reason, for his liking the Convent of the Holy
Ghost. Everything about the place pleased him, beginning
with the humble simplicity of the parlour, with its barrel
vaulted ceiling centred on the Leopard, its double gratings
for interviews, a little wooden wheel for passing messages
in and out, and a heavy door whose threshold he and the
King were the only men in the whole world allowed to cross.
He liked the look of the nuns with their wide wimples
of purest white linen in tiny pleats gleaming against the
rough black robes; he was edified at hearing for the
hundredth time the Mother Abbess describe the Blessed
One's ingenuous miracles; at her showing the corner of
the dank garden where the saintly nun had suspended in
the air a huge stone which the Devil, irritated by her
austerity, had flung at her; he was astounded at the sight
of the two famous and indecipherable letters framed on
the wall of a cell, one to the Devil from Blessed Corbèra,
to convert him to virtue, and the other the Devil's reply,
expressing, it seems, his regret at not being able to comply
with her request: the Prince liked the almond cakes which
the nuns made up from an ancient recipe, he liked listening to the Office chanted in choir, and he was even quite
happy to pay over to the community a not inconsiderable
portion of his own income, in accordance with the act of
foundation.

So that morning there were only happy people in the
two carriages moving towards the convent just outside the

town. In the first was the Prince, the Princess and their daughters Carolina and Concetta; in the second his daughter Caterina, Tancredi and Father Pirrone, both the latter of whom, of course, would stay *extra muros* and wait in the parlour during the visit, consoled by almond cakes from the wooden wheel. Concetta looked serene, though a little absent-minded, and the Prince did his best to hope that yesterday's fancies had all blown over.

Entry into an enclosed convent is never a quick matter, even for one possessing the most sacred of rights. Nuns like to show a certain reluctance, formal maybe but prolonged, which gives more flavour to however certain an admission; and, although the visit had been announced beforehand, there was a considerable wait in the parlour. Towards the end of this Tancredi unexpectedly asked the Prince, 'Uncle, can't you get me in too? After all I'm half a Salina, and I've never been here before.'

Though pleased at heart by the request, the Prince shook his head decisively. 'But, my boy, you know only I and no other man can enter here.' It was not easy, however, to put Tancredi off : 'Excuse me, Nuncle; the rule says : *The Prince of Salina may enter together with two gentlemen of his suite if the Abbess so permits.* I read it again yesterday. I'll be the gentleman in your suite, I'll be your squire, I'll be whatever you like. Do ask the Abbess, please.' He was speaking with unusual warmth; perhaps he wanted a certain person there to forget his ill-considered chatter of the night before. The Prince was flattered. 'If you're so keen on it, dear boy, I'll see . . .' But Concetta turned to her cousin with her sweetest smile : 'Tancredi, we passed a beam of wood lying in front of Ginestra's house. Go and fetch it, it'll get you in all the quicker.' Tancredi's blue eyes clouded and his face went red as a poppy, either from shame or anger. He tried to say something to the surprised Prince, but Concetta interrupted again, acidly now, and without a smile : 'Let him be, father, he's only joking; he's been in one convent already, that ought to be enough for him; it's not right for him to enter this one of ours.' With a grinding of drawn bolts the door opened.

Into the stuffy parlour entered the freshness of the cloister together with the murmur of assembled nuns. It was too late to ask questions, and Tancredi was left behind to walk up and down in front of the convent under the blazing sky.

The visit to the Holy Ghost was a great success. Don Fabrizio, from love of quiet, had refrained from asking Concetta the meaning of her words; doubtless just one of the usual tiffs between cousins; anyway the coolness between the two young people kept off bother, confabulations and decisions, so it had been welcome. On these premises the tomb of Blessed Corbèra was venerated with due respect by all, the nuns' watery coffee drunk with tolerance and the pink and greenish almond cakes crunched with satisfaction; the Princess inspected the vestment-press, Concetta talked to the nuns with her usual withdrawn kindliness and he, the Prince, left on the refectory table the ten ounces of gold that he offered every time he came. It was true that at the door Father Pirrone was found alone; but as he said that Tancredi had suddenly remembered an urgent letter and gone off on foot, no one took much notice.

On returning to the palace the Prince went up to the library, which was in the middle of the façade under the clock and lightning conductor. From the great balcony, closed against the heat, could be seen the square of Donnafugata, vast, shaded by dusty plane trees. Opposite were some house fronts of exuberant local design, rustic monstrosities in soapstone, weathered by the years, upholding amid twists and curves balconies that were too small; other houses, among them that of Don Calogero Sedàra, hid behind prim Empire fronts.

Don Fabrizio walked up and down the immense room; every now and again glancing out at the square; on one of the benches donated by himself to the commune three old men were roasting in the sun; four mules stood tethered to a tree; a dozen or so urchins chased each other, shouting and brandishing wooden swords. Under the blazing mid-summer sun the view could not have been more typical. On one of his crossings past the window, however, his eye was drawn to a figure obviously urban—slim, erect, well-dressed. He screwed up his eyes. It was Tancredi; he recognised him, although already some way off, by the sloping shoulders and slim-fitting waist of his frock coat. He had changed his clothes; he was no longer in brown as at the convent, but in Prussian blue, 'my seduction colour' as he himself called it. In one hand he held a cane with an enamel handle (doubtless the one bearing the Unicorn of the Falconeri and their motto *Semper purus*) and he was walking with cat-like tread, as if taking care not to get his shoes dusty. Ten paces behind him followed a lackey carrying a tasselled box containing a dozen yellow peaches with pink cheeks. He sidestepped a sword-waving urchin, carefully avoided a urinating mule, and reached the Sedàra's door.

3

THE TROUBLES OF DON FABRIZIO

THE RAINS had come, the rains had gone, and the sun was back on its throne like an absolute monarch kept off for a week by his subjects' barricades, and now reigning once again, choleric but under constitutional restraint. The heat braced without burning, the light domineered but let colours live; from the soil sprouted cautious clover and mint, and on faces diffident hopes.

Don Fabrizio, with his dogs Teresina and Arguto and his retainer Don Ciccio Tumeo, would spend long hours out shooting, from dawn till afternoon. The effort was out of all proportion to the results, for the most expert shot finds difficulty in hitting a target which is scarcely ever there, and it was rarely that the Prince was able to take even a brace of partridges home to the larder, or Don Ciccio to slap on his kitchen table a wild rabbit—promoted, *ipso facto* as usual in Sicily, to the rank of hare.

A big bag would anyway have been a secondary pleasure for the Prince; the joy of those days out shooting lay elsewhere, subdivided in many tiny episodes. It began with shaving in a room still dark, by candlelight that projected every gesture emphatically over the painted architecture on the ceiling; it was whetted by crossing sleeping drawing-rooms, by glimpses in the flickering light of tables with playing cards lying in disorder amid chips and empty glasses, and catching sight among them of a Jack of Spades waving a manly greeting : by passing through the motionless garden under a grey light in which the earliest birds were twisting and turning to shake the dew off their feathers; by gliding through the ivy-hung wicket gate : by escaping, in fact. And then in the street, blamelessly innocent still in the early light, he would find Don Ciccio smiling into his yellowed moustaches and swearing affectionately at the dogs; these, as they waited, were flexing their muscles under velvety fur. Venus still glimmered, like the bloom on a grape, damp and transparent, but one could already hear the rumble of the solar chariot climbing the last slope below the horizon; soon they would meet the first flocks moving towards them torpidly as tides, guided by stones thrown by leather-breeched shepherds; the wool looked soft and rosy in the early sun : then there would be obscure quarrels of precedence to be settled between sheep dogs and punctilious pointers, after which deafening interval they turned up a slope and found themselves in the immemorial silence of pastoral Sicily. All at once they were far from everything in space and still more in time. Donnafugata with its palace and its new rich was only a mile or two away, but seemed a dim memory like those landscapes sometimes glimpsed at the distant end of a railway tunnel; its troubles and splendours appeared even more insignificant than if they belonged to the past, for compared to this remote unchangeable landscape they seemed part of the future, made not of stone and flesh but of the substance of some dream of things to come, extracts from a Utopia thought up by a rustic Plato and apt to change any second into quite different forms or even not to exist at all; deprived thus of that charge of energy which everything in the past continues to possess, they could no longer be a worry.

Yes, Don Fabrizio had certainly had his worries those last two months; they had come from all directions, like ants making for a dead lizard. Some had crawled from crevices of the political situation; some been flung on him by other people's passions; and some (these had the sharpest bite) had sprung up within himself, from his irrational reactions, that is, to politics and the whims of others ('whims' was his name when irritated for what in calm he called 'pas-

sions'). He would review these worries every day, manœuvre
them, set them in column or extend them in open order
on the parade ground of his own conscience, hoping to find
in their evolutions a sense of finality that could reassure
him; and not succeeding. In former years there had been
far fewer bothers, and anyway his stay at Donnafugata had
always been a period of rest; his worries used to drop
their rifles, disperse into the windings of the valleys and
settle down there quietly, so intent on munching bread
and cheese that their warlike uniforms were forgotten and
they could be mistaken for inoffensive peasants. This year,
though, they had all stayed on parade in a body, like
mutinous troops shouting and brandishing weapons, arousing in his home the dismay of a colonel who has given the
order 'Fall out' only to find his battalion standing there in
closer and more threatening order than ever.

The arrival had been all right, with bands, fireworks,
bells, gipsy song and *Te Deum*; but afterwards! The bour-
geois revolution climbing his stairs in Don Calogero's tail-
coat, Angelica's beauty putting the shy grace of his Concetta in the shade, Tancredi rushing at the inevitable
changes and even able to deck out his realistic motives
with sensual infatuation; the scruples and deceptions of
the Plebiscite; the endless little subterfuges he had to submit to, he, the Leopard, who for years had swept away
difficulties with a wave of his paw.

Tancredi had been gone for more than a month and
was now at Caserta bivouacking in the apartments of his
King; from there every now and again he sent Don
Fabrizio letters which the latter read with alternate frowns
and smiles, then put away in the remotest drawer of his
desk. He had never written to Concetta, though he did not
forget to send her a greeting with his usual affectionate slyness; once he even wrote: 'I kiss the hands of all the little
Leopardesses and particularly Concetta's,' phrases cen-
sored by paternal prudence when the letter was read out
to the assembled family. Angelica was now visiting them
almost daily, more seductive than ever, accompanied by
her father or some old witch of a maid: officially these

visits were made to her friends the girls, but in fact their climax obviously came at the moment when she asked with apparent indifference, 'And what news of the Prince?' 'Prince' in Angelica's mouth did not, alas, mean him, Don Fabrizio, but the little Garibaldino captain; and this provoked a strange sensation in Salina, woven from the crude cotton of sensual jealousy to silken pleasure at his dear Tancredi's success; a sensation, when all was said and done, that was somewhat disagreeable. It was always he who answered this question; he would give a carefully considered account of what he knew, taking care, however, to present a well-arranged little bouquet of news from which his cautious tweezers had extracted both thorns (descriptions of many a jaunt to Naples, allusions to the lovely legs of Aurora Schwarzwald, dancer at the San Carlo) and premature buds ('send news of the Signorina Angelica'—'In Ferdinand II's study I found a Madonna by Andrea del Sarto which reminded me of the Signorina Sedàra'). So he would put together an insipid picture of Tancredi which bore very little resemblance to the original, but did at least prevent anyone saying that he himself was acting either as spoil-sport or pimp. These verbal precautions corresponded closely to his own feelings about Tancredi's considered passion, but they irritated him inasmuch as they wearied him; anyway they were only one sample of all the guile in language and behaviour he had been forced to adopt for some time; he thought with regret of the year before when he could say whatever went through his head, in the certainty that any silly remark would be treated as words from the Gospel and any unconsidered comment as princely carelessness. And now that he had begun regretting the past, he would find himself, in moments of worst humour, slithering quite a way down that perilous slope; once, as he was putting sugar in a cup of tea which Angelica was holding out to him, he realised that he was envying the chances open to a Fabrizio Salina and Tancredi Falconeri of three centuries before, who would have rid themselves of urges to bed down with the Angelicas of their day without ever going before a priest or giving a thought to such local girls' dowries (which were anyway then non-existent), or ever needing to keep respectable uncles on tenterhooks about saying or suppressing appropriate remarks. The impulse of atavistic lust (which was not really all lust, but partly sensuality stemming from laziness) stung the civilised gentleman nearing fifty so sharply that it made him blush; somewhere, at infinite removes, he had been touched by scruples which he chose to call Rousseauesque, and felt deeply ashamed; from which might be deduced an even sharper revulsion against the social circumstances in which he was so inextricably involved.

The sensation of finding himself a prisoner in a situation evolving more rapidly than foreseen was particularly acute that morning. The night before, in fact, the stage coach bearing the irregular and scanty mail to Donnafugata in its canary-yellow box had brought a letter from Tancredi.

This proclaimed its importance even before reading, written as it was on sumptuous sheets of gleaming paper and in a harmonious script scrupulously tracing full strokes down and thin strokes up. It was obviously the 'clean copy' of any number of disordered drafts. In it the Prince was not addressed by the name of 'Nuncle' which had become dear to him; the wily youth had thought of a formula, 'dearest Uncle Fabrizio', which had a number of merits; of removing any suspicion of jesting on the verge of sacred ground, proclaiming from the very first line the importance of what was to follow, of allowing the letter to be shown to anyone and also of providing a link with ancient pre-Christian beliefs which attributed a binding power to the exact invocation of a name.

'Dearest Uncle Fabrizio,' therefore, was informed that his 'most affectionate and devoted nephew' had for the last three months been a prey to the most violent love, and that neither 'the risks of war' (read: walks in the park of Caserta) nor 'the many attractions of a great city (read: the charms of the dancer Schwarzwald) had been able even for an instant to drive from his mind and heart the

image of the Signorina Angelica Sedàra (here a long procession of adjectives to exalt the beauty, grace, virtue
and intellect of his beloved); then, in neat hieroglyphics
of ink and sentiment, the letter went on to say that Tancredi had felt so conscious of his own unworthiness that
he had tried to suffocate his ardour ('long but vain have
been the hours during which, amid the clamour of
Naples or the austere company of my comrades-in-arms,
I have tried to repress my feelings'). But now love had overcome his reserve, and he was begging his dearly beloved
uncle to deign to request Signorina Angelica's 'most
esteemed father' for her hand, in his name and on his
behalf. 'You know, uncle, that all I can offer to the object
of my affections is my love, my name, and my sword.'
After this phrase, in connection with which it should not
be forgotten that romanticism was then at high noon,
Tancredi went on to long considerations of the expediency,
nay the necessity of unions between families such as the
Falconeri and the Sedàra (once he even dared write
'The House of Sedàra') being encouraged in order to bring
new blood into old families, and also to level out classes,
one of the aims of the current political movement in
Italy. This was the only part of the letter that Don Fabrizio
read with any pleasure; and not just because it confirmed
his own previsions and crowned him with the laurels of
a prophet, but also (it would be harsh to say 'above all')
because the style, with its hints of subdued irony, magic-
ally evoked his nephew's face; the jesting nasal tone,
the sparkling sly blue eyes, the mockingly polite smile.
And when he realised that this little Jacobin sally was
written out on exactly one single sheet of paper so that
if he wanted he could let others read the letter while
subtracting this revolutionary chapter, his admiration for
Tancredi's tact knew no bounds. After a brief résumé of
recent operations and an expression of the conviction that
within a year they would be in Rome, 'predestined capital
of the new Italy,' he thanked his uncle for the care and
affection given him in the past, and ended by excusing
himself for daring to confide him with this charge 'on

which my future happiness depends.' Then came greetings
(for Don Fabrizio only).

A first reading of this extraordinary composition made
Don Fabrizio's head spin : once again he noted how astound-
ingly fast all this had gone; put in modern terms he could
be said to be in the state of mind of someone to-day who
thinks he has boarded one of the easy-going old planes
pottering between Palermo and Naples, and suddenly finds
himself shut inside a Super Jet and realises he would be
at his destination almost before there was time to make
the sign of the Cross. Then the second affectionate layer
of his nature came to the top, and he rejoiced at this
decision of Tancredi which would assure him an ephemeral
carnal satisfaction and a perennial financial peace. He
paused then, for a moment, to note the youth's extraordinary self-confidence in presuming his own wish already
accepted by Angelica; but all these thoughts were swept
away eventually by a sense of humiliation at being forced
to deal with Don Calogero about a subject so intimate, and
also of vexation at having to conduct delicate negotiations
next day, with the use, what was more, of precaution and
cunning alien to his own, presumably leonine, nature.

Don Fabrizio only revealed the contents of this letter to
his wife when they were lying in bed under the pale-blue
glow from the glass-hooded oil-lamp. Maria Stella did
not say a word at first, just made a series of signs of the
Cross; then she remarked that she should have crossed herself with her left hand and not her right; after this
supreme expression of amazement she loosed the thunder-
bolts of her eloquence. Sitting up in bed, her fingers
rumpled the sheet while her words furrowed the lunar
atmosphere of the enclosed room like angry scarlet torches :
'I'd so hoped he would marry Concetta! He's a traitor,
like all liberals of his kind; first he betrayed his King, now
he betrays us! He, with that double-face of his, those
honeyed words and poisoned actions! That's what happens
when one lets people into one's home who aren't of our
own blood!' Here she let loose her cavalry charge in

family scenes—'I always said so, but no one would listen to me. I never could endure that fop! You just lost your head about him!' In reality the Princess too had been subject to Tancredi's charm, and she still loved him; but the pleasure of shouting 'I told you so' being the strongest any human being can enjoy, all truths and all feelings were swept along in its wake. 'And now he has even had the impertinence to ask you, his uncle and Prince of Salina, father of the very girl he has deceived, to carry his squalid message to that slut's rascally father! You mustn't do it, Fabrizio, you mustn't do it, you shan't do it, you mustn't do it!" Her voice went up in tone, her body began to stiffen.

Don Fabrizio, still lying on his back, gave a sideways glance to assure himself that the valerian was on the night table. The bottle was there with a silver spoon across the stopper; in the glaucous half darkness of the room they shone like a reassuring beacon built to withstand storms of hysteria. For a moment he thought of getting out of bed and fetching them; but he compromised by just sitting up too; thus he reacquired a position of prestige. 'Now, Stella, my dear, don't be silly. You don't know what you are saying. Angelica is not a slut. She may become one, but for the moment she's a girl just like any other, prettier than others, and she simply wants to make a good marriage; she may even be a little in love with Tancredi, like everyone else. She'll have money, most of which was ours; but it's now well, almost too well, taken care of by Don Calogero; and Tancredi has great need of that; he's a gentleman, he's ambitious, he's a perfect sieve with money. As for Concetta he never actually said a word to her; in fact, it's she who's treated him badly ever since we got to Donnafugata. And he's not a traitor; he follows the times, that's all, in his politics and in his private life; and anyway he's a very lovable lad, you know that as much as I do, Stella my dear.' Five huge fingers stroked the top of her tiny head. She was sobbing now; having been sensible enough to drink a sip of water, the fire of her rage had muted to self-pity. Don Fabrizio began to hope that he

would not have to get out of the warm bed, face a bare-
foot crossing of the chilly room. Then to ensure his
future peace he pretended to be angry: 'And I'll have no
shouting in my own house, in my own room, in my own
bed! None of this "You do this" and "You won't do that":
I decide; I'd already decided long before it ever crossed
your mind! That's enough now!'

The hater of shouting was himself bawling with all the
breath in his great chest. Thinking he had a table in
front of him, he banged a great fist on his own knee, hurt
himself and calmed down too.

The Princess, alarmed, was now whining in a low voice
like a frightened puppy.

'Now, let's sleep. To-morrow I'm going out shooting
and have to get up early. Enough! What's decided is
decided. Good night, Stella, my dear.' He kissed his wife
first on her forehead and then on her lips. He lay down
again and turned towards the wall. The shadow of his
recumbent form was projected on the silken walls like
the silhouette of a mountain range on a blue horizon.

Stella lay back too, and as her right leg grazed the left
leg of the Prince, she felt consoled and proud at having
for a husband a man so vital and so proud. What did Tancredi matter . . . or even Concetta . . .?

For the moment such tight-rope balancing was suspended, along with all other thought, in the archaic
and aromatic countryside—if it could be called that—
where he went shooting every morning. The term 'countryside' implies soil transformed by labour; but the scrub
clinging to the slopes was still in the very same state of
scented tangle in which it had been found by Phœnicians,
Dorians and Ionians when they disembarked in Sicily, that
America of antiquity. Don Fabrizio and Tumeo climbed up
and down, slipped and were scratched by thorns, just
as an Archedamos or Philostrates must have got tired and
scratched twenty-five centuries before. They saw the same
objects, their clothes were soaked with just as sticky a
sweat, the same indifferent breeze blew steadily from the

sea, moving myrtles and broom, spreading a smell of thyme. The dogs' sudden pauses for thought, their tension waiting for prey, was the very same as when Artemis was invoked for the chase. Reduced to these basic elements, its face washed clean of worries, life took on a tolerable aspect. That morning, shortly before reaching the top of the hill, Arguto and Teresina began the hieratic dance of dogs who have scented prey, stretching, stiffening, prudently raising paws, repressing barks; a few minutes later a tiny beige-coloured backside slid through the grass and two almost simultaneous shots ended the silent wait; at the Prince's feet Arguto placed an animal in its death throes.

It was a wild rabbit; its humble dun-coloured coat had been unable to save it. Horrible wounds lacerated snout and chest. Don Fabrizio found himself stared at by big black eyes soon overlaid by a glaucous veil; they were looking at him with no reproval, but full of tortured amazement at the whole ordering of things; the velvety ears were already cold, the vigorous paws contracting in rhythm, still-living symbol of useless flight; the animal had died tortured by anxious hopes of salvation, imagining it could still escape when it was already caught, just like so many human beings. While sympathetic fingers were still stroking that poor snout, the animal gave a last quiver and died; Don Fabrizio and Don Ciccio had had their bit of fun, the former not only the pleasure of killing but also the comfort of compassion.

When the sportsmen reached the top of the hill, there among the tamarisks and scattered cork-trees appeared the real Sicily again, the one compared to which baroque towns and orange groves are mere trifles : aridly undulating to the horizon in hillock after hillock, comfortless and irrational, with no lines that the mind could grasp, conceived apparently in a delirious moment of creation; a sea suddenly petrified at the instant when a change of wind had flung the waves into a frenzy. Donnafugata lay huddled and hidden in an anonymous fold of the ground, and not a living soul was to be seen; the only signs of the passage of man were scraggy rows of vines. Beyond the hills on one side was the indigo smudge of the sea, more mineral and barren, even, than the land. The slight breeze moved over all, universalising the smell of dung, carrion and sage, cancelling, suppressing, reordering each thing in its careless passage; it dried up the little drops of blood which were the only residue of the rabbit, far away it ruffled the locks of Garibaldi, and further still flung dust in the eyes of Neapolitan soldiers hurriedly reinforcing the battlements of Gaeta, deluded by a hope as vain as the rabbit's frenzied flight. The Prince and the organist rested under the circumscribed shadow of cork-trees; they drank tepid wine from wooden bottles with a roast chicken from Don Fabrizio's haversack, ate little cakes called *muffoletti* dusted with raw flour which Don Ciccio had brought with him, and local grapes so ugly to look at and so good to eat; with hunks of bread they satisfied the hungry dogs standing there in front of them, impassive as bailiffs bent on getting debts paid. Under the monarchic sun Don Fabrizio and Don Ciccio were dozing off.

But though a shot had killed the rabbit, though the bored rifles of General Cialdini were now dismaying the Bourbon troops at Gaeta, though the midday heat was making men doze off, nothing could stop the ants. Attracted by a few chewed grape skins spat out by Don Ciccio, along they rushed in close order, morale high at the chance of annexing this bit of garbage soaked with an organist's saliva. Up they came full of confidence, disordered but resolute; groups of three or four would stop now and again for a chat, exalting, perhaps, the ancient glories and future prosperity of ant hill Number Two under cork-tree Number Four on the top of Mount Morco; then once again they would take up their march with the others towards a buoyant future; the gleaming backs of those imperialists seemed to quiver with enthusiasm, while from their ranks no doubt rose the notes of an anthem.

By some association of ideas which it would be inopportune to pursue, the activity of these insects prevented the Prince from sleeping and reminded him of the days of the

Plebiscite about Unification through which he had lived shortly before at Donnafugata itself. Apart from a sense of amazement those days had left him many an enigma to solve; now, in sight of nature which, except for ants, obviously had no such bothers, he might perhaps find a solution for one of them. The dogs were sleeping stretched and crouched like figures in relief, the little rabbit hanging head down from a branch was swinging out diagonally under the constant surge of wind, but Tumeo, with the help of his pipe, still managed to keep his eyes open.

'And you, Don Ciccio, how did you vote on the twenty-first?'

The poor man started; taken by surprise at a moment when he was outside the stockade of precautions in which like each of his fellow townsmen he usually moved, he hesitated, not knowing what to reply.

The Prince mistook for alarm what was really only surprise, and felt irritated. 'Well, what are you afraid of? There's no one here but us, the wind and the dogs.'

The list of reassuring witnesses was not really happily chosen; wind is a gossip by definition, the Prince was half Sicilian. Only the dogs were absolutely trustworthy and that only because they lacked articulate speech. But Don Ciccio had now recovered; his peasant astuteness had suggested the right reply—nothing at all. 'Excuse me, Excellency, but there's no point in your question. You know that everyone in Donnafugata voted "yes." '

Don Fabrizio did know this; and that was why this reply merely changed a small enigma into an enigma of history. Before the voting many had come to him for advice; all of them had been exhorted, sincerely, to vote 'yes.' Don Fabrizio, in fact, could not see what else there was to do : whether treating it as a *fait accompli* or as an act merely theatrical and banal, whether taking it as historical necessity or considering the trouble these humble folk might get into if their negative attitude were known. He had noticed, though, that not all had been convinced by his words; into play had come the abstract Machiavellianism of Sicilians, which so often induced these people, with all their gener-

osity, to erect complex barricades on the most fragile of
foundations. Like clinics adept at treatment based on fundamentally false analyses of blood and urine which they
are too lazy to rectify, the Sicilians (of that time) ended by
killing off the patient, that is themselves, by a niggling
and hair-splitting rarely connected with any real understanding of the problems involved, or even of their inter-
locutors. Some of these who had made a visit *ad limina
leopardorum* considered it impossible for a Prince of
Salina to vote in favour of the Revolution (as the recent
changes were still called in those remote parts), and they
interpreted his advice as ironical, intended to effect a
result in practice opposite to his words. These pilgrims (and
they were the best) had come out of his study winking at
each other—as far as their respect for him would allow
—proud at having penetrated the meaning of the princely
words, and rubbing their hands in self-congratulation at
their own perspicacity just when this was most completely
in eclipse.

Others, on the other hand, after having listened to him,
went off looking sad and convinced that he was a turncoat
or half-wit, more than ever determined to take no notice
of what he said but to follow instead the age-old proverb
about preferring a known evil to an untried good. These
were reluctant to ratify the new national reality for
personal reasons too; either from religious faith, or from
having received favours from the former régime and not
being sharp enough to insert themselves into the new one,
or finally because during the upsets of the liberation period
they had lost a few capons and sacks of beans, and been
cuckolded either freely like Garibaldini volunteers or
forcibly like Bourbon levies. He had, in fact, the disagreeable but distinct impression that about fifteen of them
would vote 'no,' a tiny minority certainly, but noticeable
in the small electorate of Donnafugata. Taking into consideration that the people who came to him represented
the flower of the inhabitants, and that there must also be
some unconvinced among the hundreds of electors who
had not dreamt of setting foot inside the palace, the

Prince had calculated that Donnafugata's compact affirmative would be varied by about forty negative votes.

The day of the Plebiscite was windy and grey, and tired groups of youths had been seen going through the streets of the town with bits of paper covered with 'yes' stuck in the ribbons of their hats. Amid waste paper and refuse swirled by the wind they sang a few verses of *La Bella Gigugin* transformed into a kind of Arab wail, a fate to which any gay tune sung in Sicily is bound to succumb. There had also been seen two or three 'foreigners' (that is from Girgenti) installed in *Zzu* Menico's tavern, where they were declaiming Leopardi's lines on the 'magnificent and progressive destiny' of a renovated Sicily united to resurgent Italy. A few peasants were standing listening, mutely, stunned by overwork or starved by unemployment. These cleared their throats and spat continuously, but kept silent; so silent that it must have been then (as Don Fabrizio said afterwards) that the 'foreigners' decided to give Arithmetic precedence over Rhetoric in the Quadrivium arts.

The Prince went to vote about four in the afternoon, flanked on the right by Father Pirrone, on the left by Don Onofrio Rotolo; frowning and fair-skinned, he proceeded slowly towards the Town Hall, frequently putting up a hand to protect his eyes lest the breeze loaded with all the filth collected on its way should bring on the conjunctivitis to which he was subject; and he remarked to Father Pirrone that though the air would have been like a putrid pool without the wind, yet health-giving gusts did seem to drag up a lot of dirt with them. He was wearing the same black frock-coat in which two years before he had gone to pay his respects at Caserta to poor King Ferdinand, who had been lucky enough to die in time to avoid this day of dirty wind when the seal would be set on his own incapacity. But had it really been incapacity? One might as well say that a person succumbing to typhus dies of incapacity. He remembered the King busy putting up dykes against the floods of useless documents: and suddenly he realised how much unconscious appeal to pity there was in those unattractive features. Such thoughts were disagreeable, as are all those that make us understand things too late, and the Prince's face went solemn and dark as if he were following an invisible funeral car. Only the violent impact of his feet on loose stones in the street showed his internal conflict. It is superfluous to mention that the ribbon on his top hat was innocent of any piece of paper; but in the eyes of those who knew him a 'yes' and a 'no' alternated on the glistening felt.

On reaching a little room in the Town Hall used as the voting booth he was surprised to see all the members of the committee get up as his great height filled the doorway; a few peasants who had arrived before were put aside, and so without having to wait Don Fabrizio handed his 'yes' into the patriotic hands of Don Calogero Sedàra. Father Pirrone, though, did not vote at all, as he had been careful not to get himself listed as resident in the town. Don 'Nofrio, obeying the express desires of the Prince, gave his own monosyllabic opinion about the complicated Italian question; a masterpiece of concision carried through with the good grace of a child drinking castor oil. After which all were invited for 'a little glass' upstairs in the Mayor's study; but Father Pirrone and Don 'Nofrio put forward good reasons, one of abstinence, the other of stomachache, and remained below. Don Fabrizio had to face the party alone.

Behind the Mayor's writing desk gleamed a brand new portrait of Garibaldi and (already) one of King Victor Emmanuel hung, luckily, to the right; the first handsome, the second ugly; both, however, made brethren by prodigious growths of hair which nearly hid their faces altogether. On a small low table was a plate with some ancient biscuits blackened by fly droppings and a dozen little squat glasses brimming with *rosolio* wine : four red, four green, four white, the last in the centre : an ingenious symbol of the new national flag which tempered the Prince's remorse with a smile. He chose the white liquor for himself, presumably because the least indigestible and not, as some thought, in tardy homage to the Bourbon standard. Anyway, all three varieties of *rosolio* were equally sugary, sticky and revolting. His host had the good taste not to give toasts. But, as Don Calogero said, great joys are silent. Don Fabrizio was shown a letter from the authorities of Girgenti announcing to the industrious citizens of Donnafugata the concession of 2,000 lire towards sewage, a work which would be completed before the end of 1961 so the Mayor assured them, stumbling into one of those *lapsus* whose mechanism Freud was to explain many decades later; and the meeting broke up.

Before dusk the three or four easy girls of Donnafugata (there were some there too, not grouped but each hard at work on her own) appeared in the square with tricolour ribbons in their manes as protest against the exclusion of women from the vote; the poor creatures were jeered at even by the most advanced liberals and forced back to their lairs. This did not prevent the *Giornale di Trinacria* telling the people of Palermo four days later that at Donna-fugata 'some gentle representatives of the fair sex wished to show their faith in the new and brilliant destinies of their beloved Country, and demonstrated in the main square amid great acclamation from the patriotic population.'

After this the electoral booths were closed and the scrutators got to work; late that night the shutters on the balcony of the Town Hall were flung open and Don Calogero appeared with a tricolour sash over his middle, flanked by two ushers with lighted candelabra which the wind snuffed at once. To the invisible crowd in the shadows below he announced that the Plebiscite at Donna-fugata had had the following results :

Voters, 515; Voting, 512; Yes, 512; No, zero.

From the dark end of the square rose applause and hurrahs; on her little balcony Angelica, with her funereal maid, clapped lovely rapacious hands; speeches were made; adjectives loaded with superlatives and double consonants reverberated and echoed in the dark from one wall to an-other; amid thundering of fireworks messages were sent

off to the King (the new one) and to the General; a tricolour rocket or two climbed up from the village into the
blackness towards the starless sky. By eight o'clock all was
over, and nothing remained except darkness as on any other
night, always.

On the top of Monte Morco all was clear now, in bright
light; but the gloom of that night still lay stagnant deep
in Don Fabrizio's heart. His discomfort had become more
irksome, if vaguer; it had no connection at all with the
great matters of which the Plebiscite marked the start of
a solution : the major interests of the Kingdom (of the Two
Sicilies) and of his own class, his personal privileges had
come through all these events battered but still lively. In
the circumstances he could not well expect more. No, his
discomfort was not of a political nature and must have
deeper roots somewhere in one of those reasons which we
call irrational because they are buried under layers of
self-ignorance. Italy was born on that sullen night at
Donnafugata, born right there, in that forgotten little town,
just as much as in the sloth of Palermo or the clamour of
Naples; but an evil fairy, of unknown name, must have been
present; anyway Italy was born and one could only hope
that she would live on in this form; any other would be
worse. Agreed. And yet this persistent disquiet of his
must mean something; during that too brief announcement
of figures, just as during those too emphatic speeches, he
had a feeling that something, someone, had died, God
only knew in what back-alley, in what corner of the
popular conscience.

The cool air had dispersed Don Ciccio's somnolence, the
massive grandeur of the Prince dispelled his fears; all
that remained afloat now on the surface of his conscience
was resentment, useless of course but not ignoble. He stood
up, spoke in dialect and gesticulated, a pathetic puppet
who in some absurd way was right.

'I, Excellency, voted "no." "No," a hundred times "no."
I know what you told me : necessity, unity, expediency. You
may be right; I know nothing of politics. Such things

I leave to others. But Ciccio Tumeo is honest, poor though
he may be, with his trousers in holes' (and he slapped
the carefully mended patches on the buttocks of his
shooting breeches) 'and I don't forget favours done me!
Those swine in the Town Hall just swallowed up my
opinion, chewed it and then spat it out transformed as
they wanted. I said black and they made me say white!
The one time when I could say what I thought that
bloodsucker Sedàra went and annulled it, behaved as if
I'd never existed, as if I never meant a thing, me, Francesco
Tumeo La Manna son of the late Leonardo, organist of
the Mother Church at Donnafugata, a better man than
he is! To think I'd even dedicated to him a Mazurka com-
posed by me at the birth of that . . .' (he bit a finger to
rein himself in) 'that mincing daughter of his!'

At this point calm descended on Don Fabrizio, who had
finally solved the enigma; now he knew who had been
killed at Donnafugata, at a hundred other places, in the
course of that night of dirty wind : a new-born babe : good
faith; just the very child who should have been cared for
most, whose strengthening would have justified all the silly
vandalisms. Don Ciccio's negative vote, fifty similar votes
at Donnafugata, a hundred thousand 'no's' in the whole
Kingdom, would have had no effect on the result, have made
it, in fact, if anything more significant; and this maiming
of souls would have been avoided. Six months before they
used to hear a rough despotic voice saying : 'Do what I say
or you're for it!' Now there was already an impression
of such a threat being replaced by a money-lender's soapy
tones : 'But you signed it yourself, didn't you? Can't you
see? It's quite clear. You must do as we say, for here
are the I.O.U.s; your will is identical with mine.'

Don Ciccio was still thundering on : 'For you nobles
it's different. *You* might be ungrateful about an extra
estate, but *we* must be grateful for a bit of bread. It's
different again for profiteers like Sedàra with whom cheating is a law of nature. Small folk like us have to take
things as they come. You know, Excellency, that my father,
God rest his soul, was gamekeeper at the royal shoot of

Sant' Onofrio back in Ferdinand IV's time, when the English were here? It was a hard life, but the green royal livery and the silver plaque conferred authority. Queen Isabella, the Spaniard, was Duchess of Calabria then, and it was she who had me study, made me what I am now, organist of the Mother Church, honoured by your Excellency's kindness; when my mother sent off a petition to Court in our years of greatest need, back came five gold ounces, sure as death, for they were fond of us there in Naples, they knew we were decent folk and faithful subjects; when the King came he used to clap my father on the shoulder. "Don Lionà," he said, "I wish we'd more like you, devoted to the throne and to my Person." Then the officer in attendance used to hand out gold coin. Alms, they call it now, that truly royal generosity; and they call it that so as not to give any themselves; but it was just a reward for loyalty. And if those holy Kings and lovely Queens are looking down at us from heaven to-day, what'ld they say? "The son of Don Leonardo Tumeo betrayed us!" Luckily the truth is known in Paradise! Yes, Excellency, I know, people like you have told me, such things from royalty mean nothing, they're just part of the job. That may be true, in fact is true. But we got those five gold ounces, that's a fact, and they helped us through the winter. And now I could repay the debt my "no" becomes a "yes"! I used to be a "faithful subject," I've become a "filthy Bourbonite." Everyone's Savoyard nowadays! But I take "Savoyards" with coffee!' And he dipped an invisible biscuit between finger and thumb into an imaginary cup.

Don Fabrizio had always liked Don Ciccio, partly because of the compassion inspired in him by all who from youth had thought of themselves as dedicated to the Arts, and in old age, realising they had no talent, still carried on the same activity at lower levels, pocketing withered dreams; and he was also touched by the dignity of his poverty. But now he also felt a kind of admiration for him, and deep down at the very bottom of his proud conscience a voice was asking if Don Ciccio had not perhaps behaved more nobly than the Prince of Salina. And the Sedàra, all the various Sedàra, from the petty one who violated arithmetic at Donnafugata to the major ones at Palermo and Turin, had they not committed a crime by choking such consciences? Don Fabrizio could not know it then, but a great deal of the slackness and acquiescence for which the people of the South were to be criticised during the next decade, was due to the stupid annulment of the first expression of liberty ever offered them.

Don Ciccio had said his say. And now his genuine but rarely shown side of 'austere man of principle' was taken over by one much more frequent and no less genuine, that of snob. For Tumeo belonged to the zoological species of 'passive snob,' a species unjustly reviled nowadays. Of course the word 'snob' was unknown in the Sicily of 1860; but just as tuberculosis existed before Koch, so in that remote era there were people for whom to obey, imitate and above all avoid distressing those whom they considered of higher social rank than themselves was the supreme law of life; snobbery, in fact, is the opposite of envy. At that time a man of this type went under various names; he was called 'devoted,' 'attached,' 'faithful'; and life was happy for him since a nobleman's most fugitive smile was enough to flood an entire day with sun; and accompanied by such affectionate appellatives, the restorative graces were more frequent than they are to-day. Now Don Ciccio's frankly snobbish nature made him fear causing Don Fabrizio distress, and he searched diligently round for ways to disperse any frowns he might be causing on the Prince's Olympian brow; the best means to hand was suggesting they should start shooting again; and so they did. Surprised in their afternoon naps some wretched woodcock and another rabbit fell under the marksmen's fire, particularly accurate and pitiless that day as both Salina and Tumeo were identifying those innocent creatures with Don Calogero Sedàra. But the shots, the flying feathers, the shreds of skin glittering for an instant in the sun, were not enough to soothe the Prince that day; as the hours passed and return to Donnafugata drew near he felt more

and more oppressed, bothered, humiliated at the thought
of the imminent conversation with the plebeian Mayor, and
his having called in his heart those woodcock and the
rabbit 'Don Calogero' had been no use after all; though
he had already decided to swallow the horrid toad he
still felt a need for more information about his adversary,
or rather, for a sounding out of public opinion about the
step he was about to take. So for the second time that day
Don Ciccio was surprised by a sudden point-blank question.

'Listen, Don Ciccio; you see so many people, what do
they really think of Don Calogero at Donnafugata?'

Tumeo, in truth, felt he had already shown his opinion
of the Mayor quite clearly; and he was just about to say
so when into his mind came rumours he had heard about
Tancredi making up to Angelica : and he was suddenly
overwhelmed with regret at having let himself be drawn
into expressing downright judgments which must certainly
be anathema to the Prince if what he assumed was true;
in another part of his mind, meanwhile, he was congratulating himself at not having said anything positive against
Angelica; and the faint ache which he still felt in his right
forefinger had the effect of a soothing balsam.

'After all, Excellency, Don Calogero Sedàra is no
worse than lots of others who have come up in the last
few months.' The homage was moderate but enough to
allow Don Fabrizio to insist, 'You see, Don Ciccio, I'm most
interested to know the truth about Don Calogero and his
family.'

'The truth, Excellency, is that Don Calogero is very
rich, and very influential too; that he's a miser (when
his daughter was at college he and his wife used to eat a
fried egg between them), but knows how to spend when he
has to; and as every coin spent in the world must end in
someone's pocket he now finds many people dependent on
him; when he's a friend he really is a friend, one must say
that for him : he lets his land on very harsh terms and
the peasants kill themselves to pay, but a month ago he lent
fifty gold ounces to Pasquale Tripi who had helped him at

the time of the landings: without interest, too, which is
the greatest miracle ever known since Santa Rosalia
stopped the plague at Palermo. He's clever as the devil, too;
Your Excellency should have seen him last April or May;
up and down the whole district he went like a bat; by
trap, horse, mule, foot, in rain or sun; and wherever he
passed secret groups were formed, to prepare the way for
those that were to come. He's a scourge of God, Excellency,
a scourge of God. And we're only seeing the start of Don
Calogero's career. In a few months he'll be Deputy in the
Turin Parliament; in a few years, when church property
is put up for sale, he'll pay next to nothing for the estates
of Marca and Fondachello and become the biggest land-
owner in the province; that's Don Calogero, Excellency, the
new man to be: a pity he has to be like that, though.'

Don Fabrizio remembered a conversation with Father
Pirrone some months before in the sunlit observatory. What
the Jesuit had predicted had come to pass. But wasn't it
perhaps good tactics to insert himself into the new movement, make at least part use of it for a few members of his
own class? The worry of his imminent interview with Don
Calogero lessened.

'But the rest of his family, Don Ciccio, what are they
really like?'

'Excellency, no one has laid eyes on Don Calogero's wife
for years, except me. She only leaves the house to go to
early Mass, the five o'clock one, when it's empty. There's
no organ-playing at that hour; but once I got up early
just to see her. Donna Bastiana came in with her maid, and
as I was hiding behind a confessional I could not see very
much; but at the end of Mass the heat was too great for
the poor woman and she took off her black veil. Word of
honour, Excellency, she was lovely as the sun, one can't
blame Don Calogero, who's a beetle of a man, for wanting
to keep her away from others. But even in the best kept
houses secrets come out; servants talk; and it seems
Donna Bastiana is a kind of animal: she can't read or
write or tell the time by a clock, can scarcely talk; just a
beautiful mare, voluptuous and uncouth; she's incapable

even of affection for her own daughter! Good for bed and that's all.'

Don Ciccio, who, as protégé of queens and follower of princes, considered his own simple manners to be perfect, smiled with pleasure. He had found a way of getting some of his own back on the suppressor of his personality. 'Anyway,' he went on, 'one couldn't expect much else. You know whose daughter Donna Bastiana is, Excellency?' He turned, rose on tiptoe, pointed to a distant group of huts which looked as if they were slithering off the edge of the hill, nailed there just by a wretched-looking bell-tower: a crucified hamlet. 'She's the daughter of one of your peasants from Runci, Peppe Giunta he was called, so filthy and so crude that everyone called him Peppe "Mmerda" . . . excuse the word, Excellency.' Satisfied, he twisted one of Teresina's ears round a finger. 'Two years after Don Calogero had eloped with Bastiana they found him dead on the path to Rampinzeri, with twelve bullets in his back. Always lucky, is Don Calogero, for the old man was getting above himself and demanding, they say.'

Much of this was known to Don Fabrizio and had already been balanced up in his mind; but the nickname of Angelica's grandfather was new to him; it opened a profound historical perspective, and made him glimpse other abysses compared to which Don Calogero himself seemed a garden flowerbed. The Prince began to feel the ground giving way under his feet; how ever could Tancredi swallow this? And what about himself? He found himself trying to work out the relationship between the Prince of Salina, uncle of the bridegroom, and the grandfather of the bride; he found none, there wasn't any. Angelica was just Angelica, a flower of a girl, a rose merely fertilised by her grandfather's nickname. *Non olet,* he repeated, *non olet*; in fact *optime foeminam ac contuberninum olet.*

'You've mentioned everything, Don Ciccio, crude mothers and faecal grandfathers, but not what interests me: the Signorina Angelica.'

The secret of Tancredi's matrimonial intentions, although

embryonic until a few hours before, would certainly have been told then had it not luckily been camouflaged. No doubt the young man's frequent visits to Don Calogero's home had been noticed, as also his ecstatic smiles and little attentions, normal and insignificant in a city but symptoms of violent passion in the eyes of virtuous folk at Donnafugata. The main scandal had been the first; the old men cooking in the sun and the children duelling in the dust had seen all, understood all, and repeated all; and on the aphrodisiac and seductive properties of those dozen peaches had been consulted the most expert witches and abstruse treatises on potions, chiefly that by Rutilio Benincasa, the Aristotle of the rustic proletariat. Luckily there had come about a phenomenon relatively frequent amongst Sicilians; malice had masked truth; everyone had built up a puppet of a libertine Tancredi fixing his lascivous desires on Angelica; he was manœuvring to seduce her, that was all. The thought of any possible marriage between a Prince of Falconeri and a granddaughter of Peppe 'Mmerda' did not even cross the minds of these country folk, who thus rendered to feudal families a homage equivalent to that rendered by a blasphemer to God. Tancredi's departure had cut short these fantasies and they were not mentioned again. In this respect Tumeo had been like the others, so he greeted the Prince's question with the amused air assumed by older men when discoursing on the follies of the young.

'As to the Signorina, Excellency, there's nothing to say about her; she speaks for herself; her eyes, her skin, her figure are all there to be seen and appreciated by anyone. Don Tancredi has understood the language they speak, I think; or shouldn't I suggest such a thing? She has all the beauty of the mother with none of the grandfather's stink of manure; and she's intelligent, too. You've seen how those few years in Florence have transformed her completely? A real lady she's become,' went on Don Ciccio, insensitive to subtleties in such matters. 'A complete lady. When she returned from school and invited me home she played my old mazurka; badly, but it was a delight to watch her, those black locks, those eyes, those legs, that breast . . . Uuh! No stink of manure there! Her sheets must smell like paradise!'

The Prince was vexed; so touchy is the pride of class, even in a moment of decline, that these orgiastic praises of his future niece's allurements offended him; how dared Don Ciccio express himself with such lascivious lyricism about a future Princess of Falconeri? It is true, of course, that the poor man knew nothing as yet; he would have to be told all : but anyway the news would be public in three hours. He decided at once and turned to Tumeo a smile feline but friendly. 'Calm yourself, my dear Don Ciccio, calm yourself; at home I have a letter from my nephew charging me to ask for Signorina Angelica's hand in matrimony on his behalf; so from now on you will talk of her with your usual respect. You are the first to know the news, but for that privilege you must pay; when we get back to the palace you'll be locked up with Teresina in the gun-room; you'll have time to clean and oil all the guns, and you will be set at liberty only after Don Calogero's visit; I want nothing to leak out before.'

Taken by surprise like this, all Don Ciccio's snobberies and precautions collapsed together like a group of skittles hit in the middle. All that survived was age-old feeling.

'How foul, Excellency! A nephew of yours ought not to marry the daughter of those who're your enemies, who have stabbed you in the back! To try to seduce her, as I thought, was an act of conquest; this is unconditional surrender. It's the end of the Falconeri and of the Salina too.'

Having said this he bent his head and longed in anguish for the earth to open under his feet. The Prince had gone purple, even his ears, even the whites of his eyes seemed flushed with blood. He clenched his fists and took a step towards Don Ciccio. But he was a man of science, used, after all, to seeing at times the pros and cons; and anyway under that leonine aspect he was a sceptic. He had put up with so much that day already; the result of the Plebiscite, the nickname of Angelica's grandfather,

those bullets in the back. And Tumeo was right; in him
spoke clear tradition. But the man was a fool : this marriage
was not the end of everything, but the beginning of
everything. It was in the very best of traditions.

His fists unclenched; the marks of his nails were im-
pressed on his palms. 'Let's go home, Don Ciccio, there are
some things you can't understand. Now, you'll remember
what we agreed, won't you?'

And as they climbed down towards the road, it would
have been difficult to tell which of the two was Don
Quixote and which Sancho Panza.

When Don Calogero's arrival was announced at exactly
half-past four the Prince had not yet finished his toilet;
he sent a message asking the Mayor to wait a minute in
his study and went on placidly embellishing himself. He
plastered his hair with *Lemo-liscio,* Atkinson's 'Lime Juice
and Glycerine', a dense whitish lotion which arrived in
cases from London and whose name suffered the same
ethnic changes as songs : he rejected the black frock-coat
and chose instead a very pale lilac one which seemed
more in keeping with the presumably festive occasion;
he dallied a little longer to tweak out with pincers an
impudent fair hair which had succeeded in escaping
that morning in his hurried shave : he had Father Pirrone
called; before leaving the room he took off a table an
extract from the *Blätter für Himmelsforschung* and with
the rolled-up pamphlet made the sign of the Cross, a gesture of devotion which in Sicily has a non-religious meaning
more often than is realised.

As he crossed the two rooms preceding the study he
tried to imagine himself as an imposing leopard with
smooth scented skin preparing to tear a timid jackal
to pieces; but by one of those involuntary associations of
ideas which are the scourge of natures like his, he found
flicking into his memory one of those French historical
pictures in which Austrian marshals and generals, covered
with plumes and decorations, are filing in surrender past an
ironical Napoleon; they are more elegant, undoubtedly, but

it is the squat little man in the grey topcoat who is the victor; and so, put out by these inopportune memories of Mantua and Ulm, it was an irritated Leopard that entered the study.

Don Calogero was standing there, very small, very badly shaved; he would have looked like a jackal had it not been for eyes glinting intelligence; but as this intelligence of his had a material aim opposed to the abstract one to which the Prince's was supposed to tend, this was taken as a sign of slyness. Devoid of the instinct for choosing the right clothes for the occasion which was innate in the Prince, the Mayor had thought it proper to dress up almost in mourning; he was nearly as black as Father Pirrone, but while the latter was sitting in a corner with the marmoreally abstract air of priests who wish to avoid influencing the decisions of others, the Mayor's face expressed a sense of avid expectancy almost painful to behold. They plunged at once into the skirmish of insignificant words which precede great verbal battles. But it was Don Calogero who launched the main attack.

'Excellency,' he asked, 'have you had good news from Don Tancredi?' In little towns in those days the Mayor was always able to examine the post unofficially and maybe he had been warned by the unusually elegant writing paper. The Prince, when this occurred to him, began to feel annoyed.

'No, Don Calogero, no. My nephew's gone mad . . .'

But there exists a deity who is protector of princes. He is called Courtesy. And he often intervenes to prevent Leopards from unfortunate slips. But he has to be paid heavy tribute. As Pallas intervened to curb the intemperances of Odysseus, so Courtesy appeared to Don Fabrizio and stopped him on the brink of the abyss; but the Prince had to pay for his salvation by becoming explicit for just once in his life. With perfect naturalness, without a second's hesitation, he ended the phrase; '. . . mad with love for your daughter, Don Calogero. So he wrote to me yesterday.'

The Mayor preserved a surprising equanimity. He gave

a slight smile and began examining the ribbon on his hat; Father Pirrone's eyes were turned to the ceiling as if he were a master mason charged with judging its solidity. The Prince was put out : that silence on both their parts even deprived him of the petty satisfaction of arousing surprise. So it was with relief that he realised Don Calogero was about to speak.

'I knew it, Excellency, I knew it. They were seen to kiss on Tuesday, 25th of September, the day before Don Tancredi's departure. In your garden, near the fountain. Laurel hedges aren't always as thick as people think. For a month I've been waiting for your nephew to make some move, and I'd just been thinking now of coming to ask Your Excellency about his intentions.'

Don Fabrizio felt assailed by numbers of stinging hornets. First, as is proper to every man not yet decrepit, that of carnal jealousy. So Tancredi had tasted that flavour of strawberries and cream which would always be unknown to him ! Then came a sense of social humiliation at finding himself an accused instead of a bearer of good news. Third, personal vexation, that of one who thought he had everything in his control and then finds much has been happening without his knowledge. 'Don Calogero, let's not change the cards we have on the table. Remember, it was *I* who called *you*. I wished to tell you of a letter from my nephew which arrived yesterday. In it he declares his passion for your daughter, a passion of whose intensity I . . .' (Here the Prince hesitated a moment, because lies are sometimes difficult to tell before gimlets eyes like the Mayor's) '. . . I was completely ignorant till now; and at the end of it he charges me to ask you for Signorina Angelica's hand.'

Don Calagero went on smiling impassively; Father Pirrone had transformed himself from architectural expert into Moslem sage, and with four fingers of his right hand crossed in four fingers of his left was rotating his thumbs around each other, turning and changing their direction with a great display of choreographic fantasy. The silence lasted a long time; the Prince lost patience. 'Now, Don

Calogero, it is I who am waiting for you to declare your intentions.'

The Mayor's eyes had been fixed on the orange fringe of the Prince's arm-chair; for an instant he covered them with his right hand, then raised them; now they looked candid, brimming with amazed surprise, as if that action had really changed them.

'Excuse me, Prince,' (by the sudden omission of 'Excellency' Don Fabrizio knew that all was happily consummated) 'but joy and surprise had taken my words away. I'm a modern parent, though, and can give no definite answer until I have questioned the angel who is the consolation of our home. But I also know how to exercise a father's sacred rights. All that happens in Angelica's heart and mind is known to me, and I think I can say that Don Tancredi's affection, which honours us all, is sincerely returned.'

Don Fabrizio was overcome with sincere emotion; the toad had been swallowed; the chewed head and gizzards were going down his throat; he still had to crunch up the claws, but that was nothing compared to the rest; the worst was over. With this sense of liberation he began to feel his affection for Tancredi coming to the fore again, and thought of those narrow blue eyes of his glittering as they read the happy reply; he imagined, or recalled rather, the first months of a love match with the frenzies and acrobatics of the senses braced and sustained by all the hierarchies of angels, benevolent though surely surprised. And he foresaw Tancredi's security of life later on, his chances for developing talents whose wings would have been clipped by lack of money.

The nobleman rose to his feet, took a step towards the surprised Don Calogero, raised him from his arm-chair, clasped him to his breast; the Mayor's short legs were suspended in the air. For a moment that room in a remote Sicilian province looked like a Japanese print of a huge violet iris with a hairy fly hanging from a petal. When Don Calogero touched the floor again, Don Fabrizio thought, 'This won't do, I really must give him a pair of English razors.'

Father Pirrone switched off the turbine of his thumbs; he got up and squeezed the Prince's hand. 'Excellency, I evoke the protection of God on this marriage; your joy has become mine.' To Don Calogero he extended the tips of his fingers without a word. Then with a knuckle he tapped the barometer hanging on the wall : it was falling; bad weather ahead. He sat down and opened his Breviary.

'Don Calogero,' said the Prince, 'the love of these two young people is the basis, the sole foundation of their future happiness. That we all know. But we men of a certain age, men of experience, have to think of other things, too. There is no point in my telling you how illustrious is the family of Falconeri; it came to Sicily with Charles of Anjou, flourished under the Aragonese, the Spanish, the Bourbon kings (if I may name them in your presence). and I am sure that it will also prosper under the new dynasty from the mainland (which God preserve).' (It was impossible to tell how much the Prince was being ironic or how much just mistaken.) 'They were Peers of the Realm, Grandees of Spain, Knights of Santiago, and when they have a fancy to be Knights of Malta they need only raise a finger and Via Condotti turns them out a diploma all fresh from the oven, without a word of complaint. So far at least.' (This perfidious insinuation was entirely lost on Don Calogero, who was quite ignorant of the statues of the Sovereign Hierosalamitan Order of St. John.) 'I am sure that your daughter will ornament still more by her rare beauty the ancient trunk of the Falconeri and emulate by her virtue that of the saintly princesses of the line, the last of whom, my sister, God rest her soul, will certainly bless the bride and groom from Heaven.' Again Don Fabrizio felt moved, remembering his dear Giulia whose wasted life had been a perpetual sacrifice to the frenzied extravagances of Tancredi's father. 'As for the boy, you know him; and if you did not, I am here to guarantee him in every possible way. There is endless good in him, and it is not only I who say so. Isn't that true, Father Pirrone?'

The excellent Jesuit, dragged from his reading, found himself suddenly facing an unpleasant dilemma. He had been Tancredi's confessor and he knew quite a number of his little failings : none very serious, of course, but such as to detract quite a good deal from the endless goodness of which the Prince had spoken; and all such (he almost felt like saying) as to guarantee an unwavering marital infidelity. This, of course, could not actually be said both for sacramental reasons and from worldly expediency. On the other hand he liked Tancredi, and though he disapproved of the wedding with all his heart he would never say a word which could either impede it or in any way cloud its course. He took refuge in Prudence, most tractable of the cardinal virtues. 'The fund of goodness in our dear Tancredi is great indeed, Don Calogero, and, sustained by Divine Grace and by the earthly virtues of Signorina Angelica, he may one day become a good Christian husband.' The prophecy, risky but prudently conditional, passed muster.

'But, Don Calogero,' went on the Prince, chewing on the last gristly bits of toad, 'if it is pointless to tell you of the antiquity of the Falconeri, it is unfortunately also pointless, since you already know it, to tell you that my nephew's economic circumstances are not equal to the greatness of his name. Don Tancredi's father, my brother-in-law Ferdinando, was not what is called a provident parent; his magnificent scale of life, and the irresponsibility of his administrators, have gravely shaken the patrimony of my dear nephew and former ward; the great estates around Mazzara, the pistachio woods of Ravanusa, the mulberry plantations of Oliveri, the palace in Palermo, all, all have gone; that you know, Don Calogero.'

Don Calogero did indeed know that; it had been the greatest migration of swallows in living memory : a thought which still brought terror, though not prudence, to the entire Sicilian nobility, while it was a font of delight for all the Sedàras. 'During the period of my guardianship all I succeeded in saving was the villa, the one near my own, by juridical quibbles and also thanks to a sacrifice or two on my own part which I made joyfully, both in memory of my sainted sister Giulia and because of my own affection for the dear lad. It's a fine villa; the staircase was designed by Marvuglia, the drawing-rooms frescoed by Serenario; but at the moment the room in best repair can scarcely be used as a stall for goats.'

The last shreds of toad had been nastier than he had expected : but they had gone down too, in the end. Now he had only to wash out his mouth with some phrase which was pleasant as well as sincere. 'But, Don Calogero, the result of all these disasters, of all this heart-burning, has been Tancredi. There are certain things known to people like us; and maybe it is impossible to obtain the distinction, the delicacy, the fascination of a boy like him without his ancestors having romped through half a dozen fortunes. At least so it is in Sicily; it's a kind of law of nature, like those regulating earthquakes and drought.'

He paused a moment as a lackey came in bearing two lighted lamps on a tray. As they were being set in place the Prince caused a silence charged with resigned concern to reign in the study. 'Tancredi is no ordinary boy, Don Calogero,' he went on. 'He is far more than merely gentlemanly and elegant; though he has not studied much, he knows about the important things; men, women, the feel and sense of the times. He is ambitious and rightly so; he will go far; and your Angelica, Don Calogero, will be lucky to mount the ladder with him. Also, in Tancredi's company one may have moments of irritation, but never of boredom; and that means a great deal.'

It would be an exaggeration to say that the Mayor appreciated the worldly subtleties of this part of the Prince's speech; on the whole it merely confirmed him in his summary conviction of Tancredi's shrewdness and opportunism; and what he needed at home was a man astute and able, no more. He thought himself, he felt himself

to be the equal of anyone; and he was even rather sorry to
notice in his daughter a genuine affection for the handsome
youth.

'Prince, all these things I knew, and others too. And they
don't matter to me at all.' He wrapped himself round once
more in a cloak of sentimentality. 'Love, Excellency, love is
all, as I know myself.' And he may have been sincere, poor
man, if his probable definition of love were admitted. 'But
I'm a man of the world and I want to put my cards on the
table too. There's no point in talking about my daughter's
qualities; she's the blood in my heart, the liver in my
guts : I've no one else to leave what I have, and what's
mine is hers. But it's only right that the young people
should know what they can count on at once. In the
marriage contract I will assign to my daughter the estate
of Settesoli, of 644 *salmi*, that is 1010 *hectares* as they want
us to call them nowadays, all corn, first-class land, airy
and cool; and 180 *salmi* of olive groves and vineyards at
Gibildolce; and on the wedding day I will hand over to
the bridegroom twenty linen sacks each containing 10,000
ounces of gold. I'll only have a stick or two left myself,'
he added, knowing well he would not and not wanting to
be believed, 'but a daughter's a daughter. And with
that they can do up all the staircases by Marruggia and all
the ceilings by Sorcionario that exist. Angelica must be
properly housed.'

Ignorant vulgarity exuded from his every pore; even so
the two listeners were astounded; Don Fabrizio needed all
his self-control not to show surprise; Tancredi's coup was
far bigger than he had ever imagined. A sensation of revulsion came over him again, but Angelica's beauty, the
bridegroom's grace, still managed to veil in poetry the
crudeness of the contract. Father Pirrone did let his
tongue cluck on his palate; then, annoyed at having shown
his own amazement, he tried to rhyme the improvident
sound by making his chair and shoes squeak and by
crackling the leaves of his breviary but failed completely;
the impression remained.

Luckily an impromptu remark from Don Calogero, the only one in the conversation, got both of them out of the embarrassment. 'Prince,' he said, 'I know that what I am about to say will have no effect on you who descend from the loves of the Emperor Titus and Queen Berenice; but the Sedàra are noble too; till I came along we've been an unlucky lot, buried in the provinces and undistinguished, but I have the documents in order, and one day it will be known that your nephew has married the Baronessina Sedàra del Biscotto; a title granted by His Majesty Ferdinand IV on his rights from Mazzara port. I've put the papers through; there's only one link missing.'

A hundred years ago this business of a missing link, of getting such papers 'through' was an important element in the lives of many Sicilians, causing alternating exaltation and depression to thousands of respectable or not so respectable folk; but the subject is too important to be treated fleetingly, and we will content ourselves with saying here that Don Calogero's heraldic impromptu gave the Prince the incomparable artistic satisfaction of seeing a type realised in all its details; and that he gave a depressed laugh ending in a sweetish taste of nausea.

After this the conversation drifted off into a number of aimless ruts; Don Fabrizio remembered Tumeo shut up in the darkness of the gun-room; for the nth time in his life he deplored the length of country calls and ended by wrapping himself in hostile silence. Don Calogero understood, promised to return next morning with Angelica's undoubted consent, and said good-bye. He was accompanied through two of the drawing-rooms, embraced again, and began descending the stairs while the Prince, towering above, watched getting smaller this little conglomeration of ill-cut clothes, money and cunning brashness who was now to become almost part of his family.

Holding a candle in his hand he then went to free Tumeo, who was sitting resignedly in the dark smoking his pipe. 'I'm sorry, Don Ciccio, but you'll understand, I had to do it.'

'I do understand, Excellency, I do indeed. Did everything go off all right?'

'Perfectly, couldn't be better.' Tumeo mouthed some
congratulations, put the leash back on the collar of Teresina, sleeping exhausted by the hunt, and picked up the
game-bag.

'Take those woodcock of mine too, won't you? They're
not enough for us all, anyway. Good-bye, Don Ciccio,
come and see us soon. And excuse everything.' A powerful
clap on the shoulder served as sign of reconciliation and
a reminder of power; the last faithful retainer of the House
of Salina went off to his own poor rooms.

When the Prince returned to his study he found that
Father Pirrone had slipped away to avoid discussion. And
he went towards his wife's room to tell her all that had
happened. The sound of his vigorous rapid steps announced
his arrival ten yards ahead. He crossed the girls' sitting-
room; Carolina and Caterina were winding a skein of
wool, and as he passed got to their feet and smiled;
Mademoiselle Dombreuil hurriedly took off her spectacles
and replied demurely to his greeting; Concetta had her
back to him; she was embroidering and, not hearing her
father's steps, did not even turn.

4

LOVE AT DONNAFUGATA

As meetings due to the marriage contract became more frequent, Don Fabrizio found an odd admiration growing in him for Sedàra's qualities. He became used to the ill-shaven cheeks, the plebeian accent, the odd clothes and the persistent odour of stale sweat, and he began to realise the man's rare intelligence. Many problems that had seemed insoluble to the Prince were resolved in a trice by Don Calogero; free as he was from the shackles imposed on many other men by honesty, decency and plain good manners, he moved through the forest of life with the confidence of an elephant which advances in a straight line, rooting up trees and trampling down lairs, without even noticing scratches of thorns and moans from the crushed. Reared and tended in pleasant vales traversed by courteous wafts of 'please,' 'I'd be so grateful,' 'how kind,' the Prince, when chatting to Don Calogero, found himself on an open heath swept by searing winds, and although continuing in his heart to prefer defiles in the hills, he could not help admiring this vital surge which drew from the ilexes and cedars of Donnafugata chords never heard before.

Bit by bit, almost without realising it, Don Fabrizio told Don Calogero about his own affairs, which were numerous, complex and little understood by himself; this was not due to any defect of intelligence but to a kind of contemptuous indifference about matters he considered low, though deep down this attitude was really due to laziness and the ease with which he had always got out of difficulties by selling off a few more hundred of his thousands of acres.

Don Calogero's advice, after listening to the Prince's
report and mentally setting it in order, was both opportune
and immediately effective; but the eventual result of such
advice, cruelly efficient in conception, and feeble in applica-
tion by the kindly Don Fabrizio, was that as years went
by the Salina were to acquire a reputation as extortioners
of their own dependants, a reputation quite unjustified
in reality but which helped to destroy their prestige at
Donnafugata and Querceta, without in any way halting
the collapse of the family fortunes.

It is only fair to mention that more frequent contact
with the Prince had a certain effect on Sedàra too. Until
that moment he had only met aristocrats on business of
buying and selling or through their very rare and long-
brooded invitations to parties, circumstances in which the
most singular of social classes does not show at its best.
During such meetings he had formed the opinion that the
aristocracy consisted entirely of sheep-like creatures, who
existed merely in order to give up their wool to his shears
and their names and incomprehensible prestige to his
daughter. But since getting to know Tancredi during the
period after Garibaldi's landing he had found himself
dealing, unexpectedly, with a young noble as cynical as
himself, capable of striking a sharp bargain between his
own smiles and titles and the attractions and fortunes
of others, while knowing how to dress up such 'Sedàra-ish'
actions with a grace and fascination which he, Don
Calagero, felt he did not himself possess, but which in-
fluenced him without realising it and without his being
able in any way to discern its origins. When he got to
know Don Fabrizio better he found there again the
pliability and incapability for self-defence that were characteristic of his imaginary sheep-noble, but also a strength
of attraction different in tone, but similar in intensity,
to young Falconeri's; he also found a certain energy with
a tendency towards abstraction, a disposition to seek
a shape for life from within himself and not in what he
could wrest from others. This abstract energy made a deep
impression on Don Calogero, although with a direct impact

not filtered through words as has been attempted here; much of this fascination, he noticed, simply came from good manners, and he realised how agreeable can be a well-bred man, for at heart he is only someone who eliminates the unpleasant aspects of so much of the human condition and exercises a kind of profitable altruism (a formula in which the usefulness of the adjective made him tolerate the uselessness of the noun). Gradually Don Calogero came to understand that a meal in common need not necessarily be all munching and grease stains; that a conversation may well bear no resemblance to a dog fight; that to give precedence to a woman is a sign of strength and not, as he had believed, of weakness; that sometimes more can be obtained by saying 'I haven't explained myself well' than 'I can't understand a word'; and that the adoption of such tactics can result in a greatly increased yield from meals, arguments, women and questioners.

It would be rash to affirm that Don Calogero drew an immediate profit from what he had learnt; he did manage from then on to shave a little better and feel a little less aghast at the amount of soap used for laundering, no more; but from that moment there began, for him and his family, that process of continual refining which in the course of three generations transforms innocent boors into defenceless gentry.

Angelica's first visit to the Salina family as a bride-to-be was impeccably stage-managed. Her bearing was so perfect that it might have been suggested word for word by Tancredi, but this was ruled out by the slow communications of the period; one possible explanation was that he had given her some suggestions even before their official engagement: a risky hypothesis for one able to measure the young prince's foresight but not entirely absurd. Angelica arrived at six in the evening, dressed in pink and white; her soft black tresses were shadowed by a big straw hat of late summer on which bunches of artificial grapes and gilt heads of corn discreetly evoked the vineyards of

Gibildolce and the granaries of Settesoli. She sloughed off her father in the entrance hall; then with a swirl of wide skirts floated lightly up the numerous steps of the inner staircase and flung herself into the arms of Don Fabrizio; on his whiskers she implanted two big kisses which were returned with genuine affection; the Prince paused perhaps just a second longer than necessary to breathe in the scent of gardenia on adolescent cheeks. After this Angelica blushed, took half a step back : 'I'm so, so happy . . .' then came close again, stood on tiptoe, and murmured into his ear 'Nuncle !'; a highly successful line, comparable in its perfect timing to Eisenstein's business with the pram, and which, explicit and secret as it was, set the Prince's simple heart aflutter and yoked him to the lovely girl for ever. Meanwhile Don Calogero was coming up the stairs, and said how very sorry his wife was she could not be present but the night before she had slipped at home and twisted her left foot, which was most painful. 'Her ankle's like a melon, Prince.' Don Fabrizio, exhilarated by the verbal caress, and forewarned by Tumeo's revelations that his offer would never be put to the proof, said that he would give himself the pleasure of calling upon the Signora Sedàra at once, a suggestion which dismayed Don Calogero and made him, in order to reject it, think up a second indisposition of his spouse's, this time a violent headache which forced the poor woman to stay in the dark.

Meanwhile the Prince gave his arm to Angelica. They crossed a number of dark salons, just lit enough by the dim glimmer of oil lamps for them to see their way; but at the end of the splendid perspective of rooms glittered the 'Leopold' drawing-room where the rest of the family was gathered, and their procession through empty darkness towards a light centre of intimacy had the rhythm of a Masonic initiation.

The family was crowding round the door; the Princess had withdrawn her own reservations before the wrath of her husband, who had not so much rejected them as blasted them to nullity; she kissed her lovely future niece

again and again and squeezed her to her bosom with such
energy that the girl found stamped on her skin the setting
of the famous Salina ruby necklace which Maria Stella
had insisted on wearing, though it was daylight, in sign
of a major celebration. The sixteen-year-old Francesco
Paolo was pleased at having this exceptional chance of
kissing Angelica too, under the impotently jealous eyes of
his father. Concetta was particularly affectionate; her joy
was so intense that the tears even came to her eyes. The
other sisters drew close around her with noisy gaiety just
because they were not moved. Even Father Pirrone, who
in his saintly way was not insensible to female fascination
in which he saw an undeniable proof of Divine Goodness,
felt all his own opposition melt away before the warmth
of her grace (with a small 'g'); and he murmured to her :
'*Veni, spona de Libano*' (he had to check himself to avoid
other warmer verses rising to his memory). Mademoiselle
Dombreuil, as befits a governess, wept with emotion,
kneading the girl's plump shoulders in her disappointed
fingers and crying : '*Angelicà, Angelicà, pensons à la joie
de Tancrède.*' Only Bendicò, in contrast to his usual soci-
ability, crouched behind a console table and growled away
in the back of his throat until energetically called to task
by an indignant Francesco Paolo with still quivering lips.

Lighted candles had been set on twenty-four of the forty-
eight branches of the chandelier, and each of these candles,
white and at the same time ardent, seemed like a virgin in
the throes of love; the twin-coloured Murano flowers on
their stem of curved glass looked down, admired the girl
who entered, and gave her a fragile and iridescent smile.
The great fireplace was lit more in sign of joy than to warm
the tepid room, and the light of the flames quivered on
the floor, loosing intermittent gleams from the dull gold of
the furniture; it really did represent the domestic hearth,
symbol of home, and its brands were sparks of desire, its
embers ardours contained.

The Princess, who possessed to an eminent degree the
faculty of reducing emotions to a minimum common de-
nominator, began narrating sublime episodes from Tan-

credi's childhood; so insistent was she about these that
it really began to seem as if Angelica should consider herself lucky to be marrying a man who had been so reason-
able at the age of six as to submit to necessary enemas without a fuss, and bold at twelve as to have stolen a handful
of cherries. As this episode of banditry was being recalled,
Concetta burst out laughing. 'That's a habit Tancredi
hasn't yet been able to rid himself of,' she said, 'd'you
remember, papa, how a couple of months ago he took those
peaches you'd been so looking forward to?' Then she
suddenly looked dour, as if she were chairwoman of an
association for the owners of damaged orchards.

Don Fabrizio's voice quickly put such trifling in its
place : he talked of Tancredi as he now was, of the quick
attentive youth, always ready with a remark which en-
raptured those who loved him and exasperated everyone
else; he told of Tancredi's introduction to the Duchess
of Sansomething-or-other during a visit to Naples, and
how she had been so taken with him that she wanted him
to visit her morning, noon and night, whether she happened to be in her drawing-room or her bed; all because,
said she, no one knew how to tell *les petits riens* like Tancredi; and although Don Fabrizio hurriedly added that
Tancredi could have been no more than sixteen at the
time and the duchess over fifty, Angelica's eyes flashed, for
she had definite information about the habits of Palermitan
youths and strong intuitions about those of Neapolitan
duchesses.

Anyone deducing from this attitude of Angelica that
she loved Tancredi would have been mistaken; she had
too much pride and too much ambition to be capable of
that annihilation, however temporary, of one's own personality without which there is no love; apart from that
she was too young and inexperienced to be able as yet
to appreciate his genuine qualities, all subtle nuances : but
although she did not love him, she was in love with him,
a very different thing; his blue eyes, his affectionate teas-
ing, certain suddenly serious tones of his voice gave her,
even in memory, quite a definite turn, and just then her

one longing was to be enfolded by his hands; once enfolded
she would forget and substitute them, as in fact happened,
but for the moment she yearned for his clutch. So the
revelation of this possible love-affair (which was, in fact,
non-existent) gave her a twinge of that most absurd of
tortures, retrospective jealousy; a twinge soon dissipated,
however, by a cool appraisal of the advantages, erotic and
otherwise, of her marriage to Tancredi.

Don Fabrizio went on praising Tancredi. In his affection he got to the point of talking about him as a kind of
Mirabeau. 'He's begun early and well,' said he, 'and will
go far.' Angelica's smooth forehead bowed in assent.
Actually she did not care at all about Tancredi's political
future; she was one of the many girls who consider public
events as part of a separate universe and could not even
imagine that a speech by Cavour might in time, through
thousands of minute links, influence her own life and
change it. She was thinking, 'We've got the money and
that's enough for us; as to going far . . .' Such youthful
simplicities she was to discard completely when years later
she became one of the most venomous string-pullers for
Parliament and Senate.

'And then, Angelica, you have no idea yet how amusing
Tancredi is! He knows everything, sees an unexpected side
everywhere. When one's with him and he's on form, the
world seems even funnier than it usually does, sometimes
more serious, too.' That Tancredi was amusing Angelica
already knew; that he was capable of revealing new worlds
she not only hoped but had some reason to suspect ever
since that 25th of September last, day of that famous kiss,
the only one officially noted, in the shelter of that treacher-
ous laurel hedge, for it had been something much subtler
and tastier, entirely different from the only other sample
in her experience, one given her over a year before by a
gardener's boy at Poggio Cajano. But Angelica cared
very little about the wit or even the intelligence of her
fiancé, far less in any case than did sweet old Don Fabrizio—really *so* sweet, though so 'intellectual' too. In
Tancredi she saw her chance of gaining a fine position in

the noble world of Sicily, a world which to her was full
of marvels very different to those which it contained in
reality; and she also wanted him as a lively partner in bed.
If he was superior in spirit too, all the better; but she on
her part didn't bother much about that. There was always
amusement to be had. In any case those were ideas for the
future; for the moment, whether witty or stupid, she would
have liked to have had him there, stroking at least her neck
under the tresses as he had once done.

'Oh God, oh God, how I wish he were with us now!'

The exclamation moved them all, both by its evident sincerity and the ignorance that caused her to make it, and
brought that very successful first visit to an end. For
shortly afterwards Angelica and her father made their
farewells: preceded by a stable lad with a lighted lantern
the uncertain gold of whose gleams set alight the red of
fallen plane leaves, father and daughter returned to their
home, entry into which had been prevented for Peppe
'Mmerda,' by bullets tearing into his kidneys.

Now that Don Fabrizio felt serene again, he had gone
back to his habit of evening reading. In autumn, after the
Rosary, as it was now too dark to go out, the family would
gather round the fire waiting for dinner, and the Prince,
standing up, would read out to his family a modern novel
in instalments, exuding dignified benevolence from every
pore.

These were just the years when novels were helping
to form those literary myths which still dominate Euro-
pean minds to-day; but in Sicily, partly because of its
traditional impermeability to anything new, partly because
of the general ignorance of any language whatsoever, partly
also, it must be said, because of a vexatious Bourbon
censorship working through the Customs, no one had heard
of Dickens, Eliot, Sand, Flaubert or even Dumas. A
couple of Balzac's volumes had, through various subterfuges, it is true, reached the hands of Don Fabrizio, who
had appointed himself family censor; he had read them
and then lent them in disgust to a friend he didn't like,

saying that they were by a writer with a talent undoubtedly
vigorous but also wild and 'obsessed' (to-day he would have
said monomaniac); a hurried judgment, obviously, but
not without a certain acuteness. The level of these readings
was therefore somewhat low, conditioned as it was by
respect for the girls' virginal shyness, the Princess's religious scruples and the Prince's own sense of dignity, which
would have energetically rejected letting his united family
hear any 'filth.'

It was about the 10th of November and getting towards
the end of their stay at Donnafugata. The rain was pouring
down and a gale slapping gusts of rain angrily on the
window panes; in the distance could be heard a roll of
thunder; every now and again a few drops found their way
down the primitive Sicilian chimney, sizzled a moment on
the fire and dotted with black the glowing brands of olive
wood. He was reading *Angiola Maria* and that evening
had just reached the last few pages; the description of the
heroine's journey through the icy Lombard winter froze
the Sicilian hearts of the young ladies even in their warm
arm-chairs. All of a sudden there was a great scuttle in
the room next door, and in came Mimi the footman panting hard. 'Excellency,' he cried, forgetting all his style.
'Excellency, Signorino Tancredi's arrived! He's in the
court yard seeing his luggage unloaded. Think of it!
Madonna, in this weather!' And off he rushed.

Surprise swept Concetta into a time which no longer
corresponded with reality and 'Darling!' she exclaimed. But
the very sound of her own voice led her back to the comfortless present and, of course, such a brusque change from
a secret warm climate to an open frozen one was most
painful; luckily the exclamation was submerged in the
general excitement and not heard.

Preceded by Don Fabrizio's long steps they all rushed
towards the stairs; the dark drawing-rooms were hurriedly
crossed; down they went; the great gate was flung wide
on to the outer stairs and the courtyard below; the wind
rushed in, making the canvases of the portraits quiver
and sweeping with it dampness and a smell of earth;

against a sky lit by flashes of lightning the trees in the
garden swayed and rustled like torn silk. Don Fabrizio
was just about to pass through the front door, when on the
top step outside appeared a heavy shapeless mass; it was
Tancredi wrapped in the huge blue cloak of the Piedmontese Cavalry, so soaked that he must have weighed a
ton and looked quite black. 'Careful, Nuncle; don't touch
me, I'm a sponge!' The light of the lantern on the
stairs showed a glimpse of his face. He came in, undid
the chain which held the cloak at the collar, and let fall
the garment which flopped on the floor with a squelch.
He smelt like a wet dog; for the last three days he had
not taken off his boots; but to Don Fabrizio, embracing
him, he was the lad more beloved than his own sons, for
Maria Stella a dear nephew basely calumniated, for Father
Pirrone the sheep always lost and always found, for Concetta a dear ghost resembling her lost love. Even Mademoiselle Dombreuil kissed him with her mouth, so unused
to caresses, and cried, poor girl, '*Tancrède, Tancrède, pensons à la joie d'Angelicà,*' so few strings had her own bow,
forced as she always was to echo the joy of others.
Bendicò also found again its dear comrade in play, one
who knew better than anyone else how to blow into a snout
through a closed fist; but it showed its ecstasy in its own
doggy way by leaping frenziedly round the room and taking
no notice of its beloved.

It was a moving moment, this grouping of the family
around the returned youth, all the dearer as he was not
really a member of it, all the happier as he was coming
to gather both love and a sense of perennial security; a
moving moment—but a long one too. When the first trans-
ports were spent, Don Fabrizio noticed that on the threshold
were standing two other figures, also dripping and also
smiling. Tancredi noticed them too and began to laugh.
'Excuse me, all of you, but the excitement quite made
me forget. Aunt,' he said, turning to the Princess, 'I've
allowed myself to bring a dear friend, Count Carlo
Cavriaghi; anyway, you know him, he used often to come
up to the villa when he was with the general; and this

other is Lancer Moroni, my servant.' The soldier smiled
all over his dull, honest face, and stood there at attention
while the water dripped from the thick cloth of his over-
coat down on to the floor. But the young Count did not
stand at attention; taking off his soaking shapeless cap
he kissed the Princess's hand, smiled and dazzled the
girls with his little blond moustaches and his unsuppressible
slurred 'r.' 'And to think they told me that it never rained
down here! Heavens, the last two days we might have been
in the sea itself.' Then he became serious, 'But, Falconeri,
where is the Signorina Angelica? You've dragged me all
the way here from Naples to show me her. I see many a
beauty, but not her.' He turned to Don Fabrizio. 'You
know, Prince, according to him she's the Queen of Sheba!
Let's go at once to worship this creature *formosissima et
nigerrima.* Come on, you stubborn oaf!'

By such talk he brought the language of the officers'
mess into the proud hall with its double row of armoured
and beribboned ancestors; and everyone was amused.
But Don Fabrizio and Tancredi knew how things stood:
they knew Don Calogero, they knew his Beautiful Beast of
a wife, the incredible state of that rich man's home;
things unknown to candid Lombardy.

Don Fabrizio intervened. 'Listen, Count; you thought it
never rained in Sicily and now you can see it's pouring.
We wouldn't like you to think there isn't pneumonia in
Sicily too, and then find yourself in bed with a high temperature. Mimì,' he said to the footman, 'light the fire
in the Signorino Tancredi's room and in the green room of
the guest wing. Prepare the little room next door for the
soldier. And you, Count, go and get thoroughly dry and
change your clothes. I'll send you up some punch and
biscuits. And dinner is at eight, in two hours.' Cavriaghi
was too used to military service not to bow at once to
the voice of authority; he saluted and followed meekly
behind the footman. Behind him Moroni dragged along
the military boxes and curved sabres in their green flannel
wrappings.

Meanwhile Tancredi was writing, 'Dearest Angelica, I've

come, and for you. I'm head over heels in love, but also wet
as a frog, filthy as a lost dog, and hungry as a wolf.
The very minute I've cleaned myself up and consider myself
worthy of appearing before the loveliest creature in the
world, I will hurry over to you; in two hours. My respects
to your dear parents. To you . . . nothing for the moment.'
The text was submitted to the approval of the Prince;
the latter had always been an admirer of Tancredi's epis-
tolary style; he laughed, and approved in full. Donna
Bastiana would have plenty of time to catch some other
imaginary disease; and the note was at once sent opposite.

Such was the general zest and jollity that a quarter of an
hour was enough for the two young men to dry, clean up,
change uniforms and meet once again in the 'Leopold
Room' around the fire; there they drank tea and brandy
and let themselves be admired. At that period nothing
could have been less military than the families of the
Sicilian aristocracy; no Bourbon officers had ever been
seen in the drawing-rooms of Palermo, and the few Garibaldini who had penetrated them gave more the impression of picturesque scarecrows than real military men.
So those two young officers were in fact the first the
Salina girls had ever seen close to; in their double-breasted
uniforms, Tancredi's with the silver buttons of the Lancers,
Carlo's with the gilt ones of the Bersaglieri, the first with a
high black velvet collar bordered with orange, the other
with crimson, they sat stretching towards the embers legs
encased in blue cloth and black cloth. On their sleeves were
the silver and gold stars amid twirls and dashes and endless
loops; a delight for girls used only to severe frock-coats
and funereal tail-coats. The edifying novel lay upside down
behind an arm-chair.

Don Fabrizio did not quite understand; he remembered
both the young men in lobster red and very carelessly turned
out. 'But don't you Garibaldini wear red shirts any
longer?'

The two turned on him as if a snake had bitten them.
'Garibaldini, Garibaldini indeed, uncle! We were once
and now that's over! Cavriaghi and I, thanks be to God,

are officers in the regular army of His Majesty, King of Sardinia for another few months, and shortly to be of Italy. When Garibaldi's army broke up we had the choice: to go home or stay in the King's army. He and I and a lot of others went into the *real* army. We couldn't stand that rabble long, could we, Cavriaghi?'

'Heavens, what dreadful people! Good for ambushes and looting, that's all! Now we're with decent fellows, and we're proper officers!' And he plucked at his little moustache with a grimace of adolescent disgust.

'We had to drop rank, you know, Nuncle. They didn't seem to think much of our military experience. From captain I've become lieutenant again, as you see!' And he showed the two stars on his shoulder straps. 'He from being lieutenant is now second lieutenant. But we're as happy as if we'd got promotion. With these uniforms we're now respected in quite another way.'

'I should think so,' interrupted Cavriaghi, 'people aren't afraid we'll steal their chickens.'

'You should have seen what it was like from Palermo here, when we stopped at post stations to change horses! All we had to say was "Urgent orders on His Majesty's service" and horses appeared like magic; and we'd show them our orders, which were actually the bills of the Naples hotel wrapped up and sealed!'

Having had their say on military changes, they passed on to more general subjects. Concetta and Cavriaghi had sat down together a little apart and the young count showed her the present which he had brought her from Naples: Aleardo Aleardi *Canti* magnificently bound for the purpose. A princely crown was deeply incised in the dark blue leather with her initials, C.C.S. beneath. Below that again, in large, vaguely Gothic, lettering, were the words *Sempre sorda*—For ever deaf.

Concetta was amused and laughed. 'Why deaf, Count? C.C.S. hears perfectly well!'

The face of the young count flamed with boyish passion. 'Deaf, yes, deaf, Signorina, deaf to my sighs and deaf to my groans! And blind, too, blind to the begging in my

eyes! If you only know what I suffered when you left
Palermo to come here; not a wave, not a sign as the
carriage vanished down the drive. And you expect me not
to call you deaf! "Cruel" is what I really should have
written.'

His somewhat literary excitement was chilled by the
girl's reserve. 'Count, you must be very tired after your
long journey; your nerves are not quite in order : calm
yourself. Why not read me a nice poem?'

While the Bersagliere was reading out the gentle verses
in a voice charged with emotion and amid pauses full
of distress, Tancredi in front of the fireplace was taking
from his pocket a small blue satin box. 'Here's the ring,
Nuncle, the ring I'm giving to Angelica; or rather the
one you're giving her *via* me.' He pressed the clasp and
there was a dark sapphire cut in a clear octagon and
clustering close round it a multitude of tiny pure diamonds.
A slightly gloomy jewel, but in close harmony with the
funereal taste of the times, and one obviously worth
the two hundred gold ounces sent by Don Fabrizio. In
reality it had cost a good deal less; in those months of
fleeing and sacking, superb jewels were to be picked up
cheap in Naples; from the difference in price had come a
brooch, a memento for Schwarzwald. Concetta and Cavriaghi were also called to admire it, but did not move, as
the young count had already seen it and Concetta was
putting off that pleasure till later. The ring went from hand
to hand, was admired, praised, and Tancredi congratulated
on his foreseeable good taste. Don Fabrizio asked, 'But
what about the measurements; we'll have to send the ring
to Girgenti to have it cut to the right size.' Tancredi's
eyes glittered with fun. 'There's no need for that, Nuncle;
the measurement is exact; I'd taken it before.' And
Don Fabrizio was silent; here, he recognised, was a master.

The little box had done the whole round of the fireplace
and come back to the hands of Tancredi when from behind
the door was heard a subdued 'May I?' It was Angelica.
In the rush and excitement she had snatched up, to protect
her from the pouring rain, one of those huge peasants'

capes of rough cloth called *scappolare*. Wrapped in its stiff dark blue folds her body looked very slim; under the wet hood her green eyes looked anxious, bewildered, and voluptuous.

The sight of her, and the contrast between the beauty of her face and the rusticity of her clothes, was like a whip-lash to Tancredi; he got up, ran to her without a word and kissed her on the mouth. The box which he held in his right hand tickled her bent neck. Then he pressed the spring, took the ring, put it on her engagement finger; the box dropped to the ground. 'There, darling, that's for you, from your Tancredi.' Then irony broke in, 'And thank Nuncle for it, too.' Then he embraced her again; sensual anticipation made them both tremble; the room, the bystanders, seemed very far away; and he felt as if by those kisses he were taking possession of Sicily once more, of the lovely faithless land which now, after a vain revolt, had surrendered to him again, as always to his family, its carnal delights and golden crops.

As the result of this welcome arrival the family's return to Palermo was put off and there followed two weeks of enchantment. The gale which had accompanied the journey of the two officers had been the last of a series. After it came the resplendent St. Martin's summer which is the real season of pleasure in Sicily; weather luminous and blue, oasis of mildness in the harsh progression of the seasons, inveigling and leading on the senses with its sweetness, luring to secret nudities by its warmth. Not that there was any erotic nudity at the palace of Donnafugata, just an air of excited sensuality all the sharper for being carefully restrained. Eighty years before the Salina palace had been a meeting place for those obscure pleasures which appealed to the dying eighteenth century; but the severe regency of the Princess Carolina, the neo-religious fervour of the Restoration, the straightforward sensuality of Don Fabrizio had eventually caused its bizarre extravagances to be forgotten; the little powdered demons had been put to flight; they still existed, of course, but only as sleeping embryos, hibernating under piles of dust in some attic of the vast building. The lovely Angelica's entry into the palace had made them stir a little, as may be remembered; but it was the arrival of two young men in love which really awoke the instincts lying dormant in the house; and these now showed themselves everywhere, like ants woken by the sun, no longer poisonous, but livelier than ever. Even the architecture, the rococo décor itself, evoked thoughts of fleshly curves and taut erect breasts; and every opening door seemed like a curtain rustling in a bed-alcove.

Cavriaghi was in love with Concetta; but boy that he was, not only in appearance like Tancredi but deep within, his love found expression in the easy rhythms of poets such as Prati and Aleardi, and in dreaming of moonlight elopements whose logical sequence he did not dare contemplate and which anyway Concetta's 'deafness' obviated from the start. Who can tell whether in the seclusion of that green room of his he did not abandon himself to more definitive hopes? Certain it is that to the love-scenery of that autumn in Donnafugata his only contribution was the sketching in of clouds and evanescent horizons and not the creation of architectural masses. The two girls, Carolina and Caterina, however, played their parts excellently in the symphony of desires traversing the whole palace that November and mingling with the murmur of the fountains, the pawing of the horses on heat in the stables, and the tenacious burrowing of nuptial nests by wood-worms in the old furniture. The two girls were young and attractive, and though with no particular loves of their own, found themselves immersed in the currents emanating from the others; often the kiss which Concetta denied to Cavriaghi, the embrace from Angelica which left Tancredi unsatisfied would reverberate around the girls and graze their untouched bodies; and they too would find themselves dreaming about locks of hair damp with sweat, about whimpers of pleasure. Even poor Mademoiselle Dombreuil, by dint of functioning as lightning conductor, was drawn into the turbid and laughing vortex, as psychiatrists become infected and succumb to the frenzies of

their patients. When after a day of hide and seek and
moralising ambushes she lay down on her lonely bed,
she would stroke her own withered breasts and mutter indis-
criminate invocations to Tancredi, to Carlo, to Fabrizio . . .

Centre and motor of this sensual agitation were, of course,
one couple, Tancredi and Angelica. Their certain marriage,
though not very close, extended its reassuring shadow in
anticipation on the parched soil of their mutual desires.
Difference of class made Don Calogero consider their
long periods alone together as quite normal with the nobility,
and made Princess Maria Stella think habitual to those
in the Sedàra's rank of life the frequency of Angelica's
visits and a freedom of bearing which she would certainly
not have found proper in her own daughters. And so
Angelica's visits to the palace became more and more
frequent until they were almost constant, and she ended
by being only accompanied there formally by her father,
who would at once proceed to the business quarters for the
finding or weaving of hidden plots, or by a maid who
vanished into the servants' hall to drink coffee and bore
the unlucky palace domestics.

Tancredi wanted to show Angelica the whole palace
with its inextricable complex of guest rooms, state rooms,
kitchens, chapels, theatres, picture galleries, odorous saddl-
ing rooms, stables, stuffy conservatories, passages, stairs,
terraces and porticoes, and particularly of a series of
abandoned and uninhabited apartments which had not been
used for many years and formed a mysterious and intricate
labyrinth of their own. Tancredi did not realise, or he
realised perfectly well, that he was drawing the girl into the
hidden centre of the sensual cyclone; and Angelica at
that time wanted whatever Tancredi did. Their wanderings
through the seemingly limitless building were interminable;
they would set off as if for some unknown land, and
unknown indeed it was because in many of those apartments
and corners not even Don Fabrizio had ever set foot—
a cause of great satisfaction to him, for he used to say
that a house of which one knew every room wasn't worth
living in.

The two lovers embarked for Cythera on a ship made of dark and sunny rooms, of apartments sumptuous or squalid, empty or crammed with remains of heterogeneous furniture. They would set off accompanied by Cavriaghi or by Mademoiselle Dombreuil, sometimes by both (Father Pirrone with the wisdom of his Order had always refused to go); outer decency was saved. But in the palace of Donnafugata it was not difficult to mislead anyone wanting to follow; this just meant slipping into one of the very long, narrow and tortuous passages, with grilled windows which could not be passed without a sense of anguish, turning through a gallery, up some handy stairs, and the two young people were far away, invisible, alone as if on a desert island. All that remained to survey them was some faded pastoral portrait created blind by the painter's inexperience, or a shepherdess glancing down consentingly from an obliterated fresco.

Cavriaghi, in any case, soon tired, and when he found his route leading through a room he knew or some staircase down into the garden would slip off, both to please his friend and to go and sigh over Concetta's ice-cold hands. The governess would hang on longer, but not indefinitely; for some time her unanswered calls could be heard fading farther and farther away, '*Tancrède, Angelicà, où êtes-vous?*' Then silence would fall again, except for the scuffle of rats in the ceilings above, or the rustle of some centuries-old forgotten letter sent wandering by the wind over the floor; excuses for pleasant frights, for the reassuring contact of flesh to flesh. And with them always, cunning and tenacious, was Eros, drawing the young couple further and further into a game full of charm and risk. Both of them were still very near childhood, and they enjoyed the game in itself, enjoyed being followed, being lost, being found again; but when they reached each other their sharpened senses would overwhelm them, and his five fingers entwining in hers with that gesture dear to indecisive sensualists, the gentle rub of fingertips on the pale veins of the back of the hand, would shake up their whole being, prelude more insinuating caresses.

Once she had hidden behind an enormous picture propped on the floor; and for a short time *Arturo Corbera at the
Siege of Antioch* formed a protection for the girl's hopeful
anxiety; but when she was found, with her smile veined
in cobwebs and her hands veiled in dust, she was clasped
tight, and though she kept on saying again and again, 'No,
Tancredi, no,' her denial was in fact an invitation, for all
he was doing was to stare with his blue eyes into her green
ones. One luminous cold morning she was trembling in a
dress that was still summery; he squeezed her to him, to
warm her, on a sofa covered in tattered silk : her scented
breath moved the hair on his forehead; they were moments
ecstatic and painful, during which desire became a torment,
restraint upon it a delight.

The rooms in the abandoned apartments had neither a
definite layout nor a name; and like the explorers of the
New World they would baptise the rooms they crossed with
the names of their joint discoveries. A vast bedroom in
whose alcove stood the ghost of a bed adorned with a bal-
dacchino hung with skeleton ostrich feathers was remembered afterwards as 'the feather room'; a staircase with
steps of smooth crumbling slate was called by Tancredi
'the staircase of the lucky slip.' A number of times they
really did not know where they were; all this twisting and
turning, backing and following, pauses full of murmuring
contact, made them lose their way so that they had to lean
out of some paneless window to gather from an angle of
the courtyard or a view of the garden which wing of the
palace they were in. But sometimes they could not find
their way even so, as the window did not give on to one
of the great courts but on to some inner yard, anonymous
itself and never entered, marked only by the corpse of
some cat or the usual little heap of spaghetti and tomato
sauce vomited or flung there; and from another window they
would find themselves looking into the eyes of some pen-
sioned-off old maidservant. One afternoon inside a cupboard they found four *carillons,* those music-boxes which
delighted the affected simplicity of the eighteenth century.
Three of these, buried in dust and cobwebs, remained mute;

T.L.

but the last, which was more recent and shut tighter into
its dark wooden box, started up its cylinder of bristling
copper, and the little tongues of raised steel suddenly produced a delicate tune, all in clear silvery tones—the famous
Carnival of Venice; they kissed in rhythm with those notes
of disillusioned gaiety, and when their embrace loosened
were surprised to notice that the notes had ceased for
some time and their action had left no other trace than a
memory of that ghostly music.

Once the surprise was of a different kind. In one of the
rooms in the old guest wing they noticed a door hidden by
a wardrobe; the centuries-old lock soon gave way to fingers
pleasantly entwined in forcing it : behind it a long narrow
staircase wound up in gentle curves of pink marble steps.
At the top was another door, open, and covered with thick
but tattered padding; then came a charming but odd little
apartment, of six small rooms gathered round a medium-
sized drawing-room, all, including the drawing-room, with
floors of whitest marble sloping away slightly towards
a small lateral gutter. On the low ceilings were some very
unusual reliefs in coloured stucco, luckily made almost
indecipherable by damp; on the walls hung big surprised-
looking mirrors, hung too low, one shattered by a blow
almost in the middle, and each fitted with contorted rococo
candle-brackets. The windows gave on to a segregated courtyard, a kind of blind and deaf well, which let in a grey
light and had no other outlet. In every room and even
in the drawing-room were wide, too wide, sofas, showing
nails from which traces of silk had been torn away; spotty
arm-rests; on the fireplaces were delicate intricate little
marble intaglios, naked figures in paroxysm, but martyred,
by some furious hammer. The damp had marked the walls
high up and also perhaps low down at a man's height,
where it had assumed strange shapes, odd thickness,
dark tints. Tancredi, disturbed, would not let Angelica
touch a cupboard in the drawing-room wall, and opened
it himself. It was deep but empty except for a roll of dirty
stuff standing upright in a corner; inside was a bundle of
small whips, switches of bull's muscle, some with silver

handles, others wrapped half-way up in a charming old
silk, white with little blue stripes, on which could be
seen three rows of blackish marks; and metal instruments
for inexplicable purposes. Tancredi was afraid, also of himself. 'Let's go, my dear, there's nothing interesting here.'
They shut the door carefully, went down the stairs in
silence, and put the wardrobe back where it was before;
and all the rest of that day Tancredi's kisses were very
light as if given in a dream and in expiation.

After the Leopard, in fact, the whip seemed the most frequent object at Donnafugata. The day after their discovery
of the enigmatic little apartment the two lovers found another little whip. This was not actually in the secret apartment but in the venerated one called the Rooms of the
Saint-Duke, where in the middle of the seventeenth century a Salina had withdrawn as if into a private monastery,
there to do penance and prepare his own journey towards
Heaven. They were small low rooms, with floors of humble
brick, and white-washed walls, like those of the poorest
peasants. The last of these opened on to a balcony which
overlooked the yellow expanse of estate after estate, all
immersed in sad light. On one wall was a huge crucifix,
over life size; the head of the martyred God touched the
ceiling, the bleeding feet grazed the floor; the wound in
the ribs seemed like a mouth prevented by brutality from
pronouncing the words of ultimate salvation. Next to the
Divine Body there hung from a nail a lash with a short
handle, from which dangled six strips of now hardened
leather ending in six lumps of lead as big as walnuts.
This was the 'discipline' of the Saint-Duke. In that room
Giuseppe Corbera Duke of Salina had scourged himself
alone, in sight of his God and his estates, and it must have
seemed to him that the drops of his own blood were about
to rain down on the land and redeem it; in his holy exaltation it must have seemed that only through this expiatory
baptism could that earth really become his, blood of his
blood, flesh of his flesh, as the saying is. But now many
pieces of it had gone for ever and a large number of
those to be seen from up there belonged to others, to

Calogero even; to Don Calogero, thus to Angelica, thus
to his future son-in-law. This proof of ransom through
beauty, parallel to that other ransom through blood, made
Tancredi's head swim. Angelica was kneeling and kissing
the pierced feet of Christ. 'There,' said Tancredi, 'you're
like that whip there, used for the same ends.' He
showed her the whip; and since Angelica did not understand and raised her smiling head, lovely but vacuous, he
bent down and as she knelt gave her a rough kiss which
made her moan, for it bruised her lip and rasped her palate.

So the pair of them spent these days in dreamy wanderings, in the discovery of hells redeemed by love, of forgotten paradises profaned by love itself. The dangers of
stopping the game and drawing the prize became more and
more pressing for both; in the end they searched no longer,
but went off absorbed into the remotest rooms, those from
which no cry could reach anyone from the outside world.
But there never would be a cry; only invocations and low
whimpers. There they would both lie, close but innocent,
pitying each other. The most dangerous places for them were
the rooms of the old guest wing; private, in good order, each
with its neat rolled-up mattress which would spread
out again at a mere touch of the hand. One day, not
Tancredi's mind which had no say in the matter, but all his
blood had decided to put an end to it; that morning Angelica, like the beautiful bitch that she was, had said, 'I'm
your novice,' recalling to him with the clarity of an invitation their first mutual onrush of desire; and already the
woman had surrendered and offered, already the male was
about to overwhelm the man, when the church bell clanged
almost straight down on their prone bodies, adding its
own throb to the others; their interlaced mouths dis-
entangled for a smile. They came to themselves; and next
day Tancredi had to leave.

Those were the best days in the lives of Tancredi and
Angelica, lives later to be so variegated, so erring, against
the inevitable background of sorrow. But of that they
were still unaware, in their pursuit of a future which
they deemed more concrete than it turned out to be, made

of nothing but smoke and wind. When they were old and
uselessly wise their thoughts would go back to those days
with insistent regret; they had been days when desire
was always present because always overcome, when many
beds had been offered and refused, when the sensual urge,
because restrained, had for one second been sublimated in
renunciation, that is into real love. Those days were the
preparation for a marriage which, even erotically, was no
success; a preparation, however, in a way sufficient to itself,
exquisite and brief; like those overtures which outlive
the forgotten operas they belong to and hint in delicate
veiled gaiety at all the arias which later in the opera are
to be developed undeftly, and fail.

When Angelica and Tancredi returned to the world of
the living from their exile in the universe of extinct vices,
forgotten virtues and, above all, perennial desire, they were
greeted with amiable irony. 'How silly of you, children, to
get so dusty. What a state you're in, Tancredi!' would
smile Don Fabrizio; and his nephew would go off to get
himself dusted down. Cavriaghi sat astride a chair, con-
scientiously smoking a cheroot, looked at his friend washing
his face and neck, and snorted at seeing the water turn
black as coal. 'I don't deny it, Falconeri; the Signorina
Angelica is the loveliest girl I've ever seen; but that's not
a justification : heavens, do restrain yourself a bit, to-day
you've been alone together three whole hours, if you're
so much in love then get married at once and don't let
people laugh at you. You should have seen the face the
father made to-day when he came out of his office and
found you were still sailing about in that ocean of rooms!
Brakes, my dear fellow, brakes, that's what you need!
You Sicilians have so few of 'em!'
He pontificated away, enjoying inflicting his wisdom
on his older comrade, on 'deaf' Concetta's cousin. But Tancredi, as he dried his hair, was furious; to be accused of
having no brakes, he who had enough to stop a train!
On the other hand the good Bersagliere was not entirely in
the wrong; appearances had to be thought of too; though

now he had gone moralist like this from envy it was obvious that his courtship of Concetta was getting nowhere. And then Angelica! That delicious taste of blood to-day when he'd bitten the inside of her lip! That soft bending of hers under his embrace! But it was true, there was no sense in it all really. 'To-morrow we'll go and visit the church with a full escort of Father Pirrone and Mademoiselle Dombreuil!'

Angelica meanwhile was changing her dress in the girls' room. '*Mais Angélica, est-il Dieu possible de se mettre dans un tel état?*' Mademoiselle Dombreuil was wailing indignantly, as the lovely creature, in undervest and petticoats, was washing her arms and neck. The cold water subdued her excitement and she had to admit to herself that the governess was right; was it worth getting so tired and so dusty and making people smile? For what? Just to be gazed in the eyes, to be stroked by those slender fingers, little more . . . and her lip was still smarting. 'That's enough now. To-morrow we'll stay in the drawing-room with the others.' But next day those same eyes, those same fingers would cast their spell again, and the two would go back once more to their wild games of hide and seek.

The paradoxical result of all these separate but convergent resolutions was that at dinner in the evening the pair most in love were the calmest, reposing on their illusory good intentions for next day; and they would muse ironically on the love relationships of the others, however minor. Concetta had disappointed Tancredi; when at Naples he had felt a certain remorse about her and that was why he had brought Cavriaghi along with him in the hope the Milanese might replace him with his cousin. Pity also played in his foresight; in a subtle but easy-going way, astute as he was, he had seemed when he arrived almost to be commiserating with her at his own abandonment; and he pushed forward his friend. Nothing doing; Concetta unravelled her little spool of school-girl gossip and looked at the sentimental little count with icy eyes behind which there seemed almost a certain contempt. A silly girl that; no good making any more efforts. What more did she want, anyway?

Cavriaghi was a handsome lad, well set up, with a good name and flourishing dairy-farms in Brianza; in fact he was one about whom could be used that rather chilling term 'a good match.' Ah : so Concetta wanted him, Tancredi, did she? He had wanted her too once; she was less beautiful, much less rich than Angelica, but she had something in her which the girl from Donnafugata would never possess. But life is a serious matter, devil take it! Concetta must have realised that. Why had she begun treating him so badly, then? Turning on him at the Holy Ghost Convent; and so many times afterwards. The Leopard, yes, the Leopard, of course; but there must be limits even for that proud beast. 'Brakes is what you want, my dear cousin, brakes! You Sicilian girls have so few of 'em!'

Angelica, though, in her heart agreed with Concetta; Cavriaghi lacked pep; after loving Tancredi, to marry Cavriaghi would be like a drink of water after a taste of this Marsala in front of her. Concetta, of course, understood that from her own experience. But those other two sillies, Carolina and Caterina, were making fishes' eyes at Cavriaghi, wriggling and languishing every time he went near them. Well, then! With her own lack of family scruples she just could not understand why one of the two didn't try and nab the little count from Concetta for herself. 'Boys at that age are like dogs; one only has to whistle and they come straight away. Silly girls! With all those scruples and taboos and pride, in the end they won't get anyone.'

In the smoking-room, conversations between Tancredi and Cavriaghi, the only two smokers in the house and so the only exiles, also assumed a certain tone. The little count ended by confessing to his friend the failure of his own amorous hopes. 'She's too beautiful, too pure for me; she doesn't love me; it was rash of me to hope; but I'll leave here with a regret like a dagger in my heart. I've not even dared to make a definite proposal. I feel that to her I'm just a worm, and she's right. I must find myself a she-worm to put up with me.' And his nineteen years made him laugh at his own discomfiture.

From the height of his own assured happiness Tancredi tried to console him : 'You see, I've known Concetta all her life : she's the sweetest creature in the world; a mirror of all the virtues; but she's a little too reserved, too withdrawn, I'm afraid she has too high an opinion of herself; and then she's Sicilian to the very marrow : she's never left here; she might never feel at home in a place where one has to arrange a week ahead for a plate of macaroni!'

Tancredi's little joke, one of the earliest expressions of national unity, brought a smile from Cavriaghi again; pains and sorrows did not stay with him long. 'But I'd have laid in *cases* of your macaroni for her, of course! Anyway what's done is done; I only hope your uncle and aunt, who've been so sweet to me, won't take against me for having thrust myself among you pointlessly.' He was reassured quite sincerely, for Cavriaghi had made himself liked by everyone except Concetta (and perhaps liked by Concetta too, in a way) for the boisterous good humour which he combined with the most plaintive sentimentality; then they talked of something else, that is they talked of Angelica.

'You know, Falconeri, you *are* a lucky dog! To go and find a jewel like Signorina Angelica in this pigsty (excuse my calling it that, my dear fellow). What a beauty, good God, what a beauty! Lucky rascal, leading her round for hours in the remotest corners of this house as huge as our own cathedral! And not only lovely, but clever and cultured too; and good as well; one can see that in her eyes, in that sweet innocence of hers.'

Cavriaghi went on ecstatically about Angelica's goodness, under Tancredi's amused glance. 'The really good person in all this is you yourself, Cavriaghi.' The phrase slipped unnoticed over that Milanese optimism. Then, 'Listen,' said the young count, 'you'll be leaving in a few days; don't you think it's time I was introduced to the mother of the young baroness?'

This was the first time—and from a Lombard voice— that Tancredi heard his future wife called by a title. For a second he did not realise who the other was referring to. Then the prince in him rebelled. 'Baroness? what d'you mean, Cavriaghi? She's a dear, sweet creature whom I love and that's quite enough.'

That it really was 'quite enough' was not actually true; but Tancredi was perfectly sincere; with his atavistic habit of great possessions it seemed to him that the estates of Gibildolce and Settesoli, all those bags of gold, had been his since the time of Charles of Anjou, always.

'I'm sorry but I don't think you'll be able to meet Angelica's mother; she's leaving to-morrow for the vapour baths at Sciacca; she's very ill, poor thing.'

He stubbed the end of his cheroot in an ashtray. 'Let's go into the drawing-room, shall we? We've been bears here for long enough.'

One day about that time Don Fabrizio received a letter from the Prefect of Girgenti, written in a style of extreme courtesy, announcing the arrival at Donnafugata of the Cavaliere Aimone Chevalley di Monterzuolo, Secretary to the Prefecture, who wanted to talk to him, the Prince, about a subject very close to the Government's heart. Surprised, Don Fabrizio sent off his son, Francesco Paolo, to the post-station next day to receive the *missus dominicus* and invite him to stay at the palace, an act both of hospitality and of true compassion, consisting in not abandoning the body of the Piedmontese to the thousands of little creatures who would have tortured him in the cave-hostelry of *Zzu* Menico.

The post coach arrived at dusk with an armed guard on the box and a few glum faces inside. From it also alighted Chevalley di Monterzuolo, recognisable at once by his scared look and wary simper. He had been in Sicily for a month, in the most persistently native part of the island what was more, bounced there straight from his little property near Montferrat. Timid and congenitally bureaucratic, he found himself much out of his element. His head had been stuffed with the tales of brigands by which Sicilians love to test the nervous resistance of new arrivals, and for a month he had seen every usher in his office as a murderer, and every wooden paper cutter on his desk as a dagger; for a month, too, the oily cooking had upset his inside.

There he stood now, in the twilight, with his valise of beige cloth, peering at the very unpromising aspect of the street in the midst of which he had been dumped. The inscription 'Corso Vittorio Emmanuele,' whose blue letters on a white ground adorned the half-ruined house opposite him, was not enough to convince him that he was in a place which was, after all, part of his own nation; and he did not dare to ask the way from any of the peasants propped against walls like caryatids, in his certainty of not being understood and his fear of a gratuitous knife in the guts, still dear to him however upset.

When Francesco Paolo came up and introduced himself he screwed up his eyes at first as he thought himself done for : but the fair-haired youth's calm honest air reassured him a little, and when he realised that he was being invited to stay with the Salina he was both surprised and relieved. The dark journey to the palace was enlivened by a running contest between Piedmontese and Sicilian courtesies (the two most punctilious in Italy) over the valise, which in the end was borne by both knightly contenders, though very light.

On reaching the palace the bearded faces of the armed rangers standing about in the first courtyard once more disturbed the soul of Chevalley di Monterzuolo; while the distant cordiality of the Prince's greeting, together with the evident luxury of the rooms he glimpsed, flung him into contrary worries. Member of one of those families of Piedmontese squireens which live on their own land with dignity and narrow means, it was the first time he found himself a guest at a great house, and this redoubled his shyness; meanwhile the bloodthirsty anecdotes he had been told at Girgenti, the staggeringly insolent aspect of the townsfolk here, the 'bravos' (as he called them to himself) encamped in the courtyard, filled him with terror; so that he went down to dinner in the grip of contrasting fears, at finding himself in an ambience above his normal habits and at feeling an innocent traveller in a bandit's trap.

At dinner he ate well for the first time since setting foot on Sicilian shores, and the charm of the girls, the austerity of Father Pirrone and the grand manner of Don Fabrizio convinced him that the palace of Donnafugata was not the lair of Capraro the bandit, and that he would probably leave there alive. His greatest consolation was the presence of Cavriaghi, who, he was told, had been staying there for ten days and looked in excellent health and also on excellent terms with that young Falconeri, a friendship between a Sicilian and a Lombard which seemed almost miraculous to him. At the end of dinner he went up to Don Fabrizio and requested a private interview as he wished to leave again next morning; but the Prince clapped him on the shoulder and with a most Leopard-like smile exclaimed, 'Not at all, my dear Cavaliere, you're in my home now and I'll hold you as hostage for as long as I like; you won't leave to-morrow morning, and to be quite sure of it I shall deprive myself of the pleasure of a private talk with you until the afternoon.' This phrase, which would have terrified the excellent Secretary three hours before, now rather cheered him. That evening Angelica was not there, and so they played a hand of whist; at a table with Don Fabrizio, Tancredi and Father Pirrone, he won two rubbers and gained three lire and thirty-five centimes; after which he withdrew to his own room, enjoyed the cleanliness of the linen and fell into the trustful sleep of the just.

Next morning Tancredi and Cavriaghi led him around the garden, showed him the picture gallery and tapestry collection. They also trotted him a little round the town; under the honey-coloured sun of that November day it seemed less sinister than it had the night before; he even saw a smile here and there, and Chevalley di Monterzuolo began to reassure himself about rustic Sicily. Tancredi

noticed this and was at once assailed by the singular island
itch to tell foreigners tales which, however horrifying, were
unfortunately quite true. They were passing in front of a
jolly building with a façade decorated in crude stucco
work.

'That, my dear Chevalley, is the home of Baron Mútolo;
now it's closed and empty as the family live in Girgenti since
the baron's son was captured by brigands ten years ago.'

The Piedmontese began to tremble. 'Poor things, I wonder how much they paid to free him.'

'No, no, they didn't pay a thing; they were in financial
straits already and had no ready money, like everybody
else here. But they got the boy back all the same; by
instalments, though.'

'What do you mean, Prince?'

'By instalments, I said, by instalments; bit by bit. First
arrived the index finger of his right hand. A week later
his left foot; and finally in a great big basket, under a layer
of figs (it was August), the head; its eyes were staring
and there was congealed blood on the corner of the lips.
I didn't see it, I was a child then; but I'm told it wasn't
a very pretty sight. The basket was left on that very step
there, the second one up to the door, by an old woman with
a black shawl on her head; no one recognised her.'

Chevalley's eyes went rigid with horror; he had already
heard the story before this, but seeing now in the sunshine
the very step on which the bizarre gift had been put was
a different matter. His bureaucratic mind came to his
help. 'What an inept police those Bourbons had. Very
soon, when our carabinieri come along, they'll put an end
to all this.'

'No doubt, Chevalley, no doubt.'

Then they passed in front of the Civic Club, which had
its daily show of iron chairs and men in mourning under
the shade of the plane trees in the Square. Bows, smiles.
'Take a good look, Chevalley, impress the scene on your
memory; twice a year or so one of these gentlemen here
is left stone dead on his own little arm-chair; a rifle
shot in the uncertain light of dusk, and no one ever knows

who it was that shot him.' Chevalley felt the need to lean
on Cavriaghi's arm so as to sense a little northern blood
near him.

Shortly afterwards, at the top of a steep alley, through
multi-coloured festoons of drawers out to dry, they saw
the simple baroque front of a little church. 'That's Santa
Ninfa. The parish priest was killed in there five years ago
as he was saying Mass.'

'Horrors! Shooting in church!'

'Oh, no shooting, Chevalley. We are too good Catholics
for misbehaviour of that kind. They just put poison in the
communion wine; more discreet, more liturgical, I might
say. No one ever knew who did it; the priest was a most
excellent person; he had no enemies.'

Like a man who wakes up in the night to see a skeleton
sitting at the foot of the bed in his own trousers, and
saves himself from panic by forcing himself to believe it's
just a joke by drunken friends, so Chevalley took refuge
in the idea that he was having his leg pulled. 'Very amusing, Prince, really entertaining; you should write novels,
you know; you tell these stories very well.' But his voice
was trembling; Tancredi took pity on him, and although
on their way home they passed three or four places all
of which were most evocative, he abstained from telling
their tales, and talked about Bellini and Verdi, perennial
curative unctions for national wounds.

At four in the afternoon the Prince sent to tell Chevalley
that he was waiting for him in his study. This was a small
room with walls lined by glass cases containing grey
partridges with pink claws, rarities, stuffed trophies of past
shoots. One wall was ennobled by a high, narrow bookcase,
crammed full of back numbers of mathematical reviews.
Above the great arm-chair meant for visitors hung a constellation of family miniatures; Don Fabrizio's father, Prince
Paolo, dark complexioned and sensual lipped as a Moor,
with the cordon of St. Januarius diagonally across his
black court uniform; Princess Carolina as a widow, with
her fair hair heaped into a towering dressing and severe

blue eyes; the Prince's sister, Giulia, Princess of Falconeri, sitting on a bench in a garden, with the crimson splodge of a small parasol laid on the ground to her right and to her left the yellow splodge of Tancredi at three years old offering her wild flowers (Don Fabrizio had thrust this miniature into his pocket secretly while the bailiffs were making their inventory for the sale at Villa Falconeri). Beneath that was his eldest son, Paolo, in tight white leather breeches, just about to mount an arrogant horse with a curving neck and flashing eyes; then various un-identifiable uncles and aunts, covered with jewels or point-ing sorrowfully at the bust of some extinct dear one. But in the centre of the constellation, acting as a kind of Polar star, shone a bigger miniature; this was of Don Fabrizio himself at the age of about twenty, with his very young wife leaning her head on his shoulder in an act of complete loving abandon. She was dark-haired, he rosy in the blue and silver uniform of the Royal Guards, smiling with pleasure, his face framed in his first and very fair long whiskers.

Chevalley, as soon as he sat down, began explaining the mission with which he had been charged. 'After the happy annexation, I mean after the glorious union of Sicily and the Kingdom of Sardinia, the Turin Government intends to nominate a number of illustrious Sicilians as Senators of the Kingdom. The provincial authorities have been charged with drawing up a list of personalities to be pro-posed for the Central Government's examination, and eventually for the royal nomination, and, of course, at Girgenti your name was mentioned at once, Prince; a name illustrious for its antiquity, for the personal prestige of its bearer, for scientific merit; and also for the dignified and liberal attitude assumed during recent events.' The little speech had been prepared for some time; it had been even the object of a number of pencil notes in a little book which was now in the hip pocket of Chevalley's trousers. But Don Fabrizio gave no sign of life; his eyes could only just be glimpsed through his heavy lids. Motionless, the great paw with its blondish hairs completely covered a dome of St. Peter's in alabaster on the table.

Accustomed by now to the slyness of the loquacious Sicilians whenever anything is suggested to them, Chevalley did not let himself be discouraged. 'Before sending the list to Turin my superiors thought it proper to inform you in person and see if this proposal met with your approval. To ask for your assent, for which the Government much hopes, has been the object of my mission here; a mission which has also given me the honour and the pleasure of getting to know you and your family, this magnificent palace, and picturesque Donnafugata.'

Flattery always slipped off the Prince like water off leaves in fountains : it is one of the advantages enjoyed by men who are at once both proud and used to being so. 'This fellow here seems to be under the impression he's come to do me a great honour,' he was thinking. 'To me, who am what I am, among other things a Peer of the Kingdom of Sicily, which must be more or less the same as a Senator. It's true that one must value gifts in relation to those who offer them; when a peasant gives me his bit of cheese he's making me a bigger present than the Prince of Làscari when he invites me to dinner. That's obvious. The difficulty is that the cheese is nauseating. So all that remains is the heart's gratitude which can't be seen and the nose wrinkled in disgust which can be seen only too well.'

Don Fabrizio's ideas about the Senate were very vague; in spite of every effort his thoughts kept leading him back to the Roman Senate; to Senator Papirius breaking a staff on the head of an ill-mannered Gaul, to a horse, Incitatus, made a senator by Caligula, an honour which even his son Paolo might have thought excessive. He was irritated at finding recurring to him insistently a phrase which was sometimes used by Father Pirrone : '*Senatores boni viri, senatus autem mala bestia.*' Nowadays there was also an Imperial Senate in Paris, though that was only an assembly of profiteers with big salaries. There was or had been a senate in Palermo, too, though it had only been a committee of civil administrators—what administrators! Low work for a Salina. He decided to be frank. 'But Cavaliere, do explain what being a senator means; the newspapers under our last monarchy never allowed information about the constitutional systems of other Italian states to be printed, and a week's visit of mine to Turin some years ago was not enough to enlighten me. What is it? A simple title of honour? A kind of decoration, or are there legislative, deliberative functions?'

The Piedmontese, representative of the only liberal State in Italy, rose to the bait. 'But, Prince, the Senate is the High Chamber of the Kingdom! In it the flower of Italy's politicians, picked by the wisdom of the Sovereign, will examine, discuss, approve or disapprove the laws proposed by the Government for the progress of the country; it functions at the same time as spur and as brake; it incites good actions and prevents bad ones. When you have accepted a seat in it, you will represent Sicily on an equality with the other elected deputies, you will make us hear the voice of this lovely country which is only now sighting the modern world, with so many wounds to heal, so many just desires to be granted.'

Chevalley would perhaps have continued for some time in this tone if Bendicò from behind the door had not asked 'the wisdom of his Sovereign' to admit him. Don Fabrizio made as if to get to his feet and open the door, but slowly enough to allow the Piedmontese time to open it himself; Bendicò meticulously sniffed around Chevalley's trousers, after which, having decided this was a good man, the dog lay down under the window and slept.

'Just listen to me, Chevalley, will you? If it were merely a question of some honorific, of a simple title to put on a visiting card, no more, I should be pleased to accept; I feel that at this decisive moment for the future of the Italian State it is the duty of us all to support it, and to avoid any impression of disunity in the eyes of these foreign States which are watching us with alarm or hope, both of them unjustified, but that do at the moment exist.'

'Well, then, Prince, why not accept?'

'Be patient now, Chevalley, I'll explain in a moment;
we Sicilians have become accustomed, by a long, a very
long hegemony of rulers who were not of our religion
and did not speak our language, to split hairs. If we had
not done so we'd never have coped with Byzantine tax gath-
erers, with Berber Emirs, with Spanish Viceroys. Now the
bent is endemic, we're made like that. I said "support,"
I did not say "participate." In these last six months, since
your Garibaldi set foot at Marsala, too many things have
been started without our being consulted for you now
to ask a member of the old governing class to help
develop them and carry them through. I do not wish
to discuss now if what was done was good or bad; for my
part I believe much of it to have been bad; but I'd like
to tell you at once what you'll only understand after spend-
ing a year among us.

'In Sicily it doesn't matter about doing things well or
badly; the sin which we Sicilians never forgive is simply
that of "doing" at all. We are old, Chevalley, very old.
For over twenty-five centuries we've been bearing the weight
of superb and heterogeneous civilisations, all from outside, none made by ourselves, none that we could call our
own. We're as white as you are, Chevalley, and as the
Queen of England; and yet for two thousand five hundred
years we've been a colony. I don't say that in complaint;
it's our fault. But even so we're worn out and exhausted.'

Chevalley was disturbed now. 'But that is all over, isn't
it? Now Sicily is no longer a conquered land, but a free
part of a free State.'

'The intention is good, Chevalley, but it comes too late;
and I've already said that it is mainly our fault. You
talked to me a short while ago about a young Sicily sighting
the marvels of the modern world; for my part I see instead
a centenarian being dragged in a bath-chair round the
Great Exhibition in London, understanding nothing and
caring about nothing, whether it's the steel factories of
Sheffield or the cotton spinneries of Manchester, and
thinking of nothing but drowsing off again on beslobbered
pillows with a pot under the bed.'

He was still talking quietly, but the hand around St.
Peter's had tightened; later the tiny cross surmounting
the dome was found snapped. 'Sleep, my dear Chevalley,
sleep, that is what Sicilians want, and they will always hate
anyone who tries to wake them, even in order to bring
them the most wonderful of gifts: I must say, between
ourselves, that I have strong doubts whether the new kingdom will have many gifts for us in its luggage. All Sicilian
self-expression, even the most violent, is really wish-
fulfilment; our sensuality is a hankering for oblivion,
our shooting and knifing a hankering for death; our
languor, our exotic ices, a hankering for voluptuous immobility, that is for death again; our meditative air is
that of a void wanting to scrutinise the enigmas of Nirvana.
From that comes the power among us of certain people, of
those who are half awake: that is the cause of the well-
known time lag of a century in our artistic and intellectual
life; novelties attract us only when they are dead, incapable
of arousing vital currents; from that comes the extraordinary phenomenon of the constant formation of myths
which would be venerable if they were really ancient, but
which are really nothing but sinister attempts to plunge us
back into a past that attracts us only because it is dead.'

Not all of this was understood by the good Chevalley;
and the last phrase he found particularly obscure; he had
seen the variously painted carts being drawn along by
horses covered with feathers, he had heard tell of the
heroic puppet theatres, but he too had thought they were
genuine old traditions. He said, 'Aren't you exaggerating a
little, Prince? I myself have met emigrant Sicilians in Turin,
Crispi, for example, who seemed anything but asleep.'

The Prince said irritably, 'When there are so many of us
there are bound to be exceptions: in any event, I've
already mentioned some of us as half awake. As for this
young man Crispi, not I, certainly, but you perhaps may be
able to see if as an old man he doesn't fall back into our
voluptuous torpor; they all do. Anyway, I've explained
myself badly; I said Sicilians, I should have added Sicily,
the atmosphere, the climate, the landscape of Sicily. Those

are the forces which have formed our minds together with
and perhaps more than alien pressure and varied invasions :
this landscape which knows no mean between sensuous sag
and hellish drought; which is never petty, never ordinary,
never relaxed, as should be a country made for rational
beings to live in; this country of ours in which the inferno
round Randazzo is a few miles from the beauty of Taormina
Bay; this climate which inflicts us with six feverish months
at a temperature of 104. Count them, Chevalley, count
them; May, June, July, August, September, October;
six times thirty days of sun sheer down on our heads;
this summer of ours which is as long and glum as a Russian
winter and against which we struggle with less success. You
don't know it yet, but fire could be said to snow down on
us as on the accursed cities of the Bible. If a Sicilian
worked hard in any of those months he would expend
energy enough for three. Then water is either lacking
altogether or has to be carried from so far that every drop
is paid for by a drop of sweat; and when the rains come,
they are always tempestuous and set dry torrents to frenzy,
drown beasts and men on the very spot where two weeks
before both had been dying of thirst.

'This violence of landscape, this cruelty of climate, this
continual tension in everything, and even these monuments
of the past, magnificent yet incomprehensible because not
built by us and yet standing round us like lovely mute
ghosts; all those rulers who landed by main force from all
directions, who were at once obeyed, soon detested and
always misunderstood; their sole means of expression
works of art we found enigmatic and taxes we found only
too intelligible, and which they spent elsewhere. All these
things have formed our character, which is thus conditioned
by events outside our control as well as by a terrifying
insularity of mind.'

The ideological inferno evoked in this little study disturbed Chevalley even more than the bloodthirsty tales
of that morning. He tried to say something, but Don Fabrizio was now too worked up to listen.

'I don't deny that a few Sicilians may succeed in breaking the spell once off the island; but they would have to leave it very young; by twenty it's too late; the crust is formed; they will remain convinced that their country is basely calumniated like all other countries, that the civilised norm is here, the oddities elsewhere. But do please excuse me, Chevalley, I've let myself be led on and I've probably bored you. You haven't come all this way to hear Ezekiel deplore the misfortunes of Israel. Let us return to the subject of our conversation : I am most grateful to the Government for having thought of me for the Senate and I ask you to express my most sincere gratitude to them. But I cannot accept. I am a member of the old ruling class, inevitably compromised with the Bourbon régime, and bound to it by chains of decency if not of affection. I belong to an unlucky generation, swung between the old world and the new, and I find myself ill at ease in both. And what is more, as you must have realised by now, I am without illusions; what would the Senate do with me, an inexperienced legislator who lacks the faculty of self-deception, essential requisite for anyone wanting to guide others? We of our generation must draw aside and watch the capers and somersaults of the young around this ornate catafalque. Now you need young men, bright young men, with minds asking "how" rather than "why," and who are good at masking, at blending I should say, their obvious personal interests with vague public ideals.' He was silent, left St. Peter's alone. Then he went on : 'May I give you some advice to hand on to your superiors?'

'That goes without saying, Prince; it will certainly be heard with every consideration; but I still venture to hope that instead of advice you may give your consent.'

'There is a name I should like to suggest for the Senate : that of Calogero Sedàra. He has more the qualities to sit there than I have; his family, I am told, is an old one or soon will be : he has more than what you call prestige, he has power; he has outstanding practical merits instead of scientific ones; his attitude during the May crisis was not so much irreproachable as actively useful; as to illusions, I don't think he has any more than I have, but he's clever

enough to know how to create them when needed. He's
the man for you. But you must be quick, as I've heard that
he intends to put up as candidate for the Chamber of
Deputies.'

There had been much talk about Sedàra at the Prefecture. His activities both as mayor and private citizen
were well known. Chevalley gave a start; he was an honest
man and his esteem for the legislative chambers was paral-
leled by the purity of his intentions; so he thought it best
not to say a word in reply; and he did well not to compromise himself as, ten years later, Don Calogero did in fact
gain the Senate. But though honest, Chevalley was no fool;
he certainly lacked those quick wits which in Sicily usurp
the name of intelligence, but he could assess slowly and
firmly and also he had not the southern insensibility to
the distress of others. He understood Don Fabrizio's bitterness and discomfort, he reviewed for an instant the misery,
the abjection, the black indifference of which he had been
witness for the last month. During the past few hours he
had envied the Salina opulence and grandeur, but now
his mind went back tenderly to his own little vineyard,
his Monterzuolo near Casale, ugly, mediocre, but serene
and alive. And he found himself pitying this prince without
hopes as much as the children without shoes, the malaria-
ridden women, the guilty victims whose names reached his
office every morning; all were equal fundamentally, all were
comrades in misfortune segregated in the same well.

He decided to make a last effort. As he got up his
voice was charged with emotion. 'Prince, do you seriously
refuse to do all in your power to alleviate, to attempt to
remedy the state of physical squalor, of blind moral
misery in which this people of yours lies? Climate can
be overcome, the memory of evil régimes cancelled, for
the Sicilians must want to improve; if honest men withdraw the way will be open for those with no scruples and
no vision, for Sedàra and his like; and then everything will
be as before for yet more centuries. Listen to your conscience, Prince, and not to the proud truths that you have
spoken. Collaborate.'

Don Fabrizio smiled at him, took him by the hand, made him sit beside him on the sofa. 'You're a gentleman, Chevalley, and I consider it a privilege to have met you; you are right in all you say; your only mistake was saying "the Sicilians must want to improve." I'll tell you a personal anecdote. Two or three days before Garibaldi entered Palermo I was introduced to some British naval officers from one of the warships then in harbour to keep an eye on things. They had heard, I don't know how, that I own a house down on the shore facing the sea, with a terrace on its roof from which can be seen the whole circle of hills around the city; they asked to visit this house of mine and look at the landscape where Garibaldini were said to be operating, as they could get no clear idea from their ships. In fact Garibaldi was already at Gibilrossa. They came to my house, I accompanied them up on to the roof; they were simple youths in spite of their reddish whiskers. They were ecstatic about the view, the vehemence of the light; they confessed, though, that they had been horrified at the squalor, decay, filth of the streets around. I didn't explain to them that one thing was derived from the other, as I have tried to with you. Then one of them asked me what those Italian volunteers were really coming to do in Sicily. *"They are coming to teach us good manners!"* I replied in English. *"But they won't succeed, because we are gods."*

'I don't think they understood, but they laughed and went off. That is my answer to you too, my dear Chevalley; the Sicilians never want to improve for the simple reason that they think themselves perfect; their vanity is stronger than their misery; every invasion by outsiders, whether so by origin or, if Sicilian, by independence of spirit, upsets their illusion of achieved perfection, risks disturbing their satisfied waiting for nothing; having been trampled on by a dozen different peoples, they think they have an imperial past which gives them a right to a grand funeral.

'Do you really think, Chevalley, that you are the first who has hoped to canalise Sicily into the flow of universal history? I wonder how many Moslem imâms, how many of

King Roger's knights, how many Swabian scribes, how many Angevin barons, how many jurists of the Most Catholic King have conceived the same fine folly; and how many Spanish viceroys too, how many of Charles III's reforming functionaries! And who knows now what happened to them all! Sicily wanted to sleep in spite of their invocations; for why should she listen to them if she herself is rich, if she's wise, if she's civilised, if she's honest, if she's admired and envied by all, if, in a word, she is perfect?

'Now even people here are repeating what was written by Proudhon and some German Jew whose name I can't remember, that the bad state of things, here and elsewhere, is all due to feudalism; that it's my fault, as it were. Maybe. But there's been feudalism everywhere, and foreign invasions too. I don't believe that your ancestors, Chevalley, or the English squires or the French seigneurs governed Sicily any better than did the Salina. The results were different. The reason for the difference must lie in this sense of superiority that dazzles every Sicilian eye, and which we ourselves call pride while in reality it's blindness. For the moment, for a long time to come, there's nothing to be done. I'm sorry; but I cannot lift a finger in politics. It would only get bitten. These are things one can't say to a Sicilian; and if you'd said them yourself, I too would have objected.

'It's late, Chevalley; we must go and dress for dinner. For a few hours I have to act the part of a civilised man.'

Chevalley left early next morning and Don Fabrizio, who had arranged to go out shooting, was able to accompany him to the post station. With them was Don Ciccio Tumeo, carrying on his shoulders the double weight of two shotguns, his and Don Fabrizio's, and within himself the bile of his own trampled virtue.

In the livid light of five-thirty in the morning Donnafugata was deserted and seemed despairing. In front of every house the refuse of squalid meals accumulated along leprous walls; trembling dogs were routing about with a greed that was always disappointed. An occasional door was already open and the cumulative stench of sleep spread out into the street; by glimmering wicks mothers scrutinised the lids of their children for trachoma; almost all were in mourning and many had been the wives of those carcasses one stumbles over on the turns of mountain tracks. The men were coming out gripping their hoes to look for someone who might give them work, God willing; subdued silence alternated with exasperated screams of hysterical voices; away over towards the Convent of the Holy Ghost a tinny dawn was beginning to tinge leaden clouds.

Chevalley thought : 'This state of things won't last; our lively new modern administration will change it all.' The Prince was depressed. 'All this shouldn't last; but it will, always; the human "always" of course, a century, two centuries . . . and after that it will be different, but worse. We were the Leopards and Lions; those who'll take our place will be little jackals, hyenas; and the whole lot of us, Leopards, jackals and sheep, we'll all go on thinking ourselves the salt of the earth.' They thanked each other and said good-bye. Chevalley hoisted himself up on the post-carriage, propped on four wheels the colour of vomit. The horse, all hunger and sores, began its long journey.

Day had just dawned : the little light that managed to pass through quilted clouds was held up once more by the immemorial filth on the windows. Chevalley was alone; amid bumps and shakes he moistened the tip of his index finger with saliva and cleaned a pane for the width of an eye. He looked out; in front of him, under the ashen light, the landscape lurched to and fro, irredeemable.

5

FATHER PIRRONE PAYS A VISIT

FATHER PIRRONE'S origins were rustic; he had been born at San Cono, a tiny hamlet which is now, thanks to the autobus, almost a satellite-star in the solar system of Palermo, but a century ago belonged as it were to a planetary system of its own, being four or five cart-hours from the Palermo sun.

The father of our Jesuit had been overseer of two properties which the Abbey of Sant' Eleuterio thought it owned in the territory of San Cono. An overseer's job was then most perilous for the health both of soul and body, as it necessitated odd acquaintanceships and the knowledge of many a tale which might bring on ills that could suddenly stretch the patient dead beneath some rustic wall, with all those stories inside him lost irrevocably to idle curiosity. But Don Gaetano, Father Pirrone's father, had managed to avoid this occupational disease by rigorous hygiene based on discretion and a careful use of preventive remedies; and he had died peacefully of pneumonia one bright Sunday in February when a soughing wind was stripping the almond blossom. He left his widow and three children (two girls and the priest) relatively well off; like the wise man he was, he had managed to save up some of the incredibly meagre salary paid by the Abbey, and at the moment of his demise owned a few almond trees at the end of the valley, a row or two of vines on the slopes, and some stony pasturage farther up: all poor stuff, of course, but enough to confer a certain weight amid the depressed economy of San Cono. He was also owner of a small, rigidly square house, blue outside and white in, four rooms down and four up, at the very entrance of the village on the Palermo road.

Father Pirrone had left this house at the age of sixteen, when his successes at the parish school and the benevolence of the mitred Abbot of Sant' Eleuterio had set him on the road towards the archiepiscopal seminary; but every few years he had returned there, to bless the marriage of one of his sisters or to give a (in the worldly sense) superfluous absolution to the dying Don Gaetano, and he had come back now, at the end of February 1861, for the fifteenth anniversary of his father's death; on a day gusty and clear, just like that other one.

Getting there had meant a five hours' shaking in a cart with his feet dangling behind a horse's tail; but once he had overcome his nausea at the patriotic pictures newly painted on the cart panels, culminating in a rhetorical presentation of a flame-coloured Garibaldi arm in arm with an aquamarine Santa Rosalia, they had been a pleasant five hours. The valley rising from Palermo to San Cono mingles the lushness of the coast with the harshness of the interior, and is swept by sudden gusts of cleansing wind famous for being able to deviate the best-aimed bullets, so that marksmen faced with these ballistic problems preferred to go elsewhere. Then the carter, who had known the dead man well, launched out into lengthy reminiscences of his merits, reminiscences which, although not always adapted to a son's and a priest's ear, had flattered his practised listener.

His arrival was greeted with happy tears. He embraced and blessed his mother, whose deep widow's weeds set off nicely her white hair and rosy hue; and greeted his sisters and nephews, looking askance among the latter at Carmelo, who had had the bad taste to put a tricolour cockade on his cap in token of rejoicing. As soon as he got into the house he was assailed as always by sweet youthful memories. Nothing was changed, from the red brick floor to the sparse furniture; the same light entered the small narrow windows; Romeo, the dog, barking briefly in a corner, was exactly like another hound, its great-great-grandfather, his companion in violent play; and from the kitchen arose the centuries-old aroma of simmering stew of essence of tomatoes, onions and mutton, for macaroni on festive occasions. Everything expressed the serenity achieved by the dead man's labours.

Soon they moved off to church for the commemorative Mass. That day San Cono looked its best, basking almost proudly in its exhibition of different manures. Sly goats with dangling black udders and numbers of little Sicilian piglets, dark and slim as minute colts, were running among the people and up the steep tracks; and as Father Pirrone had become a kind of local glory, many women, children and even youths crowded round him to ask for his blessing or remind him of old days.

After a re-orientating gossip in the sacristy by the parish priest and attendance at Mass he moved to the tombstone in a side chapel; the women kissed the marble amid sobs, the son prayed aloud in his archaic Latin; and when they got home the macaroni was ready and much enjoyed by Father Pirrone, whose palate had not been spoilt by the culinary delicacies of Villa Salina.

Then towards evening his friends came to greet him and met in his room. A three-branched bronze lantern hung from the ceiling and spread a dim light from its oil burners; in a corner was the bed with its vari-coloured mattress and stifling pink and yellow quilt; another corner of the room, the 'barn,' was divided off by high stiff matting hiding honey-coloured corn taken weekly to the mill for the family needs; on the walls hung pock-marked engravings. St. Antony exhibiting the Divine Infant, St. Lucia her gouged-out eyes, and St. Francis Xavier haranguing crowds of plumed and naked Indians; outside, in the starry dusk, the wind blew and in its way was the only one to commemorate the dead. In the centre of the room under the lamp was a big squat brazier surrounded by a strip of polished wood on which people put their feet; all around, on hemp chairs, sat the guests. There were the parish priest, the two Schirò brothers, local landowners, and Don Piet-

rino the old herbalist; they came looking glum and remained looking glum, because, while the women were busy
below, they sat talking of politics, hoping to hear consoling
news from Father Pirrone who came from Palermo and
must know a lot as he lived with the 'nobles.' The desire for
news had been appeased and that for consolation disappointed, for their Jesuit friend, partly from sincerity and
partly also from tactics, painted for them a very black
future. The Bourbon tricolour still hung over Gaeta but
the blockade was tight and the powder magazines in the
fortress were being blown up one by one, and nothing
could be saved there now, except honour : not much, that
is; Russia was friendly but distant, Napoleon III shifty and
close, and of the risings in Basilicata and Terra di Lavoro
the Jesuit spoke little because deep down he was rather
ashamed of them. They must, he told them, face up to the
reality of this atheistic and rapacious Italian state now in
formation, to these laws of expropriation, to conscrip-
tion which would spread from Piedmont all the way down
here, like cholera. 'You'll see,' was his not very original
conclusion, 'you'll see they won't even leave us eyes to weep
with.'

These words were followed by the traditional chorus of
rustic complaints. The Schirò brothers and the herbalist
already felt the new fiscal grip; the former had had extra
contributions and additions here and there, the latter an
overwhelming shock; he had been called to the Town Hall
and told that if he didn't pay twenty lire every year he
wouldn't be allowed to sell his potions. 'But I go and gather
the grasses, these holy herbs God made, with my own
hands in the mountains, rain or shine, on certain days and
nights of the year. I dry them in the sun which belongs
to everybody and I grind them up myself, with my own
grandfather's mortar. What have you people at the Town
Hall to do with it? Why should I pay you twenty lire?
Just for nothing like that?'

The words came muffled from a toothless mouth, but
his eyes were dark with genuine rage. 'Am I right or not,
Father? You tell me !'

The Jesuit was fond of him; he remembered him as a man already grown, in fact already bent from continual wandering and stooping, when he himself had been a boy throwing stones at the birds; and he was also grateful because he knew that when the old man sold one of his potions to women he always said they would be useless without many an Ave and Gloria. But he prudently preferred to ignore what was in the potions, or the hopes with which the clients asked for them.

"You're right, Don Pietrino, a hundred times right. Why, of course! But if those people didn't take money off you and other poor souls like you, how could they afford to make war on the Pope and steal what's his?'

The conversation meandered on in the mild lamplight, quivering as the wind penetrated the heavy shutters. Father Pirrone expatiated on the future and the inevitable confiscation of ecclesiastical property; good-bye then to the mild rule of the Abbey in these parts : good-bye to the plates of soup distributed in bad winters; and when the younger Schirò had the imprudence to say that a few poor peasants might perhaps get some land of their own, his voice froze into sharp contempt. 'You'll see, Don Antonino, you'll see. The Mayor will buy everything up, pay the first instalments, and then do just what he likes. It's already happened in Piedmont!'

They ended by going off scowling even more than when they'd come, and with enough complaints to last two months. The only one to stay was the herbalist, who would not be going to bed that night as there was a new moon and he had to gather rosemary on the Pietrazzi rocks; he had brought a lantern with him and would be setting off straight from there.

'But tell me, Father, you who live with the nobles, what do they say about all these great doings? What does the Prince of Salina say, so tall and touchy and proud?'

Father Pirrone had more than once asked himself this question, and it was not an easy one to answer, particularly as he had taken little notice or interpreted as exaggeration what Don Fabrizio had told him one morning in the

Observatory nearly a year ago. He knew now, but could find no way of translating it into comprehensible terms for Don Pietrino who, though far from a fool, had more understanding of the anti-catarrhal, laxative, and even aphrodisiac properties of his herbs than of such abstractions.

'You see, Don Pietrino, the "nobles," as you call them, aren't so easy to understand. They live in a world of their own, created not directly by God but by themselves during centuries of highly specialised experiences, of their own worries and joys; they have a very strong collective memory, and so they're put out or pleased by things which wouldn't matter at all to you and me, but which to them seem vitally connected with their heritage of memories, hopes, caste fears. Divine Providence has willed that I should become a humble member of the most glorious Order in an Eternal Church whose eventual victory has been assured; you are at the other end of the scale, by which I don't mean the lowest but the most different. When you find a thick bush of marjoram or a well-filled nest of Spanish flies (you look for those too, Don Pietrino, I know) you are in direct communication with the natural world which the Lord created with undifferentiated possibilities of good and evil until man could exercise his own free will on it; and when you're consulted by evil old women and eager young girls, you are plunging back into the dark abyss of centuries that preceded the light from Golgotha.'

The old man looked at him in amazement; he had wanted to know if the Prince of Salina was satisfied or not with the latest changes, and the other was talking to him about aphrodisiacs and light from Golgotha. 'All that reading's driven him off his head, poor man.'

'But the "nobles" aren't like that; all they live by has been handled by others. They find us ecclesiastics useful to reassure them about eternal life, just as you herbalists are here to procure them soothing or stimulating drinks. And by that I don't mean they're bad people; quite the contrary. They're just different; perhaps they appear so strange to us because they have reached a stage towards which all those who are not saints are moving, that of indifference to earthly goods through surfeit. Perhaps it's because of that they take so little notice of things that are of great importance to us; those on mountains don't worry about mosquitoes in plains, nor do the people in Egypt about umbrellas. Yet the former fear landslides, the latter crocodiles, which are no worry to us. For them new fears have appeared of which we're ignorant; I've seen Don Fabrizio get quite testy, wise and serious though he is, because of a badly ironed collar to his shirt; and I know for certain that the Prince of Làscari didn't sleep for a whole night from rage because he was wrongly placed at one of the Viceroy's dinners. Now don't you think that a human being who is put out only by bad washing or protocol must be happy, and thus superior?'

Don Pietrino could understand nothing at all now : all this was getting more and more nonsensical, what with shirt collars and crocodiles. He was still upheld, though, by a basis of good rustic commonsense. 'But if that's what they're like, Father, they'll all go to Hell.'

'Why? Some will be lost, others saved, according to how they've lived in that conditioned world of theirs. Salina himself, for instance, might just scrape through; he plays his own game decently, follows the rules, doesn't cheat. God punishes those who voluntarily contravene the Divine Laws which they know and turn voluntarily down a bad road; one who goes his own way, so long as he doesn't misbehave along it, is always all right. If you, Don Pietrino, sold hemlock instead of mint, knowingly, you'd be for it; but if you thought you'd picked the right one, old Zana would die the noble death of Socrates and you'd go straight to Heaven with a cassock and wings of purest white.'

The death of Socrates was too much for the herbalist; he had given up and was fast asleep. Father Pirrone noticed this and was pleased, for now he would be able to talk freely without fear of being misunderstood; and he felt a need of talking, so as to fix into a pattern of phrases some ideas obscurely milling in his head.

'And they do a lot of good, too. If you knew, for instance, the families otherwise homeless that find shelter in those

palaces! And the owners ask for no return, not even
immunity from petty theft. They do it not from ostentation
but from a sort of obscure atavistic instinct which prevents them doing anything else. Although it may not seem
so, they are in fact less selfish than many others; the
splendour of their homes, the pomp of their receptions, have
something impersonal about them, something not unlike the
grandeur of churches and of liturgy, something which is in
fact *ad maiorem gentis gloriam,* and that redeems a great
deal : for every glass of champagne drunk by themselves
they offer fifty to others; when they treat someone badly,
as they do sometimes, it is not so much their personality
sinning as their class affirming itself. *Fata crescunt.* For
instance, Don Fabrizio has protected and educated his
nephew Tancredi and so saved a poor orphan who would
have otherwise been lost. You say that he did it because
the young man is a noble too, and that he wouldn't have
lifted a finger for anyone else. That's true, but why should
he lift a finger if sincerely, in the deep roots of his
heart, he considers all "others" to be botched attempts, china
figurines come misshapen from the potter's hands and not
worth putting to the test of fire.

'You, Don Pietrino, if you weren't asleep at this moment,
would be jumping up to tell me that the nobles are wrong
to have this contempt of others, and that all of us, equally
subject to the double slavery of love and death, are
equal before the Creator; and I would have to agree with
you. But I'd add that not only nobles are to be blamed
for despising others, since that is quite a general vice.
A university professor despises a parish schoolmaster even
if he doesn't show it, and since you're asleep I can tell
you without reticence that we clergy consider ourselves
superior to the other clergy, just as you herbalists despise
tooth-pullers who in their turn deride you. Doctors on the
other hand jeer at both tooth-pullers and herbalists, and are
themselves treated as fools by their patients who expect
to be kept alive with hearts or livers in a hopeless state;
to magistrates lawyers are just bores who try to delay
the course of law, and on the other hand literature is full

of satires against the pomposity, indolence and often worse of those very judges. The only people who also despise themselves are labourers; when they've learnt to jeer at others the circle will be closed and we'll start all over again.

'Have you ever thought, Don Pietrino, how many names of jobs have become insults? From trooper and fishwife to *reitre* or *pompier* in French? People don't think of the merits of troopers or fishwives; they just look at their marginal defects and call them all rough and profane; and as you can't hear me, I may tell you that I'm perfectly aware of the exact current meaning of the word "Jesuit."

'Then these nobles put a good face on their own disasters: I've seen one who'd decided to kill himself next day, poor man, looking beaming and happy as a boy on the eve of his first Communion; while if you, Don Pietrino, had to drink one of your own herb drinks, you'd make the village ring with your laments. To rage and mock is gentlemanly; to grumble and whine is not. In fact I could give you a recipe: if you meet a "gentleman" who's querulous, look up his family tree; you'll soon find a dead branch.

'It's a class difficult to suppress because it's in continual renewal and because if needs be it can die well, that is it can throw out a seed at the moment of death. Look at France; they let themselves be massacred with elegance there and now they're back as before. I say as before, because it is differences of attitude, not estates and feudal rights, which make a noble.

'They tell me that in Paris nowadays there are Polish counts who've been forced into exile and poverty by revolts and despotism; they drive cabs, but frown so at their middle-class customers that the poor things get into the cab, without knowing why, as humbly as dogs in church.

'And I can tell you too, Don Pietrino, that if, as has often happened before, this class were to vanish, an equivalent one would be formed straight away with the same qualities and the same defects; it might not be based on blood any more, but possibly on . . . on, say, length of time in a place, or pretended knowledge of some text presumed sacred.'

T.L.

At this point his mother's steps were heard on the wooden stairs; she laughed as she came in. 'Who d'you think you're talking to, son? Can't you see your ıı asleep?'

Father Pirrone looked a little abashed; he did not reply but just said, 'I'll go outside with him now. Poor man, he's got to spend all night out in the cold.' He took the wick from the lantern and lit it from one of the ceiling lamps, getting up on tiptoe and splashing his cassock with oil; then he put it back and shut its little gate. Don Pietrino was sailing in dreams; saliva was dribbling from a lip and spreading over his collar. It took some time to wake him up. 'Excuse me, Father, but you were saying such confusing things.' They smiled, went downstairs, and out. Night submerged the little house, the village, the valley; the nearby mountains could just be seen, surely as always; the wind had calmed but it was very cold; the stars were glittering away, producing thousands of degrees of heat which were not enough to warm one poor old man. 'Poor Don Pietrino! Would you like me to go and get you another cloak?'

'Thank you, I'm used to it. We'll meet to-morrow, then you'll tell me what the Prince of Salina feels about the Revolution.'

'I can tell you that at once and in a few words; he says there's been no revolution and that all will go on as it did before.'

'More fool he! Doesn't it seem a revolution to you when the Mayor wants me to pay for a grass God created and which I gather myself? Or have you gone off your head too?'

The light of the lantern went jerking off and eventually vanished into shadows thick as felt.

Father Pirrone thought what a mess the world must seem to one who knew neither mathematics nor theology. 'Oh, Lord, only Thy Omniscience could have devised so many complications.'

Another sample of these complications faced him next

morning. When he went down, ready to say Mass in the parish church, he found his sister Sarina chopping onions in the kitchen. The tears in her eyes seemed bigger than her activity warranted.

'What is it, Sarina? Any trouble? Don't let it depress you; the Lord afflicts and consoles.'

His affectionate tone dissipated the remains of the poor woman's reserve; she began sobbing loudly, with her face on the greasy table-top. Among the sobs could always be heard the same words, 'Angelina, Angelina . . . If Vincenzino knew he'd kill them both . . . Angelina . . . He'd kill them both!'

His hands thrust into his wide black sash, with only his thumbs showing. Father Pirrone stood looking at her. It wasn't difficult to understand; Angelina was Sarina's adolescent daughter; Vincenzino, whose fury was so feared, was her father and his brother-in-law; the only unknown part of the equation was the name of the other person involved, Angelina's presumed lover.

The Jesuit had seen her for the first time the day before as a full-grown girl, after having left her a snivelling child seven years before. She seemed about eighteen and was very plain indeed, with the jutting mouth of so many peasant girls around these parts, and frightened dog's eyes. He had noticed her on his arrival and in his heart in fact made rather uncharitable comparisons between her, plebeian as the diminutive of her own name, and Angelica, sumptuous as that name from Ariosto, who had recently disturbed the peace of the Salina household.

The trouble must be serious and here he was right in the middle of it; he remembered what Don Fabrizio had once said : every time one sees a relative one finds a thorn; then he was sorry for having remembered that. He extracted his right hand from his sash, took off his hat and clapped his sister's quivering shoulder. 'Come on now, Sarina, don't do that! Luckily, I'm here. Crying's no use. Where is Vincenzino?' Vincenzino had gone off to Rimato to see the Schiròs' ranger. All the better; they could talk things over without fear of surprise. Between sobs, sucked tears and nose snuffling, out the whole squalid story came; Angelina (or rather 'Ncilina) had let herself be seduced; the disaster had happened during St. Martin's Summer; she used to go to meet her lover in Donna Nunziata's hayloft; now she'd been with child three months; in a panic she had confessed all to her mother; soon her belly would begin showing and Vincenzo would raise hell. 'He'll kill me too, he will, because I didn't tell him; he's what they call "a man of honour!" '

In fact with his low forehead, ornamental quiffs of hair on the temples, lurching walk and perpetual swelling of the right trouser pocket where he kept a knife, it was obvious at once that Vincenzino was 'a man of honour,' one of those violent cretins capable of any havoc.

Now Sarina was overcome by a new fit of sobbing, stronger than the first because she'd been seized by re-newed remorse for having been unworthy of her husband, that mirror of chivalry.

'Sarina, Sarina, stop it now! Don't do that! The young man must marry her, he will marry her. I'll go to his home, talk to him and his family, everything will be all right. Then Vincenzo will know only about the engagement and his precious honour will remain intact. But I must know who the man is. If you know, tell me.'

His sister raised her head; her eyes now showed another fear, no longer the animal one of the knife thrusts, but a more restricted, keener one which the brother could not for the moment place.

'It was Santino Pirrone! Turi's son! And he did it out of spite, spite against me, against our mother, against our father's memory! I've never spoken to him, they all said he was a good boy—but he's a swine, a true son of that double-dishonoured father of his. I remembered afterwards; I always used to see him passing here in November with two friends and a red geranium behind his ear. Red of hell, that was, red of hell!'

The Jesuit took a chair and sat down next to the poor woman. Obviously he would have to be late for Mass. This

was serious. Turi, the father of the seducer Santino, was
an uncle of his; the brother, in fact the elder brother, of
his dead father. Twenty years ago he had worked together
with the dead man in his job as overseer, just at the
moment of the latter's greatest and most meritorious
activity. Later the brothers had quarrelled, one of those
family quarrels we all know with deeply entangled roots,
impossible to cure because neither side speaks out clearly,
each having much to hide. The fact was that when the
dead man acquired the little almond grove, his brother
Turi had said that half of it really belonged to him because
half the money for it, or half the work, he had put in himself; but the deeds bore only the name of the dead Gaetano.
Turi stormed up and down the roads of San Cono foaming
at the mouth. The dead man's prestige was in danger,
friends came between and the worst was avoided; the
almond grove remained Gaetano's property, but the gulf
between the two branches of the Pirrone family became
unbridgeable; Turi did not even go to his brother's funeral
and was referred to simply as the 'swine,' in his sister's
house. The Jesuit had been told of all this by letters dic-
tated to the parish priest and had formed some ideas of
his own about it which he did not express from filial
reverence. The little almond grove now belonged to
Sarina.

It was all quite obvious; no love or passion played any
part; just a dirty trick to revenge another dirty trick.
But it could be set right; the Jesuit thanked Providence for
having brought him to San Cono at that very time. 'Listen,
Sarina, I'll settle all this in a couple of hours, but you've
got to help me; half of Chibbaro' (that was the almond
grove) 'must go as 'Ncilina's dowry. There's no other way
out of it; the silly girl has been the ruin of you.' And he
thought how the Lord to bring about His justice can
even use bitches in heat.

Sarina lost her temper. 'Half of Chibbaro! To that swine,
never! Better dead!'

'All right. Then after Mass I'll go and talk to Vincen-

zino. Don't be afraid, I'll try and calm him down.' He
put his hat back on his head and his hands into his belt;
and waited patiently, sure of himself.

Any version of Vincenzino's furies, even though revised
and expurgated by a Jesuit priest, was always beyond poor
Sarina, who began weeping for the third time; gradually her
sobs lessened and then stopped. She got up: 'May God's
will be done; you fix it, it's beyond me. But our lovely
Chibbaro! All that sweat of our father's!'

Her tears were just about to start again, but the priest
had already gone.

After celebrating the Divine Sacrifice and accepting coffee
from the parish priest, the Jesuit went straight to his Uncle
Turi's home. He had never been there but knew it was a
shack at the very top of the village near Mastro Ciccu
the blacksmith's. He soon found it, and as there were no
windows and the door was open to let in a little sun, he
stopped on the threshold. In the darkness inside he could
see heaps of mules' harness, saddle-bags, sacks; Don Turi
earned his living as a mule driver, now helped by his son.

'*Dorâzio!*' called Father Pirrone. This was an abbrevia-
tion of the form of *Deo Gratias* (*agamus*) used by clerics
asking permission to enter. An old man's voice shouted,
'Who is it?' and someone got up at the back of the room
and came towards the door. 'It's your nephew, Father
Saverio Pirrone. I wanted to talk to you if I may.'

It was not much of a surprise for Turi; a visit by
Father Pirrone or some representative must have been
expected for at least two months. Uncle Turi was a vigorous, straight-backed old man baked through and through
by sun and hail, with the sinister furrows on his face which
troubles trace on people who are not good.

'Come in,' he said without a smile. He stood aside and
even went grudgingly through the action of kissing the
priest's hand. Father Pirrone sat down on one of the
big wooden saddles. The place looked very wretched
indeed: two chickens were grubbing away in a corner

and everything smelt of manure, wet washing and evil
poverty.

'Uncle, we've not met for years, but that's not all my
fault; I'm seldom at home, as you know, but you never
come near my mother, your sister-in-law; I'm sorry to hear
that.'

'I'll never set foot in that house again. Just passing it
turns my stomach! Turi Pirrone never forgets an injury,
even after twenty years!'

'Oh, yes, of course, yes indeed. But here I am to-day
like the dove from Noah's Ark, to assure you that the flood
is over. I'm very glad to be here and I was very happy
yesterday when they told me at home that your son
Santino is engaged to my niece Angelina; they are two
fine young people, I'm told, and their union will put an
end to the quarrel between our families which, if I may
say so, has always grieved me.'

Turi's face expressed a surprise too obvious not to be
false. 'If it weren't for your habit, Father, I'd say you
were lying. You must have been listening to tales from
those females of yours. Santino has never spoken to
Angelina in his life : he's far too good a son to go against
his father's wish.'

The Jesuit admired the old man's astuteness and the
smoothness of his lying.

'Apparently, uncle, I've been misinformed; why, they
told me that you'd agreed on the dowry and would both
be coming to our place to-day to make it official. But the
nonsense these idle females talk! Even if it's not true,
though, it does show what's in those good hearts of theirs.
Well, uncle, there's no point in my staying here; I'm going
straight home to reprove my sister. Very pleased to find
you so well.'

The old man's face was beginning to show a certain
greedy interest. 'Wait, Father. Give us another laugh with
this gossip of yours; what dowry were the females talking
of?'

'Oh, I don't know! I think I heard something about

half of Chibbaro! 'Ncilina, they said, was very dear to them and no sacrifice was too much to ensure peace in the family!'

Don Turi stopped laughing. He got up, 'Santino!' he began bawling as loudly as if calling a recalcitrant mule. And as no one came he shouted louder still, 'Santino, blood of the Madonna, where are you?' Then, when he saw Father Pirrone quiver, he put a hand over his mouth with a gesture unexpectedly servile.

Santino was seeing to the animals in the adjacent yard. He entered shyly, with a curry-comb in his hand. He was a fine-looking lad of twenty-two, tall and slim like his father, with eyes not yet embittered. He had seen the Jesuit pass through the village the day before as had everyone else and he recognised him at once. 'This is Santino. And this is your cousin Father Saverio Pirrone. You can thank God the Reverend Father is here, or I'd have cut your ears off. What's all this love-making without your own father knowing? Children are born for their parents and not to run after skirts.'

The young man looked ashamed, perhaps not from disobedience but because of his father's past consent, and did not know what to say; he got out of the difficulty by putting the curry-comb on the floor and going to kiss the priest's hand. The latter showed his teeth in a smile and sketched a benediction. 'God bless you, my son, though I don't think you deserve it.'

The old man continued, 'As your cousin here has gone on begging me I've given my consent in the end. Why didn't you tell me before, though? Now clean yourself up and we'll go down to Angelina's now.'

'A moment, uncle, just a moment.' It occurred to Father Pirrone that he ought to say a word to the 'man of honour' who knew nothing as yet. 'Back home they'll be sure to want to get things ready; anyway they told me they'd be expecting you at seven this evening. Come then, and it'll be a pleasure to see you.' And off he went, embraced by father and son.

When Father Pirrone got back to the little square

house he found his brother-in-law Vincenzino already
home, so all he could do to reassure his sister was wink
at her from behind her proud husband's back; but as they
were both Sicilians that was quite enough. Then he told
his brother-in-law that he wanted to talk to him, and the
two went off to the scraggy little pergola at the back. The
swaying edge of the Jesuit's cassock traced a kind of
uncrossable mobile frontier around him; the fat buttocks
of the 'man of honour' waggled, perennial symbol of threatening pride. Their conversation was actually quite different
from what the priest had foreseen. Once assured of the
imminence of 'Ncilina's marriage, the 'man of honour'
showed complete indifference about what her behaviour
had been. But at the first mention of the proposed dowry
his eyes rolled, the veins in his temples swelled and the
lurch in his walk became more marked; from his mouth
came a gurgle of low obscene oaths and announcements of
murderous intentions; his hand, which had not made a
single gesture in defence of his daughter's honour, began
clutching the right pocket of his trousers to show that in
defence of his almond trees he was ready to spill the very
last drop of other people's blood.

Father Pirrone let the stream of abuse run out, merely
making quick signs of the Cross at the frequent curses;
of the gesture announcing a massacre he took no notice
at all. During a pause he put in : 'Of course I want to
contribute to a general settlement too. You know the
private agreement ensuring me the ownership of whatever
was due to me from our father's estate? I'll send that
back to you from Palermo, torn up.'

This balsam had an immediate effect. Vincenzino, intent
on computing the value of the anticipated inheritance, was
silent; and through the cold sunny air came the cracked
notes of a song which had suddenly burst from 'Ncilina
as she swept out her uncle's room.

In the afternoon Uncle Turi and Santino came to pay
their visit, quite spruced up and wearing very white shirts.
The engaged couple sat on chairs side by side and broke
out now and again into loud wordless giggles in each other's

faces. They were really pleased, she at 'settling' herself and having this big handsome male at her disposal, he at following his father's advice and now owning not only half an almond grove but a slave too. And no one now found the red geranium he had put in his buttonhole to have any connection with hell.

Two days later Father Pirrone left for Palermo. As he jogged along he went over impressions that were not entirely pleasant; that brutish love-affair come to fruition in St. Martin's Summer, that wretched half almond grove reacquired by means of calculated courtship, seemed to him the rustic poverty-struck equivalent of other events recently witnessed. Nobles were reserved and incomprehensible, peasants explicit and clear; but the Devil twisted them both round his little finger all the same.

At the Villa Salina he found the Prince in excellent spirits. Don Fabrizio asked if he had enjoyed his four days away and if he had remembered to give his mother his, the Prince's, greetings. He knew her, in fact; she had stayed at the villa six years before and pleased both the Prince and Princess by her serene widowhood. The Jesuit had entirely forgotten about the greetings and was silent; then he said that his mother and sister had charged him with bearing His Excellency their respects, which was a fib rather than a lie. 'Excellency,' he added then, 'I wanted to ask you if you could give orders for me to have a carriage to-morrow; I must go to the Archbishopric to ask for a dispensation; a niece of mine has got engaged to her cousin.'

'Of course, Father Pirrone, of course, if you wish; but I have to go down to Palermo myself the day after to-morrow, you could come with me—or are you really in such a rush?'

6

A BALL

THE PRINCESS Maria Stella climbed into the carriage, sat
down on the blue satin cushions and gathered around her
as many rustling folds of her dress as she could. Meanwhile
Concetta and Carolina were also getting in; they sat down
in front of her, their identical pink dresses exhaling a faint
scent of violets. Then a heavy foot on the running board
made the barouche heel over on its high springs; Don
Fabrizio was getting in too. The carriage was crammed,
waves of silk, hoops of three crinolines, billowed, clashed,
mingled almost to the height of their heads; beneath was
a tight press of foot-gear, the girls' silken slippers, the
Princess's russet ones, the Prince's patent leather pumps:
each suffered from the other's feet and could find nowhere to
put his own.

The mounting steps were folded, the footman given his
orders. 'To Palazzo Ponteleone.' He got back on to the
box, the groom holding the horses' bridles moved aside,
the coachman gave an imperceptible click of his tongue, and
the barouche slid into motion.

They were going to a ball.

Palermo at the moment was passing through one of its
intermittent periods of social gaiety; there were balls everywhere. After the coming of the Piedmontese, after the
Aspromonte affair, now that spectres of violence and
spoliation had fled, the few hundred people who made up
'the world' never tired of meeting each other, always the
same ones, to exchange congratulations on still existing.

So frequent were the various and yet identical parties

that the Prince and Princess of Salina had moved to their town palace for three weeks so as not to have to make the long drive from San Lorenzo almost every night. The ladies' dresses would arrive from Naples in long black cases like coffins, and there would be an hysterical coming and going of milliners, hairdressers and shoemakers; of exasperated servants carrying excited notes to fitters. The Ponteleone ball was to be one of the most important of that short season; important for all concerned because of the standing of the family, the splendour of the palace and the number of guests; particularly important for the Salina who would be presenting to 'society' Angelica, their nephew's lovely bride-to-be. It was still only half-past ten, rather early to appear at a ball if one is Prince of Salina, whose arrival should be timed for when a fête is at its height. But this time they had to be early if they wanted to be there for the entry of the Sedàras, who were the sort of people ('they don't *know* yet, poor things') to take literally the times on the gleaming invitation card. It had taken a good deal of trouble to get one of those cards sent to them; no one knew them, and the Princess Maria Stella had been obliged to make a visit to Margherita Ponteleone ten days before; all had gone smoothly, of course, but even so it had been one of those little thorns that Tancredi's engagement had inserted into the Leopard's delicate paws.

The short drive to Palazzo Ponteleone took them through a tangle of dark alleys, and they went at walking pace: Via Salina, Via Valverde, down the Bambinai slope, so gay in daytime with its little shops of waxen figures, so dreary by night. The horseshoes sounded muffled amid the dark houses asleep or pretending to sleep.

The girls, incomprehensible beings for whom a ball is fun and not a tedious worldly duty, were chatting away gaily in low voices; the Princess Maria Stella felt her bag to assure herself she'd brought her little bottle of sal volatile; Don Fabrizio was enjoying in anticipation the effect of Angelica's beauty on all those who did not know her and of Tancredi's luck on all those who knew him too well. But a shadow lay across his contentment; what about Don Calogero's tail-coat? Certainly not like the one worn at Donnafugata; he had been put into the hands of Tancredi, who had dragged him off to the best tailor and even been present at fittings. Officially the result had seemed to satisfy him the other day; but in confidence he had said, 'The coat is the best we can do; Angelica's father lacks *chic*.' That was undeniable; but Tancredi had guaranteed a perfect shave and decently polished shoes. That was something.

Where the Bambinai slope comes out by the apse of San Domenico the carriage stopped; there was a faint tinkle and round the corner appeared a priest bearing a ciborium with the Blessed Sacrament; behind, a young acolyte held over him a white canopy embroidered in gold; in front another bore a big lighted candle in his left hand and in his right a little silver bell which he was shaking with obvious enjoyment. These were the Last Sacraments; in one of those barred houses someone was in a death agony. Don Fabrizio got out and knelt on the pavement, the ladies made the sign of the Cross, the tinkling faded into the alleys tumbling down towards San Giacomo, and the barouche, with its occupants given a salutary warning, set off again towards its destination, now close by.

They arrived, they alighted in the portico; the coach vanished into the immensity of the courtyard, whence came the sound of pawing horses and the gleams of equipages arrived before.

The great stairs were of rough material but superb proportions; from every step country plants spread rustic scents; on the landing between flights the amaranthine liveries of two footmen, motionless under their powder, set a note of bright colour in the pearly grey surroundings. From two high little grated windows came a gurgle of laughter and childish murmurs; the small Ponteleone grandchildren, excluded from the party, were looking on, making fun of the guests. The ladies smoothed down silken folds; Don Fabrizio, *gibus* under an arm, was head and shoulders above them, although a step behind. At the door of the first drawing-room they met their host and hostess; he, Don Diego, white-haired and paunchy, saved from looking plebeian only by his caustic eyes, she, Donna Margherita, with, between coruscating tiara and triple row of emeralds, the hooked features of an old priest.

'You've come early! All the better! But don't worry, *your* guests haven't appeared yet.' A new thorn pierced the sensitive fingertips of the Leopard. 'Tancredi's here already too.' There in the opposite corner of the drawing-room was standing their nephew, black and slim as an adder, surrounded by three or four young men whom he was making roar with laughter at little tales that were quite certainly indecent; but his eyes, restless as ever, were fixed on the entrance door. Dancing had already begun and through three, four, five ante-chambers came notes of an orchestra from the ballroom.

'We're also expecting Colonel Pallavicino, who did so well at Aspromonte.'

This phrase from the Prince of Ponteleone was not as simple as it sounded. On the surface it was a remark without political meaning, mere praise for the tact, the delicacy, the respect, the tenderness almost with which the Colonel had got a bullet fired into General Garibaldi's foot; and for the accompaniment too, the bowing, kneeling and hand-kissing of the wounded Hero lying under a chestnut tree on a Calabrian hillside, smiling from emotion and not from irony as he might well have done (for Garibaldi, alas, lacked a sense of humour).

At an intermediate stage of the princely psyche the phrase had a technical meaning and was intended to praise the Colonel for the aptness of his dispositions, the timely deployment of his battalions, and his ability to carry out successfully against the same adversary what Landi had so unaccountably failed to do at Calatafimi. At heart, though, Ponteleone thought that the Colonel 'did so well' by managing to stop, defeat, wound and capture Garibaldi, in so doing saving the compromise so laboriously achieved between the old state of things and the new.

Evoked, created almost by the approving words and still

more approving thoughts, the Colonel now appeared at
the top of the stairs. He was moving amid a tinkle of
epaulettes, chains and spurs in his well-padded, double-
breasted uniform, a plumed hat under his arm and his left
wrist propped on a curved sabre. He was a man of the world
with graceful manners, well-versed, as all Europe knew by
now, in hand-kissing dense with meaning; every lady whose
fingers were brushed by his perfumed moustaches that night
was able to re-evoke from first-hand knowledge the historical incident so highly praised in the popular press.

After sustaining the shower of praise poured over him
by the Ponteleone, after shaking the two fingers held out
to him by Don Fabrizio, Pallavicino merged into the
scented froth of a group of ladies. His consciously virile
features emerged above snowy white shoulders, and an
occasional phrase came over. 'I sobbed, countess, sobbed
like a child'; or 'He looked fine and serene as an arch-
angel.' The male sentimentality enchanted ladies reassured
already by the musketry of his Bersaglieri.

Angelica and Don Calogero were late, and the Salina
family were thinking of plunging into the other rooms
when Tancredi was seen to detach himself from his little
group and move like a dart towards the entrance: the
expected pair had arrived. Above the ordered swirl of her
pink crinoline Angelica's white shoulders merged into
strong soft arms; her head looked small and proud on its
smooth youthful neck adorned with intentionally modest
pearls. And when from the opening of her long kid glove
she drew a hand which though not small was perfectly
shaped, on it was seen glittering the Neapolitan sapphire.

In her wake came Don Calogero, a rat escorting a rose:
though his clothes had no elegance this time they were at
least decent. His only mistake was wearing in his buttonhole the Cross of the Order of the Crown of Italy recently
conferred on him; but this soon vanished into one of the
secret pockets in Tancredi's tail-coat.

Her fiancé had already taught Angelica to be impassive,
that fundamental of distinction ('You can be expansive
and noisy only with me, my dear; with all others you must

be the future Princess of Falconeri, superior to many, equal to all'), and so she greeted her hostess with a totally unspontaneous but highly successful mixture of virginal modesty, neo-aristocratic hauteur and youthful grace.

The Palermitans are Italians after all, and so particularly responsive to the appeal of beauty and the prestige of money; apart from which Tancredi, however attractive, being also notoriously penniless, was considered an undesirable match (mistakenly, as was seen afterwards when too late); and so he was appreciated more by married women than by marriageable girls. This merging of merits and demerits now had the effect of Angelica being received with unexpected warmth. One or two young men might well have regretted not having dug up for themselves so lovely an amphora brimming with coin : but Donnafugata was a fief of Don Fabrizio's, and if he had found that treasure there and then passed it to his beloved Tancredi, one could no more be jealous of that than of his finding a sulphur mine on his land; it was his property, there was nothing to be said.

But even this transient resentment melted before the rays of those eyes. At one moment there was quite a press of young men wanting to be introduced and to ask for a dance; to each one of them Angelica dispensed a smile from her strawberry lips, to each she showed her card in which every polka, mazurka and waltz was followed by the possessive signature : Falconeri. There was also a general attempt by young ladies to get on familiar terms; and after an hour Angelica found herself quite at her ease among people who had not the slightest idea of her mother's crudity or her father's rapacity.

Her bearing did not contradict itself for an instant; never was she seen wandering about alone with head in the clouds, never did her arms move from her body, never was her voice raised above the murmur (quite high anyway) of the other ladies. For Tancredi had told her the day before, 'Now darling, we (and so you too now) are more attached to our houses and furniture than we are to anything else;

and nothing offends us more than carelessness about those; so look at everything and praise everything; anyway Palazzo Ponteleone is worth it; but as you're not just a girl from the provinces whom everything surprises, always put a little reserve into your praise; admire, but always compare with some arch-type seen before and known to be outstanding.' The long visits to the palace at Donnafugata had taught Angelica a great deal, so that evening she admired every tapestry, but said that the ones in Palazzo Pitti had a finer border; she praised a Madonna by Dolci but remembered that the Grand Duke's had a more expressive melancholy; even of the slice of tart brought her by an attentive young gentleman she said that it was excellent, almost as good as that of 'Monsù Gaston,' the Salina chef. And as Monsù Gaston was positively the Raphael of cooks, and the tapestries of Palazzo Pitti the Monsù Gaston of hangings, no one could complain, in fact everyone was flattered by the comparison; and so from that evening she began to acquire the reputation of a polite but inflexible art expert which was to accompany her quite unwarrantably throughout her long life.

While Angelica reaped laurels, Maria Stella gossiped on a sofa with two old friends, and Concetta and Caroline froze with their shyness the politest partners. Don Fabrizio was wandering round the rooms; he kissed the hands of ladies he met, numbed the shoulders of men he wanted to greet, but could feel ill-humour creeping slowly over him. First of all he didn't like the house; the Ponteleone hadn't done it up for seventy years, it was still the same as in the time of Queen Maria Carolina, and he, who considered himself to have modern tastes, was indignant. 'Good God, with Diego's income it wouldn't take long to sweep away all these consoles, all these tarnished mirrors! Then order some decent rosewood and plush furniture, and so live in comfort himself and stop making his guests go round catacombs like these. I'll tell him so in the end.' But he never told Diego, for these opinions only stemmed from his mood and his tendency to contradiction; they were soon forgotten and he himself never changed a thing either at San Lorenzo or Donnafugata. Meanwhile, however, they served to increase his disquiet.

The women at the ball did not please him either. Two or three among the older ones had been his mistresses, and seeing them now, weighed down by years and daughters-in-law, it was an effort to imagine them as they were twenty years before, and he was annoyed at the thought of having thrown away his best years in chasing (and catching) such slatterns. The younger women weren't up to much either, except for one or two : the youthful Duchess of Palma, whose grey eyes and gentle reserve he admired, Tutú Làscari also, with whom, had he been younger, he might well have found himself in unique and exquisite harmony. But the others . . . it was a good thing that Angelica had emerged from the shades of Donnafugata to show these Palermitans what a really lovely woman was like.

There was something to be said for his strictures; what with the frequent marriages between cousins in recent years due to sexual lethargy and territorial calculations, with the dearth of proteins and overabundance of starch in the food, with the total lack of fresh air and movement, the drawing-rooms were now filled with a mob of girls incredibly short, improbably dark, unbearably giggly. They were sitting around in huddles, letting out an occasional hoot at an alarmed young man, and destined, apparently, to act only as background to three or four lovely creatures such as the fair-haired Maria Palma, and the exquisite Eleonora Giardinelli, who glided by like swans over a frog-filled pool.

The more of them he saw the more put out he felt; his mind, conditioned by long periods of solitude and abstract thought, at one moment, as he was passing through a long gallery where a numerous colony of these creatures had gathered on the central *pouf,* got into a kind of hallucination; he felt like a keeper in a zoo looking after some hundred female monkeys; any moment he expected to see them clamber up the chandeliers and hang there by their tails, swinging to and fro, showing off their behinds and loosing a stream of nuts, shrieks and grins at pacific visitors below.

A religious evocation, oddly enough, drew him away from this zoologic vision. For from the group of crinolined monkeys rose a monotonous, continuous sacred cry. 'Maria! Maria!' the poor creatures were perpetually exclaiming. 'Maria, what a lovely house!' 'Maria, what a handsome man Colonel Pallavicino is!' 'Maria, how my feet are aching!' 'Maria, I'm so hungry! When does the supper-room open?' The name of the Virgin, invoked by that virginal choir, echoed throughout the gallery and changed the monkeys back into women, for the *ouistiti* of the Brazilian forests had not yet, as far as he knew, been converted to Catholicism.

Slightly nauseated, the Prince passed into the room next door, where were encamped the rival and hostile tribe of men; the younger were off dancing and those now there were only the older ones, all of them his friends. He sat down a little among them; there, instead of the name of the Queen of Heaven being taken in vain, the air was turgid with commonplaces. Among these men Don Fabrizio was considered an 'eccentric'; his interest in mathematics was taken almost as sinful perversion, and had he not been actually Prince of Salina and known as an excellent horseman, a tireless shot and a fair womaniser, his parallaxes and telescopes might have exposed him to the risk of outlawry. Even so they did not say much to him, for his cold blue eyes, glimpsed under the heavy lids, put would-be talkers off, and he often found himself isolated, not, as he thought, from respect, but from fear.

He got up; his melancholy had now changed to black gloom. He had been wrong to come to this ball; Stella, Angelica, his daughters, could easily have coped with it alone, and he at this moment would have been happily ensconced in his study next to the terrace in Valla Salina, listening to the tinkling of the fountain and trying to catch

comets by their tails. 'Anyway, I'm here now; it would be
rude to leave. Let's go and have a look at the dancing.'

The ballroom was all golden; smoothed on cornices,
stippled on door-frames, damascened pale, almost silvery,
over darker gold on door panels and on the shutters which
covered and annulled the windows, conferring on the
room the look of some superb jewel-case shut off from an
unworthy world. It was not the flashy gilding which decor-
ators slap on nowadays, but a faded gold, pale as the hair
of certain nordic children, determinedly hiding its value
under a muted use of precious material intended to let
beauty be seen and cost forgotten. Here and there on the
panels were knots of rococo flowers in a colour so faint
as to seem just an ephemeral pink reflected from the chandeliers.

That solar hue, that variegation of gleam and shade,
made Don Fabrizio's heart ache as he stood black and stiff
in a doorway : this eminently patrician room reminded him
of country things; the chromatic scale was the same as
that of the vast wheat fields around Donnafugata, rapt,
begging for pity from the tyrannous sun; in this room,
too, as on his estates in mid August, the harvest had been
gathered long ago and stacked elsewhere, leaving, as here
now, a sole reminder in the colour of burnt up useless
stubble. The notes of the waltz in the warm air seemed
to him but a stylisation of the incessant winds harping their
own sorrows on those parched surfaces, to-day, yesterday,
to-morrow, for ever and for ever. The crowd of dancers
among whom he could count so many near to him in
blood if not in heart, began to seem unreal, made of the
raw material of lapsed memories, more labile even than
that of disturbing dreams. From the ceiling the gods, reclining on gilded couches, gazed down smiling and inexor-
able as a summer sky. They thought themselves eternal;
but a bomb manufactured in Pittsburgh, Penn., was to
prove the contrary in 1943.

'Fine, Prince, fine! They don't do things like this nowadays, with gold leaf at its present price!' Sedàra was

standing beside him; his quick eyes were moving over the room, insensible to its charm, intent on its monetary value.

Quite suddenly Don Fabrizio felt a loathing for him; to the rise of this man and a hundred others like him, to their obscure intrigues and their tenacious greed and avarice, was due the sense of death looming darkly over these palaces; it was due to him and his colleagues, to their rancour and sense of inferiority, their incapacity for putting out blooms, that the black clothes of the men dancing reminded Don Fabrizio of crows veering to and fro above lost valleys in search of putrid prey. He felt like giving a sharp reply and telling him to get out of his way. But he couldn't; the man was a guest, he was the father of that dear girl Angelica; and maybe, too, he was just as unhappy as others.

'Fine, Don Calogero, fine. But our young couple's the finest of all.' Tancredi and Angelica were passing in front of them at that moment, his gloved right hand on her waist, their outspread arms interlaced, their eyes gazing into each other's. The black of his tail-coat, the pink of her interweaving dress, looked like some unusual jewel. They were the most moving sight there, two young people in love dancing together, blind to each other's defects, deaf to the warnings of fate, deluding themselves that the whole course of their lives would be as smooth as the ballroom floor, unknowing actors set to play the parts of Juliet and Romeo by a director who had concealed the fact that tomb and poison were already in the script. Neither was good, each self-interested, turgid with secret aims; yet there was something sweet and touching about them both; those murky but ingenuous ambitions of theirs were obliterated by the words of jesting tenderness he was murmuring in her ear, by the scent of her hair, by the mutual clasp of those bodies destined to die.

The two young people drew away, other couples passed, less handsome, just as moving, each submerged in their passing blindness. Don Fabrizio felt his heart thaw; his disgust gave way to compassion for all these ephemeral beings out to enjoy the tiny ray of light granted them between two shades, before the cradle, after the last spasms. How could one inveigh against those sure to die? It would be as vile as those fish-vendors insulting the condemned in the Piazza del Mercato sixty years before. Even the female monkeys on the *poufs,* even those old boobies of friends were poor wretches, condemned and touching as the cattle lowing through city streets at night on their way to the slaughter-house; to the ears of each of them would one day come that tinkle he had heard three hours before behind San Domenico. Nothing could be decently hated except eternity.

And then these people filling the rooms, all these faded women, all these stupid men, these two vainglorious sexes were part of his blood, part of himself; only they could really understand him, only with them could he be at ease. 'I may be more intelligent, I'm certainly more cultivated than they are, but I come from the same stock, with them I must make common cause.'

He noticed Don Calogero talking to Giovanni Finale about a possible rise in the price of cheese and how in the hope of this beatific event his eyes had gone liquid and gentle. Don Fabrizio could slip away without remorse.

Till that moment accumulated irritation had given him energy; now with relaxed nerves weariness overcame him; it was already two o'clock. He looked round for a place where he could sit down quietly, far from men, beloved and brothers, all right in their way, but always tiresome. He soon found it; the library, small, silent, lit and empty. He sat down, then got up to drink some water which he found on a side table. 'Only water is really good,' he thought like a true Sicilian; and did not dry the drops left on his lips. He sat down again; he liked the library and soon felt at his ease there; it did not oppose his taking possession for it was impersonal as are rooms little used; Ponteleone was not a type to waste his time in there. He began looking at a picture opposite him, a good copy of Greuze's *Death of the Just Man*; the old man was expiring on his bed amid welters of clean linen, surrounded by afflicted grandsons, and by granddaughters raising arms

towards the ceiling. The girls were pretty, and provoking :
and the disorder of their clothes suggested sex more than
sorrow; they, it was obvious at once, were the real subject
of the picture. Even so Don Fabrizio was surprised for a
second at Diego always having this melancholy scene
before his eyes; then he reassured himself by thinking
that the other probably entered that room only once or
twice a year.

Immediately afterwards he asked himself if his own
death would be like that; probably it would, apart from
the sheets being less impeccable (he knew that the sheets
of those in their death agony are always dirty with spittle,
ejections, medicine marks . . .) and it was to be hoped that
Concetta, Carolina and his other women folk would be
more decently clad. But the same, more or less. As always
the thought of his own death calmed him as much as that
of others disturbed him : was it perhaps because, when all
was said and done, his own death would in the first place
mean that of the whole world?

From this he went on to think that he must see to re-
pairing the tomb of his ancestors at the Capuchins. A pity
corpses could no longer be hung up by the neck in the
crypt and watched slowly mummifying; he'd look magnificent on that wall, tall and big as he was, terrifying girls
by the set smile on his parchment face, by his long, long
white nankeen trousers. But no, they'd dress him up in
party clothes, perhaps in this very evening coat he was
wearing now. . . .

The door opened. 'Nuncle, you're looking wonderful
this evening. Black suits you perfectly. But what are you
looking at? Are you paying court to death?'

Tancredi was arm in arm with Angelica; both of them
were still under the sensual influence of the dance, and
were tired. Angelica sat down and asked Tancredi for a
handkerchief to mop her brow; Don Fabrizio gave her his.
The two young people looked at the picture with complete
lack of interest. For both of them death was purely an
intellectual concept, a facet of knowledge as it were and no
more, not an experience which pierced the marrow of

their bones. Death, oh, yes, it existed of course, but was
something that happened to others. The thought occurred
to Don Fabrizio that it was inner ignorance of this supreme
consolation which makes the young feel sorrows much more
sharply than the old; the latter are nearer the safety
exit.

'Prince,' said Angelica, 'we'd heard you were here; we
came to have a little rest, but also to ask you something.
I hope you won't refuse it.' Her eyes were full of sly
laughter, her hand was resting on Don Fabrizio's sleeve.
'I wanted to ask you to dance the next mazurka with me.
Do say yes, now, don't be naughty; we all know you used
to be a great dancer.' The Prince was very pleased and
felt suddenly quite spry. The Capuchins' crypt indeed!
His hairy cheeks quivered with pleasure. The idea of the
mazurka rather alarmed him, though; that military dance,
all heel-banging and turns, was not for his joints. To
kneel before Angelica would be a pleasure, but what if he
found it difficult to get up afterwards?

'Thank you, my dear girl : you're making me feel young
again. I'll be happy to obey you; but not the mazurka;
grant me the first waltz.'

'You see, Tancredi, how good Nuncle is? No nonsense
about him, like you. You know, Prince, he didn't want me
to ask you; he's jealous.'

Tancredi laughed. 'When one has such a smart good-
looking uncle one's quite right to be jealous. Anyway
this time I won't oppose it.' They all three smiled, and
Don Fabrizio could not make out if they had thought up
this suggestion to please him or to mock him. It didn't
matter; they were dear creatures all the same.

As he was going out Angelica slid a finger over the cover
of an arm-chair. 'Pretty, these; a good colour, but those
at your home, Prince . . .' The ship was taking its usual
course.

Tancredi intervened. 'That's enough, Angelica. We both
love you quite apart from your knowledge of furniture.
Leave the chairs alone and come and dance.'

As he was going into the ballroom, Don Fabrizio saw

that Sedàra was still talking to Giovanni Finale. He heard
market terms; they were comparing the prices of wheat.
The Prince foresaw an invitation soon to Margarossa, the
estate which was ruining Finale by his agricultural experi-
ments.

Angelica and Don Fabrizio made a magnificent couple.
The Prince's huge feet moved with surprising delicacy
and never were his partner's satin slippers in danger of
being grazed. His great paw held her waist with vigorous
firmness, his chin leant on the black waves of her hair;
from Angelica's bust rose a delicate scent of *bouquet à la
Maréchale,* and above all an aroma of young smooth skin.
A phrase of Tumeo came back to him : 'Her sheets
must smell like paradise.' A crude, vulgar phrase, but
accurate. Lucky Tancredi . . .
She talked. Her natural vanity was as appeased as her
tenacious ambition. 'I'm so happy, Nuncle. Everyone's been
so kind, so sweet. Tancredi's an angel; and you're an angel,
too. I owe all this to you, Nuncle; even Tancredi. For if
you hadn't agreed, I don't know what would have happened.'
'I've nothing to do with it, my dear; all this is due
to yourself alone.'
It was true; no Tancredi could ever have resisted that
beauty united to that income. He would have married her
whatever happened. A twinge crossed his heart : the thought
of Concetta's haughty yet defeated eyes. But that was a
brief little pain; at every twirl a year fell from his shoulders; soon he felt back at the age of twenty, when in that
very same ballroom he had danced with Stella before he
knew disappointment, boredom and the rest. For a second,
that night, death seemed to him once more 'something that
happens to others.'
So absorbed was he in memories which dovetailed so
well with his present feelings that he did not notice how
all of a sudden he and Angelica were dancing alone.
Instigated, perhaps, by Tancredi, the other couples had
stopped and were watching; the two Ponteleone were there

too, looking touched; they were old and perhaps understood. Stella was old too, but she was gazing on dully
from beneath a doorway. When the band stopped there
was nearly a round of applause; but Fabrizio had too
leonine an air for anyone to risk such an impropriety.

When the waltz was over Angelica suggested that Don
Fabrizio should come and take supper at her and Tancredi's
table. He would have much liked to, but at that moment
the memories of his own youth were too vivid for him not
to realise how tiresome supper with an old uncle would
have been then, with Stella only a yard or so away. Lovers
want to be alone, or at least with strangers; never with
older people, worst of all with relations.

'Thank you, Angelica, but I'm not hungry. I'll take
something standing up. Go with Tancredi, don't worry
about me.'

He waited a moment for the two young people to draw
away, then he too went into the supper room. A long, narrow
table was set at the end, lit by the famous twelve silver-
gilt candelabra given to Diego's grandfather by the Court
of Madrid at the end of his embassy in Spain; on tall
pedestals of gleaming metal six alternating figures of athletes
and women held above their heads silver-gilt shafts crowned
by the flames of twelve candles. The sculptor had hinted
skilfully at the serene ease of the men and the graceful
effort of the girls in upholding the disproportionate weight.
Twelve pieces of first-class quality . . . 'I wonder how
much land they're worth,' that wretch Sedàra would have
said. Don Fabrizio remembered Diego showing him one day
the cases for each of these candles, vast green morocco
affairs with the tripartite shield of Ponteleone and the
entwined initials of the donors stamped on the sides in
gold.

Beneath the candelabra, beneath the five tiers bearing
towards the distant ceiling pyramids of home-made cakes
that were never touched, spread the monotonous opulence
of buffets at big balls : coralline lobsters boiled alive, waxy
chaud-froids of veal, steely-lined fish immersed in sauce,

turkeys gilded by the ovens' heat, rosy *foie-gras* under gelatine armour, boned woodcocks reclining on amber toast decorated with their own chopped guts, dawn-tinted galantine, and a dozen other cruel, coloured delights. At the end of the table two monumental silver tureens held limpid soup, the tint of burnt amber. To prepare this supper the cooks must have sweated away in the vast kitchens from the night before.

'Dear me, what an amount! Donna Margherita knows how to do things well. But it's not for me!'

Scorning the table of drinks, glittering with crystal and silver on the right, he moved left towards that of the sweet-meats. Huge sorrel *babas, Mont Blancs* snowy with whipped cream, cakes speckled with white almonds and green pistachio nuts, hillocks of chocolate-covered pastry, brown and rich as the top soil of the Catanian plain from which, in fact, through many a twist and turn they had come, pink ices, champagne ices, coffee ices, all *parfaits* and falling apart with a squelch at a knife cleft; a melody in major of crystallised cherries, acid notes of yellow pine-apple, and green pistachio paste of those cakes called 'Triumphs of Gluttony,' shameless 'Virgins' cakes' shaped like breasts. Don Fabrizio asked for some of these, and as he held them on his plate looked like a profane carica-ture of Saint Agatha claiming her own sliced-off breasts. 'Why ever didn't the Holy Office forbid these puddings when it had the chance? "Triumphs of Gluttony" indeed! (Gluttony, mortal sin!) Saint Agatha's sliced-off teats sold by convents, devoured at dances! Well! Well!'

Round the room smelling of vanilla, wine, *chypre,* wan-dered Don Fabrizio looking for a place. Tancredi saw him from his table and clapped a hand on a chair to show there was room there; next to him was Angelica, peering at the back of a silver dish to see if her hair was in place. Don Fabrizio shook his head in smiling refusal. He went on looking; from a table he heard the satisfied voice of Pallavicino, 'The most moving moment of my life . . .' By him was an empty place. What a bore the man was! Wouldn't it be better, after all, to listen to Angelica's

refreshing if forced cordiality, to Tancredi's dry wit?
No : better bore oneself than bore others.

With a word of apology he sat down next to the
Colonel, who got up as he arrived—a small sop to Salina
pride. As he savoured the subtle mixture of blancmange,
pistachio and cinnamon in the puddings he had chosen,
Don Fabrizio began conversing with Pallavicino and realised
that, beyond those sugary phrases meant perhaps only for
ladies, the man was anything but a fool. He too was a
'gentleman,' and the fundamental scepticism of his class,
smothered usually by the impetuous Bersaglieri flames
on his lapel, came peering out again now that he found
himself in surroundings like those into which he was born,
away from the inevitable rhetoric of barracks and admirers.

'Now the Left wants to string me up because last August
I ordered my men to open fire on the General. But can you
tell me, Prince, what else I could have done in view of the
written orders I was carrying? I must confess though,
when at Aspromonte I found myself facing that mob of a
few hundred ragamuffins, some looking like out-and-out
fanatics, others scowling like professional agitators, I was
pleased my instructions coincided so with my own feelings.
If I hadn't given orders to fire those people would have
hacked us to pieces, my soldiers and me; that wouldn't have
mattered much, of course. But in the end it would have
meant French and Austrian intervention, and that would
have had endless repercussions, including the collapse of
this Italian Kingdom of ours which has got itself put together in some miraculous way, quite how I can't for the
life of me understand. And I can tell you another thing in
confidence : those musket shots of ours were a particular
help to . . . Garibaldi himself ! They freed him from the
rabble hanging round him, all those creatures like Zam-
bianchi who were making use of him for ends that may
have been generous but were certainly inept, with the
Tuileries or Palazzo Farnese behind them. Very different
types those were to the ones who landed with him at
Marsala, who did believe, the best of them, that Italy could

be created by repeating 1848. And he knows that, the General does, for when I was making him the genuflection that has caused so much comment, he shook my hand with a warmth that must surely be unusual towards a man who's just fired a bullet into one's foot a few minutes before. And d'you know what he said to me in a low voice, he who was the one really decent person on the whole wretched mountainside? "Thank you, Colonel." Thank you for what, I ask you? For laming him for life? Obviously not; but for having brought home to him so clearly the bluster, the cowardice, worse maybe, of those followers of his.'

'Forgive me saying so, Colonel, but don't you think all the hand-kissing, cap-doffing and compliments went a little far?'

'No, frankly. For they were all genuine acts of respect. You should have seen him, that poor great man, stretched out under a chestnut tree, suffering in body and still more in mind. A sad sight! He showed himself plainly as what he's always been, a child, in spite of beard and wrinkles, a simple adventurous little boy; it was difficult for me not to feel moved at having had to shoot at him. Why shouldn't I, anyway? Usually I kiss only ladies' hands; on that occasion, Prince, I was kissing a hand for the salvation of the Kingdom, also a lady to whom we soldiers owe homage.'

A footman passed; Don Fabrizio told him to bring a slice of *Mont Blanc* and a glass of champagne. 'And you, Colonel, aren't you taking anything?'

'Nothing to eat, thank you. Perhaps I'll drink a glass of champagne too.'

Then he went on, obviously unable to take his mind off a memory which, consisting as it did of a little shooting and a lot of skill, was exactly the sort that attracts men of his type. 'The General's men, as my Bersaglieri disarmed them, were cursing away, and d'you know who at? At him, the only one of them who'd actually paid in his own person. Foul, but natural really; they saw that childlike yet large personality, the only one capable of covering up their obscure intrigues, slipping out of their grasp. And if my own courtesies were superfluous, I'd be pleased even so at having done them; we in Italy can never go too far with sentiment and hand-kissing; they're the most effective political arguments we have.'

He drank the wine brought him, but that seemed to increase his bitterness even more. 'Have you been on the mainland since the Kingdom was founded? You're lucky. It's not a pretty sight. Never have we been so disunited as since we've been reunited. Turin doesn't want to cease being a capital. Milan finds our administration inferior to the Austrians', Florence is afraid the works of art there will be carried off, Naples is moaning about the industries she's lost and here, here in Sicily, some huge irrational disaster is growing up . . . For the moment, due partly to your humble servant, no one mentions red shirts any more; but they'll be back again. When they've vanished, others of different colours will come; and then red ones once again. And how will it end? There's Italy's Lucky Star, they say. But you know better than me, Prince, that even fixed stars are so only in appearance.' Perhaps he was a little tipsy, making such prophecies. But at such disquieting prospects Don Fabrizio felt his heart contract.

The ball went on for a long time still, until six in the morning; all were exhausted and wishing they had been in bed for at least three hours; but to leave early was like proclaiming the party a failure and offending the host and hostess who had taken *such* a lot of trouble, poor dears.

The ladies' faces were livid, their dresses crushed, their breaths heavy. 'Maria! How tired I am! Maria! How sleepy!' Above their disordered cravats the faces of the men were yellow and lined, their mouths stained with bitter saliva. Their visits to a disordered little room near the band alcove became more frequent; in it were disposed a row of twenty vast vats; by that time nearly all were brimful, some spilling over. Sensing that the dance was nearing its end, the sleepy servants were no longer changing the candles in chandeliers, and the short stubs diffused a different, smoky, ill-omened light. In the empty supper room where only dirty plates, glasses with dregs of wine which the servants, glancing around, would hurriedly drain; through the cracks in the shutters filtered a plebeian light of dawn.

The party was crumbling away and around Donna Margherita there was already a group saying good-bye. 'Heavenly! A dream! Like the old days!' Tancredi was hard put to wake Don Calogero who, with head flung back, had gone off to sleep on an arm-chair apart; his trousers were rucked up to his knees and above his silken socks showed the ends of his drawers, a most rustic sight. Even Colonel Pallavicino had circles under his eyes, declaring, though, to whoever wished to listen, that he was not going home and would move straight from Palazzo Ponteleone to his headquarters; such in fact was the iron tradition followed by officers invited to a ball.

When the family had settled into its carriage (the dew had made the cushions damp) Don Fabrizio said that he would walk home; a little fresh air would do him good, he had a slight headache. The truth is that he wanted to draw a little comfort from gazing at the stars. There were still one or two up there, at the zenith. As always, seeing them revived him; they were distant, they were omnipotent and at the same time they were docile to his calculations; just the contrary to humans, always too near, so weak and yet so quarrelsome.

There was already a little movement in the streets, a cart or two with rubbish heaped four times the height of the tiny grey donkey dragging it along. A long open wagon came by stacked with bulls killed shortly before at the slaughter-house, already quartered and exhibiting their intimate mechanism with the shamelessness of death. At intervals a big thick red drop fell on to the paving-stones.

At the cross-roads he glimpsed the sky to the east, above the sea. There was Venus, wrapped in her turban of autumn mist. She was always faithful, always awaiting a Don Fabrizio on his early morning outings, at Donnafugata before a shoot, now after a ball.

Don Fabrizio sighed. When would she decide to give him an appointment less ephemeral, far from stumps and blood, in her own region of perennial certitude?

7

DEATH OF A PRINCE

JULY, 1883

DON FABRIZIO had always known that sensation. For a dozen years or so he had been feeling as if the vital fluid, the faculty of existing, life itself in fact and perhaps even the will to go on living, were ebbing out of him slowly but steadily, as grains of sand cluster and then line up one by one, unhurried, unceasing, before the narrow neck of an hour-glass. In some moments of intense activity or concentration this sense of continual loss would vanish, to reappear impassively in brief instants of silence or introspection; just as a constant buzzing in the ears or ticking of a pendulum superimpose themselves when all else is silent, assuring us of always being there, watchful, even when we do not hear them.

With the slightest effort of attention he used to notice at all other times too, the rustling of the grains of sand as they slid lightly away, the instants of time escaping from his mind and leaving him for ever. But this sensation was not, at first, linked to any physical discomfort. On the contrary this imperceptible loss of vitality was itself the proof, the condition so to say, of a sense of living; and for him, accustomed to scrutinising limitless outer space and to probing vast inner abysses, the sensation was in no way disagreeable; this continuous whittling away of his personality seemed linked to a vague presage of the rebuilding elsewhere of a personality (thanks be to God) less conscious and yet broader. Those tiny grains of sand were not lost; they were vanishing, but accumulating elsewhere to cement some more lasting pile. Though 'pile,' he had reflected, was not the exact word, for it suggested weight; nor was 'grain of sand' either for that matter. They were more like the tiny particles of water vapour exhaled from a narrow pond, mounting then into the sky to great clouds, light and free.

Sometimes he was surprised that the vital reservoir could still contain anything at all after all those years of loss. 'Not even were it big as a Pyramid . . .' On other occasions, more frequent, he had felt a kind of pride at being the only one to notice this continual escape, while no one around him seemed to sense it in the same way; and this had made him feel a certain contempt for others, as an old soldier despises a conscript who deludes himself that sizzling bullets are just harmless flies. Such things are never confessed, no one knows why, but left for others to sense; and no one around him had ever sensed them at all, none of his daughters with their dreams of a world beyond the tomb identical with this life, all complete with judges, cooks and convents; not even Stella who, though devoured by the canker of diabetes, had still clung pitiably to this vale of tears.

Perhaps only Tancredi had understood for an instant, when he had said with that subdued irony of his, 'You, Nuncle, are courting death.' Now the courtship was ended; the lovely lady had said a definite 'yes' to an elopement, to a reserved compartment on the train.

For this was different now, quite different. Sitting in an arm-chair, his long legs wrapped in a blanket, on the balcony of the Hotel Trinacria, he felt life flowing from him in great pressing waves with a spiritual roar like that of the Rhine Falls. It was noon on a Monday at the end of July, and away in front of him spread the sea of Palermo, compact, oily, inert, improbably motionless, crouching like a dog trying to make itself invisible at its master's threats; but up there the static perpendicular sun was straddling it and lashing at it pitilessly. The silence was absolute. Under the high, high light Don Fabrizio heard no other sound but that inner one of the life gushing from him.

He had arrived that morning, a few hours before, from Naples, where he had gone to consult a specialist, Professor Sémmola. Accompanied by his forty-year-old daughter, Concetta, and his grandson Fabrizietto, he had had a dreary journey, slow as a funeral procession. The bustle of the port of departure and that of arrival at Naples, the acrid smell of the cabin, the incessant clamour of that paranoiac city, had exasperated him with the querulous exasperation which tires and prostrates the very weak while arousing an equivalent exasperation in good folk with years of life ahead. He had insisted on returning by land; a sudden decision which the doctor had tried to oppose : but he had been adamant, and so overwhelming was the shadow of his prestige still that he had had his way.

The result was that he had been forced to spend thirty-six hours cooped up in a scorching hot box, suffocated by the smoke of tunnels repetitive as feverish dreams, blinded by the sun in open patches stark as sad realities, humiliated by the innumerable squalid services he had to ask of his alarmed grandson. They crossed evil-looking landscapes, accursed mountain ranges, torpid malarial plains, those landscapes of Calabria and Basilicata which seemed barbarous to him while they were actually just like those of Sicily. The railway line had not yet been completed; in its last tract near Reggio it made a wide detour through Metaponto across lunar deserts called sarcastically by the athletic and voluptuous names of Croton and Cybaris. Then, at Messina, after the deceitful smile of the Straits had been given a lie by the parched slopes of Cape Pelorus, there was another detour, long and cruel as legal arrears. They had gone down to Catania, clambered up again towards Castro Giovanni; the locomotive, as it panted up those fabulous slopes, seemed about to die like an over-forced horse; then after a noisy descent they reached Palermo. On the arrival platform were the usual masks of family faces with painted smiles of pleasure at the journey's happy outcome. It was in fact from the would-be consoling smiles of those awaiting him at the station, from their pretence—a bad pretence—at an air of gaiety, that there

suddenly came home to him what had been the real diag-
nosis of Sémmola, who to him had spoken only reassuring
phrases; and it was then, after getting down from the train,
as he was embracing his daughter-in-law buried in widow's
weeds, his children showing their teeth in smiles, Tancredi with anxious eyes, Angelica with silken bodice tight
over mature breasts, it was then that he heard the crash
of the cascade.

Probably he fainted, for he did not remember how he
had reached the carriage; he found himself lying in it with
his legs contracted, only Tancredi with him. The carriage
had not yet moved, and from outside came voices of his
family in confabulation. 'It's nothing.' 'The journey was
too long.' 'Any of us might faint in this heat.' 'It would be
too tiring for him to go up to the villa.' He was perfectly
lucid again now : he noticed a serious conversation going
on between Concetta and Francesco Paolo, Tancredi's
elegance, his brown and beige check suit, his brown bowler;
and he noticed too how for once his nephew's smile was
not mocking but touched with sad affection; from this he
got the bitter-sweet sensation that his nephew loved him
and also knew him to be done for, since that perpetual irony
had been driven off by tenderness. The carriage moved off
and turned to the right. 'But where are we going, Tancredi?' His own voice surprised him. It seemed to echo
that inner booming.

'Nuncle, we're going to the Hotel Trinacria; you're
tired and the villa's a long way; you can have a night's
rest and get home to-morrow. Don't you think so?'

'Then let's go to our place by the sea, that's even
nearer.'

But it wasn't possible; the house was not in order, as he
knew well; it was only used for occasional luncheons by
the sea; there wasn't even a bed in it.

'You'll be better at the hotel, uncle; you'll have every
comfort there.' They were treating him like a new-born
baby; and he had just about a new-born baby's strength.

The first comfort he found at the hotel was a doctor,
called in a hurry, perhaps during his black-out. But it was

not the one who always treated him, Doctor Cataliotti, with big white cravat under smiling face and rich gold spectacles; this was a poor devil, doctor to the slum quarter around, impotent witness of a thousand wretched death-agonies. Above a torn frock-coat stretched his long, haggard face stubbled with white hair, the disillusioned face of a famished intellectual; when he took a chainless watch from his pocket, the false gilt showed marks of verdigris. He too was a poor goat-skin flask worn through by the jostle of the mule path and scattering without realising its last drops of oil. He felt the pulse-beats, prescribed camphor drops, showed his decayed teeth in a smile meant to be reassuring and which was pitiable instead, and shuffled off.

The drops soon arrived from a chemist nearby; they did him good; he felt a little less weak, but the impetus of escaping time did not lessen.

Don Fabrizio looked at himself in the wardrobe mirror: he recognised his own suit more than himself; very tall and emaciated, with sunken cheeks and three days' growth of beard; he looked like one of those maniac Englishmen who amble round the vignettes in books by Jules Verne which he used to give Fabrizietto as Christmas presents. A Leopard in very bad trim. Why, he wondered, did God not want anyone to die with their own face on? For the same happens to us all: we all die with a mask on our features; even the young; even that blood-daubed soldier, even Paolo, when he'd been raised from the cobbles with taut crumpled features as passers-by rushed in the dust after his runaway horse. And if in him, an old man, the crash of escaping life was so powerful, what a tumult there must have been as the brimming reservoirs emptied in a second out of those poor young bodies.

An absurd rule of enforced camouflage—he would have liked to contravene it as much as he could; but he felt that he was unable, that to hold up a razor would have been like holding up his own desk, before. 'Call a barber, will you?' he said to Francesco Paolo. But at once he thought, 'No. It's a rule of the game; hateful but formal. They'll shave me afterwards.' And he said out loud, 'It doesn't matter; we'll think about that later.' The idea of the utter abandon of his corpse, with a barber crouched over it, did not disturb him.

A waiter came in with a basin of warm water and a sponge, took off his coat and shirt and washed his face and hands, as one washes a child, as one washes the dead. Smuts from the day and a half's train journey turned the water a funereal black. The low room was suffocating; the heat fomented smells, brought out the mustiness of ill-dusted plush; the ghosts of dozens of crushed cockroaches were manifested in a faint medicinal odour; by the night table tenacious memories of stale and varied urine over-cast the room. He had the shutters opened; the hotel was in shadow, but a blinding light was reflected from the metallic sea; better, though, than that prison stink. He asked for an arm-chair to be taken on the balcony; lean-ing on someone's arm he dragged himself out, and sat down after those few steps with the sensation of relief he used to feel once on sitting down after four hours of shooting in the mountains. 'Tell everyone to leave me in peace; I feel better; I want to sleep.' He did feel sleepy; but he found that to give way to drowsiness now would be as absurd as eating a slice of cake immediately before a longed-for banquet. He smiled. 'I've always been a wise gourmet.' And he sat there, immersed in that great outer silence, in that terrifying inner rumble.

He could turn his head to the left; beside Monte Pelle-grino could be seen a cleft in the circle of hills and, beyond, two hillocks at whose feet lay his home. Unreachable to him as this was, it seemed very far away; he thought of his own observatory, of the telescopes now destined to years of dust; of poor Father Pirrone, who was dust too; of the paintings of his estates, of the monkeys on the hangings, of the big brass bedstead in which his dear Stella had died; of all those things which now seemed to him humble how-ever precious, just braided metal, woven threads and canvas corded with sap and earth, which he had kept alive and would shortly be plunged, through no fault of their

own, into a limbo of abandon and oblivion. His heart
tightened, he forgot his own agony thinking of the imminent
end of those poor dear things. The inert row of houses behind him, the wall of hills, the sun-scourged distance,
prevented him thinking clearly even of Donnafugata; it
seemed like a house in a dream, no longer his; all he had
of his own now was this exhausted body, those slate tiles
under his feet, that surging of dark water towards the
abyss. He was alone, a shipwrecked man adrift on a raft,
prey of untameable currents.

There were his sons, of course. The only one who resembled him, Giovanni, was no longer here. Every couple
of years he sent greetings from London; he had ceased
dealing with coal and moved on to diamonds; just after
Stella's death a short letter had come addressed to her and
soon after a little parcel with a bracelet. Ah, yes. He too had
'courted death,' in fact by leaving everything he had done
his best to organise for himself as much of death as he could
while actually going on living. But the others . . . There
were his grandchildren, too, of course; Fabrizietto, youngest
of the Salina, so handsome, so lively, so dear . . .

So odious. With his double dose of Màlvica blood, with
his good-time instincts, with his tendency to middle-class
smartness. It was useless to try and avoid the thought, but
the last of the Salina was really he himself, this gaunt giant
now dying on a hotel balcony. For the significance of a
noble family lies entirely in its traditions, that is in its
vital memories; and he was the last to have any unusual
memories, anything different from those of other families.
Fabrizietto would only have banal ones like his school-
fellows, of snacks, of spiteful little jokes against teachers,
horses bought with an eye more to price than quality;
and the meaning of his name would change more and more
to empty pomp, embittered by the gad-fly thought that
others could outdo him in outward show. He would go
hunting for a rich marriage when that would have become
a commonplace routine and no longer a predatory adven-
ture like Tancredi's. The tapestries of Donnafugata, the
almond groves of Ragattisi, even, who knew, the fountain of

Amphitrite, might suffer a grotesque metamorphosis from
the age-old muted things they had been into pots of quickly-
swallowed *foie gras,* or can-can girls transient as their own
rouge. And he himself would be only a memory of a
choleric old grandfather who had collapsed one July afternoon just in time to prevent the boy going off to Livorno
for sea-bathing. He had said that the Salina would always
remain the Salina. He had been wrong. The last Salina was
himself. That fellow Garibaldi, that bearded Vulcan had
won after all.

From the room next door, open on to the same balcony,
Concetta's voice reached him, 'We simply must; he's got
to be called. I should never forgive myself if he weren't.'
He understood at once; they were talking of a priest.
For a moment he had an idea of refusing, of lying, of
starting to shout that he was perfectly well, that he needed
nothing. But soon he realised how ridiculous all that would
be : he was the Prince of Salina and as a Prince of Salina
he must die with a priest by his side. Concetta was right.
Why should he avoid what was longed for by thousands
of other dying people? And he fell silent, waiting to hear
the little bell with the Last Sacraments. It soon came;
the parish church of the Pietà was almost opposite. The
gay silvery tinkle came climbing up the stairs, flowed along
the passage, became sharp as the door opened; preceded
by the hotel manager, a Swiss, flustered at having a dying
man on his hands, in came Father Balsamo, the parish
priest, bearing the Blessed Sacrament in a leather-sheathed
pyx. Tancredi and Fabrizietto raised the arm-chair, bore
it back into the room; the others were kneeling. He signed
more than said, 'Away, away.' He wanted to confess.
Things should be done properly or not at all. Everyone
went out, but when he was about to speak he realised he had
nothing to say; he could remember some definite sins,
but they seemed so petty as not to be worth bothering
a worthy priest about on a hot day. Not that he felt
himself innocent; but his whole life was blameworthy, not
this or that single act : and now he no longer had time to
say so. His eyes must have expressed an uneasiness which

the priest took for contrition; as in fact in a sense it was. He was absolved; his chin seemed to be propped on his chest, for the priest had to kneel down to place the Host between his lips. Then there was a murmur of the immemorial syllables which smooth the way, and the priest withdrew.

The arm-chair was not pulled back on to the balcony. Fabrizietto and Tancredi sat down next to him and held each of his hands; the boy was staring at him with the natural curiosity of one present at his first death agony and no more; this dying person was not a man, he was a grandfather, which is a very different thing. Tancredi squeezed his hand tightly and talked to him, talked a great deal, talked gaily; he explained projects with which he was associated, commented on political developments; he was a Deputy, had been promised the Legation in Lisbon, knew many a secret and savoury tale. His nasal voice, his subtle vocabulary sketched a futile arabesque over the ever noisier surging away of the waters of life. The Prince was grateful for the gossip; and he squeezed Tancredi's hand with a great effort though with almost no perceptible result. He was grateful, but did not listen. He was making up a general balance sheet of his whole life, trying to sort out of the immense ash-heap of liabilities the golden flecks of happy moments. These were : two weeks before his marriage, six weeks after; half an hour when Paolo was born, when he felt proud at having prolonged by a twig the Salina tree (the pride had been misplaced, he knew that now, but there had been some genuine self-respect in it); a few talks with Giovanni before the latter vanished (a few monologues, if the truth were told, during which he had thought to find in the boy a kindred mind); and many hours in the observatory, absorbed in abstract calculations and the pursuit of the unreachable. Could those latter hours be really put down to the credit side of life? Were they not some sort of anticipatory gift of the beatitudes after death? It didn't matter, they had existed.

Below in the street, between the hotel and the sea, a barrel-organ had halted and was playing away in the avid

hope of touching the hearts of foreigners who, at that
season, were not there. It was grinding out *You who opened
Your Wings to God* from 'Lucia di Lammermoor.' What
remained of Don Fabrizio thought of all the rancour
mingling with all the torture, at that moment, throughout
Italy, from mechanical music of this kind. Tancredi,
intuitive as ever, ran to the balcony, threw down a coin,
waved for the barrel-organ to stop. The outer silence closed
in again, the clamour within him grew huge.

Tancredi. Yes, much on the credit side came from Tancredi; that sympathy of his, all the more precious for being
ironic; the aesthetic pleasure of watching him manœuvre
amid the shoals of life, the bantering affection whose
touch was so right. Then dogs; Fufi, the fat pug of his
childhood, the impetuous poodle Tom, confidant and friend,
Speedy's gentle eyes, Bendicò's delicious nonsense, the
caressing paws of Pop, the pointer at that moment search-
ing for him under bushes and garden chairs and never to
see him again; then a horse or two, these already more
distant and detached. There were the first few hours of
returns to Donnafugata, the sense of tradition and the
perennial expressed in stone and water, of time congealed;
a few care-free shoots, a cosy massacre or two of hares
and partridges, some good laughs with Tumeo, a few
minutes of compunction at the convent amid odours of
must and confectionery. Anything else? Yes, there were
other things : but these were only grains of gold mixed with
earth : moments of satisfaction when he had made some
biting reply to a fool, of content when he had realised that
in Concetta's beauty and character was prolonged the true
Salina strain; a few seconds of frenzied passion; the
surprise of Arago's letter spontaneously congratulating him
on the accuracy of his difficult calculations about Huxley's
comet. And—why not?—the public thrill of being given a
medal at the Sorbonne, the exquisite sensation of one or two
fine silk cravats, the smell of some macerated leathers, the
gay voluptuous air of a few women passed in the street,
of one glimpsed even yesterday at the station of Catania,
in a brown travelling dress and suède gloves, mingling

amid the crowds and seeming to search for his exhausted face through the dirty compartment window. What a noise that crowd was making! 'Sandwiches!' '*Il Corriere dell' Isola.*' And then the panting of the tired breathless train . . . and that appalling sun as they arrived, those lying faces, the crashing cataracts. . . .

In the glowing dark he tried to count how much time he had really lived. His brain could not cope with the simple calculation any more; three months, three weeks, a total of six months, six by eight, eighty-four . . . forty-eight thousand . . . 840,000. He summed up. 'I'm seventy-three years old, and all in all I may have lived, really lived, a total of two . . . three at the most.' And the pains, the boredom, how long had they been? Useless to try and make himself count those; the whole of the rest; seventy years.

He felt his hand no longer being squeezed. Tancredi got up hurriedly and went out . . . Now it was not a river erupting over him but an ocean, tempestuous, all foam and raging white-flecked waves. . . .

He must have had another stroke for suddenly he realised that he was lying stretched on the bed. Someone was feeling his pulse; from the window came the blinding implacable reflection of the sea; in the room could be heard a faint hiss; it was his own death-rattle, but he did not know it. Around him was a little crowd, a group of strangers staring at him with frightened expressions. Gradually he recognised them : Concetta, Francesco Paolo, Carolina, Tancredi, Fabrizietto. The person holding his pulse was Doctor Cataliotti; he tried to smile a greeting at the latter but no one seemed to notice; all were weeping except Concetta; even Tancredi, who was saying : 'Uncle, dearest Nuncle!'

Suddenly amid the group appeared a young woman; slim, in brown travelling dress and wide bustle, with a straw hat trimmed with a speckled veil which could not hide the sly charm of her face. She slid a little suède-gloved hand between one elbow and another of the weeping kneelers, apologised, drew closer. It was she, the creature for ever yearned for, coming to fetch him; strange that one so young should yield to him; the time for the train's departure must be very close. When she was face to face with him she raised her veil, and there, chaste but ready for possession, she looked lovelier than she ever had when glimpsed in stellar space.

The crashing of the sea subsided altogether.

8

RELICS

ANYONE PAYING a visit to the old Salina ladies would be apt to find at least one priest's hat on the hall chairs. All three were spinsters and their household had been rent by secret struggles for power, so that each one, a strong character in her own way, wanted a separate confessor of her own. It was still the custom in that year, 1910, for confessions to take place at home, and these penitents' scruples required frequent repetition. Add to this little platoon of confessors the chaplain who came every morning to celebrate Mass in the private chapel, the Jesuit in charge of the general spiritual direction of the household, the monks and priests who came to draw alms for this or that parish or good work, and it will be readily understood why there was such an incessant coming and going of clerics, and why the ante-chamber of Villa Salina was often reminiscent of one of those Roman shops around Piazza della Minerva which display in their windows every imaginable ecclesiastical headgear, from flaming red for Cardinals to cindery black for country priests.

On that particular afternoon of May 1910 the parade of hats was quite unprecedented. The presence of the Vicar-General of the Archdiocese of Palermo was announced by his huge hat of fine beaver in a delicate shade of fuchsia, placed on a separate chair, with next to it a single glove, the right hand one, in woven silk of the same delicate hue; his secretary's of gleaming long-haired black plush, the crown circled by a narrow violet cord; those of two Jesuit Fathers, subdued tenebrous felts, symbols of modesty and reserve. The chaplain's headgear lay on an isolated chair, as was proper for a person undergoing inquiry.

The meeting that day was no unimportant matter. In accordance with Papal instructions the Cardinal Archbishop had begun an inspection of the private chapels of his arch- diocese, to reassure himself about the merits of those allowed to hold services there, the conformity of liturgy and decoration with the canons of the Church, and the authen- ticity of relics venerated in them. The Salina chapel was the best known in the city and one of the first which his Eminence proposed to visit. And it was in order to arrange for this event, fixed for next morning, that Monsignor the Vicar-General had called at Villa Salina. Unfortunate rumours about that chapel, seeped through many a filter, had reached the archiepiscopal Curia; not, of course, any- thing about the merits of the owners or of their right to carry out their religious duties in their own home; such subjects were beyond discussion. Nor was there any doubt thrown on the propriety or continuity of services held there, for these were as near perfection as may be, except per- haps for an overwhelming and perfectly comprehensible re- luctance on the part of the Salina ladies to let anyone be present at the sacred rites who was outside their close family circle. The Cardinal's attention had been drawn to a picture venerated in the Villa, and to the relics, the dozens of relics, exposed in the chapel. There were the most disturbing rumours about the authenticity of these, and it was desired that their genuineness be proved. The chaplain, an ecclesiastic of some culture and high hopes, had been reprimanded severely for not having kept the old ladies sufficiently on the alert; he had had, as it were, a 'dressing-down of the tonsure.'

The meeting was taking place in the main drawing-room of the Villa, the one of the monkeys and cockatoos. On a sofa covered with blue material interwoven with pink, a purchase of thirty years earlier that clashed with the evanes- cent tints of the precious wall-hangings, sat the Signorina Concetta with Monsignor the Vicar-General on her right; on each side of the sofa in two similar arm-chairs were the

Signorina Carolina and one of the Jesuits, Father Corti, while the Signorina Caterina, whose legs were paralysed, was in a wheel chair, and the other ecclesiastics had to be content with chairs covered in the same material as the walls, which seemed then far less valuable than the envied arm-chairs.

The three sisters were all around seventy, and Concetta was not the eldest; but the struggle for power which has been hinted at earlier had ended some time ago with the rout of her adversaries, so no one would now have dared contest her functions as mistress of the house.

She still showed the vestiges of past beauty; heavy and imposing in her stiff clothes of black watered silk, she wore her snow-white hair raised on her head so as to show her almost unfurrowed brow; this, together with contemptuous eyes and a resentful line above her nose, gave her an air that was authoritarian, almost imperial; so much so that a nephew of hers, having caught sight in some book or other of a picture of a famous Czarina, used to call her in private 'Catherine the Great'; an unsuitable name made quite innocent by the complete purity of Concetta's life and her nephew's total ignorance of Russian history.

The conversation lasted an hour, coffee had been taken and it was getting late. Monsignor reassumed his arguments : 'It is His Eminence's paternal wish that Mass celebrated in private should conform to the purest rites of Holy Mother Church, and that is why in his pastoral care he is visiting your chapel first, for he knows your house to be a beacon for the laity of Palermo and he desires that the authenticity of all objects venerated there should bring even more edification to yourselves and to all devout souls.' Concetta was silent, but Carolina, the elder sister, exploded, 'Now we're to appear as accused before our friends, are we? The idea of inspecting our chapel, excuse me for saying so, Monsignor, should never have so much as passed through His Eminence's head.'

Monsignor laughed, amused. 'Signorina, you cannot imagine how gratifying your vehemence is to me; as the

expression of a simple and absolute faith, most acceptable
to the Church and certainly to Our Lord Himself; and
only in order to make this faith flower yet more abundantly
and to purify it has the Holy Father recommended these
inspections, which have already been taking place for
some months throughout the Catholic world.'

The reference to the Holy Father was not, actually, very
opportune; Carolina was one of those Catholics who consider themselves to be in closer possession of religious truths
than the Pope himself; and a few moderate declarations of
Pius X, the abolition of some secondary feast days in particular, had already exasperated her. 'This Pope would do
better to mind his own business.' Then she began to wonder
if she hadn't gone too far, crossed herself and muttered a
Gloria Patri.

Concetta intervened. 'Don't let yourself be drawn into
saying things you don't think, Carolina. Or what sort of
impression will Monsignor take away with him?'

The latter was actually smiling more than ever; here
before him, he was thinking, was a little girl grown old in
narrow ideas and arid acts of piety. Benignly he indulged
her.

'Monsignor will take away the impression of having been
in the company of three devout ladies,' said he.

Father Corti, the Jesuit, tried to relax the tension. 'I,
Monsignor, am among those who can best confirm your
words; Father Pirrone, whose memory is venerated by all
that knew him, often used to tell me when I was a novice
of the devout atmosphere in which the ladies grew up:
the name of Salina should anyway be a guarantee for
that.'

Monsignor wanted to get down to facts. 'Well, Signorina
Concetta, now everything's clear, I should like, with your
permission, to visit the chapel in order to prepare His Eminence for the marvels of faith he will see to-morrow morning.'

In Prince Fabrizio's time there had been no chapel in the
Villa; the whole family used to go out to church on feast

days, and even Father Pirrone had to walk quite a step
every morning to say his own Mass. But after the death of
Prince Fabrizio, when, as a result of various complications
of inheritance which would be boring to narrate, the Villa
became the exclusive property of the three sisters, they at
once thought of setting up their own oratory. They chose
an out-of-the-way drawing-room, which with its half
columns of imitation granite stuck into the walls was vaguely
reminiscent of a Roman basilica; they obliterated an unsuitable mythological fresco from the centre of the ceiling;
decked up an altar. And all was ready.

When Monsignor entered, the chapel was lit by the late
afternoon sun, which fell full on the altar and the picture
above so venerated by the Salina ladies. It was a painting
in the style of Cremona, and represented a slim and very
attractive young woman with eyes turned to heaven and
an abundance of brown hair scattered in gracious disorder
on half-bare shoulders; in her right hand she was gripping
a crumpled letter, with an expression of anxious expectancy
not unconnected to a certain sparkle in her glistening eyes;
behind her was a green and gentle Lombard landscape. No
Holy Child, no crowns, no snakes, no stars, none in fact
of those symbols which usually accompany the image of
Mary; the painter must have trusted that virginal expression as being enough to recognise her by. Monsignor drew
nearer, went up one of the altar steps and stood there,
without crossing himself, looking at the picture for a minute
or two, his face all smiling admiration as if he were an
art critic. Behind him the sisters made signs of the Cross
and murmured an *Ave Maria*.

Then the prelate came down the steps again, turned
round and said, 'A fine painting, that; very expressive.'

'A miraculous icon, Monsignor, most miraculous!' explained Caterina, poor ill creature, leaning from her am-
bulating instrument of torture.

'It has done so many miracles!' Carolina pressed on. 'It
represents the Madonna of the Letter. The Virgin is on the
point of consigning the holy missive invoking her Divine
Son's protection on the people of Messina; a protection

which has been gloriously conceded, as is shown by the
many miracles during the earthquake of two years ago.'

'A fine picture, Signorina; whatever it represents it's a
pretty thing and should be treated carefully.' Then he
turned to the relics; seventy-four of them, they completely
covered the two walls on each side of the altar. Each was
enclosed in a frame which also contained a card with
information about it and a number referring to the documents of authentication. These documents themselves, many
voluminous and hung with seals, were locked into a damask-
covered chest in a corner of the chapel. There were frames
of worked and smooth silver, frames of bronze and coral,
frames of tortoiseshell; in filigree, rare woods, box-wood,
in red and blue velvet; large, tiny, square, octagonal, round,
oval; frames worth a fortune and frames bought at the
Bocconi stores; all collected by those devoted souls in their
religious exaltation as custodians of supernatural treasures.

The real creator of this collection had been Carolina;
she had found somewhere a certain Donna Rosa, a huge
old woman, half-nun, with useful connections in all the
churches, convents and charity foundations of Palermo
and its surroundings. It had been this Donna Rosa who
had brought up to Villa Salina every few months a relic
of a saint wrapped in tissue paper. She had managed,
she would say, to get some dilapidated parish or decayed
family to part with it. The name of the seller was not given
merely because of understandable, in fact praiseworthy, discretion; and anyway there were the proofs of authenticity
which she brought and always handed over, clear as daylight, written out in Latin or mysterious characters she
called Greek or Syriac. Concetta, administrator and bursar,
would pay. Then came a search and adaptation of frames.
And once again the impassive Concetta would pay. There
was a period, a couple of years ago, when the collecting
mania even disturbed Caterina and Carolina's sleep; in
the morning they would recount to each other dreams of
miraculous discoveries, with the hope that they would be
realised, as did indeed sometimes happen after the dreams
had been confided to Donna Rosa. What Concetta dreamt

no one knew. Then Donna Rosa died and the influx of relics stopped almost completely; anyway, by then, there was a certain superfluity.

Monsignor glanced rather hurriedly at one or two of the nearest frames. 'Treasures,' he said, 'treasures! What lovely frames!' Then congratulating them on the fine 'display' (such was his word), and promising to return next day with His Eminence ('yes, at nine exactly') he genuflected, crossed himself towards a modest Madonna of Pompeii hung on a side wall, and left the oratory. Soon the seats were bereft of hats, and the ecclesiastics climbed into the three carriages from the Archbishopric, with their black horses, which had awaited them in the courtyard. Monsignor made a point of asking the chaplain, Father Titta, to share his own carriage, much to the latter's solace. The carriages moved off, and Monsignor was silent; they drove by the sumptuous Villa Falconeri, with its flowering bougainvillaea drooping over the walls of the splendidly kept gardens; and when they reached the slope down to Palermo amid the orange groves, Monsignor spoke. 'And so you, Father Titta, have actually said Mass for years in front of the picture of that girl? That girl with a rendezvous and waiting for her lover? Now don't tell me you too believed it was a holy icon.'

'Monsignor, I am to blame, I know. But it's not easy to gainsay the Signorina Carolina. That you cannot know.'

Monsignor shivered at the memory. 'My son, you've put your finger on it; and that will be taken into consideration.'

Carolina had gone off to pour out her rage in a letter to Chiara, her married sister in Naples; Caterina, tired by the long and painful conversation, had been put to bed; Concetta went back to her own solitary room. This was one of those rooms (so numerous that one might be tempted to say it of all rooms) which have two faces, one with a mask that they show to ignorant visitors, the other which is only revealed to those in the know, the owner in particular to whom all its squalid essence is manifest. This particular room was airy and looked over the broad garden; in a

corner was a high bed with four pillows (Concetta suffered
from heart trouble and had to sleep almost sitting up);
no carpets, but a fine white floor with intricate yellow tiles;
a valuable money chest with dozens of little drawers
covered with hardstone and worked stucco : the desk, central table and all the furniture in breezy local inlay work,
with figures of huntsmen, dogs and game in amber-colour
on a rose-wood background : furniture considered by Concetta herself as antiquated and even in bad taste and which,
sold at auction after her death, is to-day the pride of a pros-
perous shipping agent when his wife serves cocktails to en-
vious friends. On the walls were portraits, water colours,
sacred images. All was clean, all ordered. Two things only,
perhaps, might have appeared unusual : in the corner opposite the bed towered four enormous wooden cases painted in
green, each with a big padlock; and in front of these,
on the floor, was a heap of mangy fur. To the lips of an
ingenuous visitor the little room might have brought a smile,
so suggestive was it of an old maid's affectionate care.

To one who knew the facts—Concetta herself—it was an
inferno of mummified memories. The four green cases contained dozens of day and night shirts, dressing-gowns, pillow-
cases, sheets carefully divided into 'best' and 'second-best';
the trousseau collected by Concetta herself fifty years before.
Now those padlocks were never opened for fear incongru-
ous demons might leap out, and under the ubiquitous
Palermo damp the contents grew yellow and decayed, useless for ever and for anyone. The portraits were of dead
people no longer loved, the photographs of friends who
had hurt her in their lifetime, the only reason they were
not forgotten in death; the water-colours showed houses
and places most of which had been sold, or rather stupidly
bartered away by spendthrift nephews. Anyone looking
carefully into the heap of moth-eaten fur would have noticed two erect ears, a snout of black wood, and two aston-
ished eyes of yellow glass; it was Bendicò, dead for forty-
five years, embalmed for forty-five years, nest now of
spiders' webs and moth, detested by the servants who had
been imploring Concetta for dozens of years to have it

thrown on the rubbish heap; but she always refused, reluctant to detach herself from the only memory of her past which aroused no distressing sensations.

But the distressing sensations of to-day (at a certain age every day punctually produces its own) all referred to che present. Much less devout than Carolina, much more sensitive than Caterina, Concetta had understood the meaning of the Vicar-General's visit and foreseen the consequences; orders to take away all or nearly all the relics, the changing of the picture above the altar, an eventual reconsecration of the chapel. She had never really believed in the authenticity of these relics, and had paid up with the indifference of a father settling a bill for toys which are of no interest to himself but help to keep the children quiet. To her the removal of these objects was a matter of indifference; what did touch her, the day's real thorn, was the appalling figure the Salina family would now cut with ecclesiastical authorities, and soon with the entire city. The Church kept its secrets much better than anyone else in Sicily, but that did not mean much yet; all would be spread round in a month or two; as everything spreads on this island which should have as its symbol not the Trinacria but the Ear of Dionysius at Syracuse which makes the lightest sigh resound for fifty yards. And the Church's esteem meant a lot to her. The prestige of her name had slowly disappeared, the family fortune, divided and subdivided, was at best equivalent to that of any number of other lesser families and very much smaller than that of some rich industrialists. But in the Church, in their relations with it, the Salina had maintained their pre-eminence. What a reception His Eminence had given the three sisters when they went to make their Christmas visit! Would that happen now?

A maid entered : 'Excellency, the Princess is just arriving. Her motor-car is in the courtyard.' Concetta got up, tidied her hair, threw a black lace shawl over her shoulders, resumed her imperial air, and reached the entrance hall just as Angelica was climbing the last steps of the outer staircase. She suffered from varicose veins; her legs, which had always been a little short, scarcely upheld her, and she was climbing up leaning on the arm of her own footman whose black topcoat swept the stairs. 'Concetta, darling!' 'Angelica, dear! It's so long since we've met!' In fact only five days had gone by since her last visit, but the intimacy between the two cousins, an intimacy similar in closeness and feeling to that which was to bind Italians and Austrians in their opposing trenches a few years later, was such that five days really could seem a long time.

Angelica, now nearly seventy, still showed many traces of beauty; the illness which was to transform her into a wretched spectre three years later was already active, but still secreted deep in her blood; her green eyes were what they had been before, only slightly dulled by the years, and the wrinkles on her neck were hidden by the soft black folds of the hood and veil which she, a widow for the last three years, wore not without a certain nostalgic coquetry. 'You see,' she said to Concetta as they moved entwined towards a drawing-room, 'you see, with these imminent celebrations of the fiftieth anniversary of The Thousand there's never a minute's peace. Just imagine, a few days ago they told me I'd been put on the Committee of Honour; a homage to dear Tancredi's memory, of course, but such a lot for me to do! Finding lodgings for veterans coming from all over Italy, arranging invitations for the grandstand without offending anyone; taking care to invite the mayor of every commune in the island. Oh, by the way, dear: the Mayor of Salina is a clerical and has refused to march past; so I thought at once of your nephew, of Fabrizio; he came to visit me, and I pinned him down there and then. He couldn't refuse. So at the end of the month we'll see him filing past dressed to the nines down Via Libertà in front of a big placard with "Salina" on it in letters a foot high. Don't you think it's a good idea? A Salina rendering homage to Garibaldi! A fusion of old and new in Sicily! I've thought of you too, darling; here's your invitation for the grandstand, right next to the royal box.' And she pulled out of her Parisian bag a piece of cardboard in

Garibaldi red, the very same colour as the strip of silk worn for a time by Tancredi above his collar. 'Carolina and Caterina won't be too pleased,' she went on in her arbitrary way, 'but I only had one place; anyway you have more right to it than they have; you were Tancredi's favourite cousin.'

She talked a lot and she talked well; forty years of living with Tancredi, however tempestuous and interrupted, had been more than long enough to rub off the last traces of Donnafugata accent and manners; she had camouflaged herself even to the point of copying that graceful twining of the fingers which had been one of Tancredi's characteristics. She read a lot; on her table the latest books by Anatole France and Bourget alternated with D'Annunzio and Serao; and she had the reputation in the drawing-rooms of Palermo of being an expert on the architecture of the Châteaux of the Loire, about which she would often discourse with somewhat hazy enthusiasm, contrasting, perhaps unconsciously, their Renaissance serenity with the restless baroque of the palace at Donnafugata, against which she nurtured an aversion inexplicable to anyone who knew nothing of her meek and slighted youth.

'But what a head I have, my dear! I was forgetting to tell you that Senator Tassoni will soon be coming here; he's staying with me at Villa Falconeri and wants to meet you; he was a great friend of poor Tancredi's, a comrade-in-arms too, and he's heard Tancredi talk of you, it seems. Our dear Tancredi!' The handkerchief with its narrow black border came out of her bag, and she dried a tear in eyes that were still fine.

Concetta had been inserting, as always, an occasional phrase of her own into Angelica's continual flow; but at the name of Tassoni she was silent. Once again she saw a scene, very distant but quite clear, as if through the other end of a telescope : the big white table surrounded by all those people now dead; near her Tancredi, dead too— as anyway, really, she was herself; his brutal anecdote, Angelica's hysterical laughter, her own no less hysterical tears. It had been the turning-point of her life, that; the road she had taken then had led her here, to this desert not even inhabited by extinct love or spent rancour.

'Oh, I've heard of the bother you're having with the Curia. What a nuisance they are! But why didn't you tell me before? I could have done something; the Cardinal is always very good to me. I'm afraid that it's too late now. But I'll pull some strings. Anyway, it'll all blow over.'

Senator Tassoni, who arrived soon after, was a brisk and spruce old man. His wealth, which was great and growing, had been acquired by competition and hard struggle, and instead of making him flabby it had kept him in a state of continual energy which now seemed to conquer the years and made him almost fiery. From the few months spent with Garibaldi's southern army he had acquired a military bearing destined never to be discarded. Blended with courtesy it formed a philtre which had gained him many successes in the past, and which now, joined to the number of his securities, was of great use for getting his own way with the boards of banks and cotton factories; half Italy and a great part of the Balkan countries sewed on their own buttons with thread made by Tassoni & Co.

'Signorina,' he was saying to Concetta as he sat beside her on a low stool suitable for a page, which was just why he had chosen it, 'Signorina, a dream of my distant youth is now being realised. How often in those icy nights camping out on the Volturno or around the ramparts of besieged Gaeta, how often our unforgettable Tancredi used to talk of you! I seemed to know you already, to have frequented this house amid whose walls his untamed youth was passed, and I am happy to be able, though with such delay, to lay my homage at the feet of her who was the consolation of one of the purest heroes of our Risorgimento.'

Concetta was unused to conversations with people she had not known since infancy; she was also no lover of literature; so she had no immunity against rhetoric and was in fact open to its fascination. The senator's words moved her; she forgot that old anecdote of half a century ago, she no longer saw in Tassoni a violator of convents, a jeerer at poor terrified nuns, but an old man, Tancredi's sincere friend who talked of him with true affection, one who brought to her a shadow, a message from the dead man across the morass of time which the dead can so seldom cross. 'And what did my dear cousin tell you about me?' she asked in a low voice, with a shyness that brought to life once more the eighteen-year-old-girl from that bundle of black silk and white hair.

'Ah, so many things! He talked of you almost as much as of Donna Angelica! She for him was love, you were the image of his sweet youth, that youth which for us soldiers passes so soon.'

Again an icy hand froze her old heart; but now Tassoni had raised his voice, and turned to Angelica. 'D'you remember, Princess, what he said at Vienna ten years ago?' He turned back towards Concetta to explain. 'I was there with the Italian delegation for the Trade Treaty; Tancredi put me up at the embassy like the warm-hearted friend and comrade he was, with that great gentleman's affability of his. Perhaps seeing a comrade-in-arms again in that hostile city had moved him, for he told us so much about his past. In the back of a box at the Opera, between one act and another of *Don Giovanni*, he confessed, in his incomparably ironic way, a sin, an unpardonable sin, which he said he'd committed against you, yes, against you, Signorina.' He interrupted himself a second to gain time to set his surprise. 'He told us how one evening, during dinner at Donnafugata, he had allowed himself to invent a story and tell it to you; a tale of war connected with the fighting round Palermo; and how you believed it and were offended because the story was rather outspoken for the customs of fifty years ago. You had reproved him. "She was so sweet," said he, "as she fixed me with those angry eyes of hers and as her lips swelled with anger so prettily, like a puppy's; she was so sweet that if I hadn't controlled myself I'd have kissed here there and then in front of twenty people and that terrible old uncle of mine!" You, Signorina, will have forgotten it; but Tancredi remembered it well, he had such delicacy of feeling; he also remembered it because it happened on the very day he met Donna Angelica for the first time.' And he sketched towards the Princess one of those gestures of homage, with his right hand dropping away through the air, whose Goldoniesque tradition was preserved then only among Senators of the Kingdom.

The conversation continued for some time, but it could not be said that Concetta took any great part in it. The sudden revelation penetrated into her mind slowly and did not make her suffer much at first. But when the visitors had said good-bye and left and she was alone, she began seeing more clearly and so suffering more. The spectres of the past had been exorcised for years; though they were of course to be found hidden in everything, and it was they that made food taste bitter and company seem boring : but it was a long time since they had shown their faces; now they came leaping out, with the ghastly grins of irreparable wrongs. It would, of course, be absurd to say that Concetta still loved Tancredi; love's eternity lasts but a year or two, not fifty. But as one who has recovered from smallpox fifty years before still bears its marks on the face although he may have forgotten the pain of the disease, so she bore in her own oppressed life now the wounds of a bitter disappointment that had become almost part of history, so much part in fact that its fiftieth anniversary was being celebrated officially.

Until to-day, on the rare occasions when she thought over what had happened at Donnafugata that distant summer, she had felt upheld by a sense of martyrdom, of wrong endured, of resentment against a father who had neglected her, and of torturing emotion on account of that other dead man. Now, however, these second-hand feelings which had formed the skeleton of her whole mode of thought were also collapsing. There had been no enemies, just one single adversary, herself; her future had been killed by her own imprudence, by the reckless Salina pride; and now, just at the moment when her memories had come alive again after so many years, she found herself even without the solace of being able to blame her own unhappiness on others, a solace which is the last protective device of the desperate.

If Tassoni had told the truth, then the long hours spent in savouring her hatred before her father's picture, her hiding of every photograph of Tancredi so as not to be forced to hate him too, had been stupidity—worse, cruel injustice; and she suffered now at the memory of Tancredi's warm and imploring tone as he had begged his uncle to allow him into that convent; they had been words of love towards her, words not understood, routed by her pride which at her harshness had drawn back with their tails between their legs like whipped puppies. From the timeless depth of her being a black pain came welling to spatter her all over at that revelation of the truth.

But was it the truth? Nowhere has truth so short a life as in Sicily; a fact has scarcely happened five minutes before its genuine kernel has vanished, been camouflaged, embellished, disfigured, annihilated by imagination and self-interest; shame, fear, generosity, malice, opportunism, charity, all the passions, good as well as evil, fling themselves on the fact and tear it to pieces; very soon it has vanished altogether. And poor Concetta was hoping to find the truth of feelings that had never been expressed but only glimpsed half a century before! The truth no longer existed. Precarious fact, though, had been replaced by irrefutable pain.

Meanwhile Angelica and the Senator were driving the short distance back to Villa Falconeri. Tassoni was worried : 'Angelica,' he said (they had had a very short affair thirty years before, and kept the intimacy, for which there is no substitute, conferred by a few hours spent between the same pair of sheets), 'I'm afraid I disturbed your cousin in some way; did you notice how silent she was towards the end of the visit? I hope I didn't, she's such a dear.'

'I should think you have hurt her, Vittorio,' said Angelica, exasperated by a double though imaginary jealousy, 'she was madly in love with Tancredi; but he never took any

notice of her.' And so a new spadeful of soil fell on the
tumulus of truth.

The Cardinal of Palermo was a truly holy man; and
even now after he has been dead a long time his charity and
his faith are still remembered. While he was alive, though,
things were different; he was not a Sicilian, he was not
even a southerner or a Roman; and many years before
he had tried to leaven with nordic activity the inert and
heavy dough of the island's spiritual life in general and the
clergy's in particular. Flanked by two or three secretaries
from his own parts he had deluded himself, those first years,
that he could remove abuses and clear the soil of its more
flagrant stumbling-blocks. But soon he had to realise that
he was, as it were, firing into cotton-wool; the little hole
made at the moment was covered after a few seconds by
thousands of tiny fibres and all remained as before, the
only additions being cost of powder, ridicule at useless effort
and deterioration of material. Like everyone who in those
days wanted to change anything in the Sicilian character he
soon acquired the reputation of being a fool (which in the
circumstances was exact) and had to content himself with
doing good works, which only diminished his popularity still
further if they involved those benefited in making the slightest effort themselves, such as, for instance, visiting the
Archipiscopal palace.

So the aged prelate who set out on the morning of the
fourteenth of May to visit Villa Salina was a good man
but a disillusioned one, who had in the end assumed towards those in his own diocese an attitude of contemptuous pity (which was sometimes, after all, unjust). This
made him adopt brusque and cutting ways that dragged
him even farther into the swamps of unpopularity.

The three Salina sisters were, as we know, deeply
offended by the inspection of their chapel; but, childish
and above all feminine in mind, they also drew a certain
undeniable satisfaction from the thought of receiving in
their home a Prince of the Church, at being able to show
him the grandeur of the Salina which in good faith they

thought still intact, and above all at seeing a kind of sumptuous red bird moving round their rooms for half an hour and admiring the varied and harmonising tones of its different purples and heavy shot silk. But the poor creatures were destined to be disappointed even of this last modest hope. When they, having descended the external staircase, saw His Eminence alight from his carriage, they realised that he was in informal dress. Only the tiny purple buttons on the severe black cassock indicated his high rank; in spite of his expression of injured goodness, the Cardinal was no more imposing than the Archpriest of Donnafugata, He was polite but cold, mingling almost too ably a show of respect for the Salina name and the individual virtues of the ladies themselves with a contempt for their inept and formalised devotions. To the Vicar-General's exclamations about the beauty of the decorations in the rooms they passed he did not answer a word; he refused to accept any of the refreshments prepared for him ('Thank you, Signorina, only a little water; to-day is the eve of my Holy Patron's feast-day'), he did not even sit down. He went to the chapel, bowed a second before the Madonna of Pompeii, made a hurried inspection of the relics. Then he blessed with pastoral benignity the mistresses of the house and the servants kneeling in the entrance hall, and said to Concetta, who bore on her face the signs of a sleepless night, 'Signorina, for three or four days no Divine Service can be held in the chapel, but I will see that it is re-consecrated as soon as possible. It seems to me that the picture of the Madonna of Pompeii could well take the place of the one now above the altar, which can join the fine works of art I have admired while passing through your rooms. As for the relics, I am leaving behind Don Pacchiotti, my secretary and a most competent priest; he will examine the documents and tell you the results of his researches; and what he decides will be as if I had decided it myself.'

Benignly he let everyone kiss his ring, then climbed into the heavy carriage together with his small suite.

The carriages had not yet reached the Falconeri turning before Carolina, with cheeks taut and darting eyes, exclaimed 'This Pope must be a Turk,' while Caterina had to be given smelling salts. Meanwhile Concetta was chatting calmly to Don Pacchiotti, who had in the end accepted a cup of coffee and a *baba*.

Then the priest asked for the keys of the case of documents, requested permission and withdrew into the chapel, after first taking from his bag a small hammer and saw, a screw-driver, a magnifying glass and a couple of pencils. He had been a pupil of the Vatican School of Palaeography; and he was also Piedmontese. His labours were long and meticulous; the servants who passed by the chapel door heard the knocks of a hammer, the squeak of screws, and sighs. Three hours later he re-emerged with his cassock full of dust and his hands black, but with a pleased look and a serene expression on his bespectacled face. He apologised for carrying a big wicker basket. 'I took the liberty of appropriating this to put in what I'd discarded; may I set it down here?' And he placed his burden in a corner; it was overflowing with torn papers and cards, little boxes containing bits of bone and gristle. 'I am happy to say that I have found five relics which are perfectly authentic and worthy of being objects of devotion. The rest are there,' he said, pointing at the basket. 'Could you tell me, Signorina, where I can brush myself down and wash my hands?'

Five minutes later he reappeared and dried his hands on a big towel on whose border pranced a Leopard in red thread. 'I forgot to say that the frames are all laid out on the chapel table; some of them are really lovely.' He said good-bye. 'Ladies, my respects.' But Caterina refused to kiss his hand.

'And what are we to do with the things in the basket?'

'Just whatever you like, ladies; keep them or throw them on the rubbish heap; they have no value whatsoever.' And when Concetta wanted to order a carriage to drive him back, he said, 'Don't worry about that, Signorina; I'll lunch with the Oratorians a few steps away; I don't neec a thing.' And putting his instruments back into his bag off he went on light feet.

Concetta withdrew to her room; she felt no emotion whatsoever; she seemed to be living in a world familiar yet alien, which had already ceded all the impulses it could give and consisted now only of pure forms. The portrait of her father was just a few square inches of canvas, the green cases just a few square yards of wood. Later she was brought a letter. The envelope had a black seal with a big coronet in relief.

'Darling Concetta, I've heard of His Eminence's visit and am so glad a few relics could be saved. I hope to get the Vicar-General to come and say the first Mass in the reconsecrated chapel. Senator Tassoni is leaving to-morrow and recommends himself to your *bon souvenir*. I'll be coming over to visit you soon. Meanwhile a warm embrace to you and to Carolina and Caterina too. Ever, Angelica.'

Still she could feel nothing; inner emptiness was total; but she did sense an unpleasant atmosphere exhaling from the heap of furs. That was to-day's distress: even poor Bendicò was hinting at bitter memories. She rang the bell. 'Annetta,' she said, 'this dog has really become too moth-eaten and dusty. Take it out, throw it away.'

As the carcass was dragged off, the glass eyes stared at her with the humble reproach of things discarded in the hope of final riddance. A few minutes later what remained of Bendicò was flung into a corner of the yard visited every day by the dustman. During the flight down from the window its form recomposed itself for an instant; in the air there seemed to be dancing a quadruped with long whiskers, its right foreleg raised in imprecation. Then all found peace in a little heap of livid dust.

THE END